BOOKS BY TINA FOLSOM

Ace on the Run (Code Name Stargate, Book 1)

Fox in plain Sight (Code Name Stargate, Book 2)

Yankee in the Wind (Code Name Stargate, Book 3)

Tiger on the Prowl (Code Name Stargate, Book 4)

Samson's Lovely Mortal (Scanguards Vampires, Book 1)

Amaury's Hellion (Scanguards Vampires, Book 2)

Gabriel's Mate (Scanguards Vampires, Book 3)

Yvette's Haven (Scanguards Vampires, Book 4)

Zane's Redemption (Scanguards Vampires, Book 5)

Quinn's Undying Rose (Scanguards Vampires, Book 6)

Oliver's Hunger (Scanguards Vampires, Book 7)

Thomas's Choice (Scanguards Vampires, Book 8)

Silent Bite (Scanguards Vampires, Book 8 1/2)

Cain's Identity (Scanguards Vampires, Book 9)

Luther's Return (Scanguards Vampires, Book 10)

Blake's Pursuit (Scanguards Vampires, Book 11)

Fateful Reunion (Scanguards Vampires, Book 11 1/2)

John's Yearning (Scanguards Vampires, Book 12)

Ryder's Storm (Scanguards Vampires, Book 13)

Damian's Conquest (Scanguards Vampires, Book 14)

Grayson's Challenge (Scanguards Vampires, Book 15)

Lover Uncloaked (Stealth Guardians, Book 1)

Master Unchained (Stealth Guardians, Book 2)

Warrior Unraveled (Stealth Guardians, Book 3)

Guardian Undone (Stealth Guardians, Book 4)

Immortal Unveiled (Stealth Guardians, Book 5)

Protector Unmatched (Stealth Guardians, Book 6)

Demon Unleashed (Stealth Guardians, Book 7)

A Touch of Greek (Out of Olympus, Book 1)

A Scent of Greek (Out of Olympus, Book 2)

A Taste of Greek (Out of Olympus, Book 3)

A Hush of Greek (Out of Olympus, Book 4)

Venice Vampyr (Novellas 1 – 4)

Teasing (The Hamptons Bachelor Club, Book 1)

Enticing (The Hamptons Bachelor Club, Book 2)

Beguiling (The Hamptons Bachelor Club, Book 3)

Scorching (The Hamptons Bachelor Club, Book 4)

Alluring (The Hamptons Bachelor Club, Book 5)

Sizzling (The Hamptons Bachelor Club, Book 6)

WARRIOR UNRAVELED

STEALTH GUARDIANS #3

TINA FOLSOM

PROLOGUE

Zoltan stared into the fireplace in his study, a fiery pit fed by lava from deep underground. It bubbled up, releasing hot air into the cavernous room illuminated by gas-burning lamps lining the walls. The walls around him were made of black lava stone, like many of the caves in the Underworld.

But unlike the other caves that had been fashioned into rooms and living quarters for him and his demons centuries ago, this room was soundproof. There wasn't a single crack in the walls, not a single crevice that might catch and carry sound miles away. This was where he conducted business, and he'd made sure he was safe from being overheard.

Because there was a traitor among them. A demon who was vying for his throne.

He'd found out only a short while ago from his personal guard and right hand Vintoq that one of his subjects was working against him during his latest attempt to turn the city of Baltimore into a demon stronghold. Somebody had ambitions to take over as the Great One.

Now it was more important than ever to deliver a devastating blow to their enemies, the Stealth Guardians. Because if Zoltan could prove to his demons that they were better off with him, that he could lead them to victory over the Stealth Guardians and thus over mankind, they would back him and rat out the traitor.

But if he showed weakness now, it would be his end. And just like Zoltan had killed the last Great One for his throne when he'd shown weakness, some traitorous demon could dispatch Zoltan just as easily.

What he needed now was a quick strike against those slippery immortal guardians. A strike that would prove that he was smarter than any of his underlings. That he alone was capable of devising a strategy for victory.

But things weren't looking good. And that infuriated him. So much so that he needed to let it out or it would eat him up from the inside.

His gaze fell onto a narrow side table that was covered with his trophies: items he'd taken from his kills. Jewelry, weapons, watches. He looked at it often, reminding himself of what he'd achieved in the time since he'd become the Great One. But right now, the sight gave him no satisfaction. All it did was remind him that he hadn't yet reached his goal.

With an angry curse, he swiped his arm over the table, flinging his trophies to the ground. Watches shattered, a dagger clattered against the wall, the hilt separating from the blade, a pearl necklace broke into pieces, sending individual pearls rolling over the uneven stone floor.

Zoltan stomped on the loose pearls, crushing them with the same force he wished to use against the Stealth Guardians. There was satisfaction in this needless destruction, so he turned to the other trophies. When he reached the broken dagger, he stopped. Something caught his eye.

Zoltan crouched down and picked up the two pieces. Something was sticking out from inside the hilt. He pulled on it, freeing it from the broken weapon.

For a long moment, he stared at it in disbelief, shocked to realize what he was holding in his hand: the key to destroying the Stealth Guardians.

1

———

S*everal days later*
  Heads would roll tonight.

Virginia stepped into the portal and concentrated on her destination.

The members of the Baltimore compound had broken the rules one too many times. She—better than anybody—knew what could happen when rules were broken. Even an hour's hesitation to set things right could mean the difference between life and death. The difference between danger and safety. Between love and hate.

The guardians in Baltimore had to learn this. And learn it fast.

One single broken rule had cost her everything she'd ever held dear. One broken rule had changed her life. She wouldn't allow history to be repeated.

Never again on her watch.

She wasn't an ex-enforcer for nothing. Just because she'd risen to become a member of the Council of Nine, the ruling body of the Stealth Guardians, didn't mean she'd forgotten her training. First and foremost, she was a warrior, a warrior who understood that the rules existed for a reason: to keep their kind safe. And nobody broke those rules without being punished. Not if she had anything to say about it. Which she did.

To intimidate the guardians at the compound and to demand instant respect, she'd dressed in the uniform of the enforcers: black leather pants, black T-shirt, black leather jacket with silver buttons adorned with the symbol of an ancient dagger. Her tall black boots reached to her knees and gleamed like a shiny new toy. At her hip sat a dagger forged in the Dark Days—the only kind of weapon capable of killing a demon.

Arrived at the compound, Virginia stepped out of the portal that had transported her thousands of miles in only a few seconds and took in her surroundings. She was in one of the sublevels of the Baltimore compound, and though she'd never been here, finding her way wasn't difficult. All compounds had a similar layout.

She made her way toward the compound's command center, but it was quiet there. The computers on the console were on standby, another violation she could add to her ever-growing list. She grunted in disapproval, then turned as she heard voices coming from the compound's living area, more precisely the kitchen. She marched toward it. Outside the door, she stopped for a short moment. With a deep breath and a steely resolve, she opened the door.

"Tessa did it," one of the guardians said.

She recognized him immediately, though she'd never met him. She'd studied the files of all the guardians assigned to this compound and committed the information to memory.

The guardian who'd spoken, Aiden, put his arm around his wife, Leila, a human authorized to live at the compound thanks to her unbreakable bond with Aiden. He added, "We should celebrate."

At the words, Virginia wanted to snort. Instead, she kicked the door shut behind her.

"Celebrate what?"

All eyes snapped to her. Good! She loved to make an entrance. She had everybody's undivided attention now.

"The fact that this compound constantly ignores our rules?" she continued. "Or maybe that your security protocols are so loose that a witch was able to breach your defenses? Or maybe the fact that you just don't give a damn that no human charges are allowed here? Enlighten me!"

Virginia narrowed her eyes at the assembled: Aiden, Leila, Enya, Hamish, Manus, Pearce, and Logan, as well as two people who weren't authorized to be at the compound. The human charge and the witch.

"And you are?" Hamish asked, his chin tipped up defiantly.

Figured that he was the ringleader. In a millisecond, she recalled the details of his file and the notes she'd made in the margins after reading it cover to cover: rebellious, stubborn, insubordinate. But also innovative, quick on his feet, and exceptional in hand-to-hand combat.

"Virginia Robson, newest member of the Council of Nine," she announced.

A few mumbled curses reached her ears. As she'd expected.

"Oh crap," Manus choked out.

Yes, they all knew the name and the reputation that came with it. And she was proud of that reputation.

"To what do we owe your visit?" Hamish asked.

"You must be Hamish. I would have expected better from you than bringing a human charge into the compound." Her jaw tightened. "Not to speak of letting a witch run wild here."

Her gaze shot to the couch where the witch in question stood as if paralyzed. For the first time, she looked beyond the aura that identified him as a preternatural creature. She took in the features of the man. Tall with dark hair and a lean, yet strong, body. Not unattractive. In fact, not unattractive at all. On the contrary. There was something about him that made her heart beat just a tiny bit faster. Annoyed at her reaction, she tore her eyes from him.

"But all this is about to change. I'm here to clean up."

She noticed how Hamish pulled his human charge closer.

"Starting with the human." Virginia pointed at Tessa. She'd read her file, too. A talented politician, a public servant who hadn't forgotten what it meant to serve the public. A rarity. Nevertheless, rules were rules.

"She has no right to be here. You've compromised the security of this compound by having brought her here. We'll have to abandon this place and relocate everybody. You'll answer for this before the Council of Nine."

"He didn't do anything wrong!" Tessa blurted.

How dare the human raise her voice to her? "What did you say?"

"I have the same right to be here as Leila, Aiden's wife." A stubborn lift of her chin.

Virginia tilted her head to the side, suspicion rising like dense fog in the Outer Hebrides. "Are you telling me that you're Hamish's mate?"

"Yes."

This changed everything. As his mate, she had every right to be here—*if* it was true. "And why has the council not been informed of this?"

Anybody else would have missed the quick but silent exchange between Tessa and Hamish, and the slight hesitation before Hamish replied. But Virginia didn't. She was trained to notice.

"It only just happened. I was about to inform the council but we had to deal with a demon attack instead," Hamish claimed. "I apologize for my tardiness."

For now, Virginia couldn't refute the statement. It was rare that she was wrong. And something was definitely wrong. She could smell it. It stank like the rotting corpse of a demon.

"Very well. I suppose congratulations are in order," she ground out through clenched teeth.

If it turned out the two weren't bonded—something she could ascertain at a later time—she would haul Hamish before the council and let him have it. Nobody pulled the wool over her eyes.

"Thank you," Hamish said, his voice icy. "If you don't mind then, my mate and I would like to retire. It's been a long night."

"Not so fast!" Virginia snapped. "There's still the matter of the witch."

"Name's Wesley." The witch grinned and walked toward her.

Did he think his charming smile would stop her from doing her job? Apparently, the cocky bastard thought she'd come to chat as if they were old friends. Never mind that the way he looked at her with his baby-blue eyes shaved off a few layers of her protective armor. Never mind that sweat was collecting on her palms. And never fucking mind that low in her groin, a second beat mirrored her heart, pounding an urgent rhythm of desire and need against a drum that only she could hear.

Fuck! She was well past *rasen*, well past the period in a Stealth Guardian's life when the call of mating season clouded a warrior's judgment. She'd never mated, and instead chosen to serve her kind in other ways. She couldn't allow *rasen* to catch up with her now.

"Stay where you are!"

To underscore her demand, Virginia placed her hand on her dagger, letting the cool obsidian handle calm her.

The witch stopped walking. "Whatever you want. Anything, really."

She tried to ignore his eyes running over her body as if he were a sculptor taking measurements. Instead, she noticed his lips parting in appreciation. She didn't dare look at the other Stealth Guardians. Would they notice what was going on between her and the witch? She had to stop this now, or everything she'd built for herself, her reputation, her iron will, would wash away just like the green blood of the last demon she'd killed had washed down a storm drain.

"You'll be interrogated. In the meantime, you'll be locked up."

"Wesley helped us with our mission," Hamish said from behind her. "Without him, we might have never been able to thwart the demons' plans to destroy Tessa's political future. He's no danger to any of us."

Virginia tossed a dismissive look over her shoulder, glad to have a genuine reason to tear her gaze from the witch. "That remains to be seen. Anybody breaching our defenses is a danger." She turned fully, scorching the guardians with her glare. "And you and your compound mates should have notified the Council of Nine immediately when the breach occurred. We had to find out from a guardian at another compound. This has not gone unnoticed. Together with the previous infractions of your motley crew, you've exhausted the council's patience."

Behind her she heard a sigh coming from the witch. "Oh, listen, Virginia, I—"

She spun around and glared at him. "That's Ms. Robson to you!" Because if she allowed him to address her in any other fashion, a familiarity could develop between them—one she couldn't allow. If that happened, she might as well stab herself with her own dagger and twist the blade for good measure.

"Ms. Robson then." He shrugged as if he didn't care what he called her. "Listen, it's really not their fault. Don't punish them for what I did."

Before she realized it, she was nose to nose with him. "You, witch, listen to me. I'm the one giving the orders. If you think you can wrap me around your little finger like you've clearly done with these dimwits, you're wrong. I'm your worst nightmare."

The warning didn't have the desired effect.

The witch grinned.

2

———————

Nightmare? More like a wet dream.

Wesley couldn't stop his imagination from taking him on a wild ride. Virginia was everything he'd ever dreamed of in a woman.

Long legs, strong and toned. A slim waist, flaring hips, firm boobs. Just the right curves everywhere. Hazel eyes with flecks of green, luscious plump lips. And then that hair. Flaming red. Like the smoldering embers of a fire.

And every time she lashed an insult at him, her voice sent a not unpleasant shiver down his spine. Not unpleasant at all.

Did she realize that her commanding nature was a huge turn-on? Or was she oblivious to the fact that he was about five seconds away from jumping her bones?

Virginia wouldn't be an easy conquest, that was certain. She would be a challenge, but he didn't mind. She was worth it. Worth the extra effort to get her into bed. Or on any flat surface. Horizontal or vertical. He didn't care.

As long as he was inside her and she was panting in ecstasy.

Because one thing was certain: he was in lust!

"What are you grinning at?"

Another spear of heat raced from his neck to his tailbone faster than a vampire could extend his fangs.

Fuck! Didn't this siren have any idea what her voice did to him? She might as well tie him up, strip him bare, and have her way with him.

"I asked you a question!"

He met her hard gaze. "Nothing. I always look like that."

"Hmm." She whipped her head to the other Stealth Guardians. "I'm locking him up until the council is convened and ready to interrogate him. I'll transport him to the council compound myself when it's time."

"That isn't necessary," Aiden dared to say.

She shot him down with one look. "I'll decide what's necessary. You and your comrades have shown poor judgment. He's my prisoner now. He'll be locked in a lead cell."

Aiden's expression turned to stone. He motioned to the door in mock-polite fashion. "Would you like me to show you the way?"

"I don't need directions," she hissed and spun around, grabbing Wesley's biceps.

Despite her firm grip, he didn't mind the touch. "Well, it's just you and me then, I guess."

She shoved him in the direction of the door, emphasizing her command by lifting her chin.

"I'd say, ladies first, but I suppose you'd rather I walk ahead of you?" He pivoted toward the door, without waiting for an answer. He opened the door, then glanced over his shoulder. "Oh, and guys, I'll have coffee and pancakes for breakfast. Black, no sugar. Appreciate it."

"Move it, witch," Virginia interrupted and marched toward him.

"Your wish is my command, Ms. Robson," he answered and stepped into the corridor, Virginia right behind him. The door slammed a second later, and her heels clickety-clacked on the stone floor. They were alone, which suited him just fine. He slowed his walk so she was only a step or two behind him.

"So, what are you planning to do with me?" he asked casually.

For a moment he thought she wouldn't answer, but then she said, "Are you deaf? You'll be brought before the council and interrogated."

He glanced over his shoulder, slowing even more so she was only a foot behind him. "What if I'd rather be interrogated by you?"

"You have no choice in the matter!" She nudged him not too gently. "Keep moving. The cell is in the basement."

"I'm well acquainted with it." Though he had no intention of spending the night there. Nevertheless, he picked up the pace and started heading down the first staircase. When he reached the landing, he stopped and turned.

"Listen, why don't you interrogate me now, and get it over with? You'll see very quickly that I'm no threat whatsoever. I'll even let you tie me up." He ran his eyes over her, contemplating the endless possibilities a little bondage session presented. "If that's what you're into."

The last word had barely left his lips when Virginia gripped his biceps and slammed him against the stone wall. The crushing impact forced all air from his lungs, making him gasp.

"You think this is a joke?"

He snatched a quick breath. His admiration for the female Stealth Guardian had just risen by a hundred points. She was no pushover. Not a woman who would be won over with a few easy compliments. She was hard as nails, and if she pressed him against the wall a little longer, her thighs touching his, her forearms pinning his torso to the stone, one part of his anatomy would be just as hard.

"No, I don't think this is a joke," Wes said as calmly as he could. "But you must admit, you're going about this a little heavy-handed, aren't you?"

Her eyes narrowed in displeasure, and she applied more pressure—not only to his chest, but also to his lower body. He had to suppress a moan, clenching his jaw to hide the fact that her treatment wasn't having the intended effect on him. Instead of intimidating him and putting him in his place, she was turning him on.

"I'm happy to answer any questions you have. I swear I'm only here to seek an alliance between your race and the company I work for. My boss at Scanguards might be a vampire, but he—"

"A vampire? You work with vampires?"

Genuine surprise made the green flecks in her irises shine like fireflies. For the first time since meeting her, her protective shell showed a hairline crack.

"I already explained all this to Aiden and the others. Guess nobody's passed the information on to you." He knew full well that neither Hamish nor Aiden had had a chance yet to talk to their superiors, but there was something about Virginia that made him want to provoke her so she lost her cool.

"Give me the summary!" she demanded.

Considering that she made no move to release him—and he did enjoy feeling her body pressed to his—he decided to go with the extended version.

"Well, since you're asking..."

She growled like a tigress.

Fuck! Pull yourself together, man!

"I was born the second of three children to a witch—"

"You do know what a summary is, don't you? Let me translate it for you: the short version!"

"This is the short version. Witch's honor."

"For the last time: summarize!"

"Fine." He attempted a shrug, but she still had him pinned too tightly. "My siblings and I were meant to be the Power of Three. A witch betrayed us. My brother Haven gave up his mortal life, became a vampire. Ergo: Power of Three went poof. Result: vampires became our allies. The end."

～

"You suck at summarizing."

Virginia let go of him and took a step back. If she'd had to spend one more second pressing her body against his, she would have forgotten why she was here and tossed the impertinent witch to the floor to ride him.

Damn it!

She'd treated plenty prisoners the way she handled Wesley, but never had she experienced any kind of sexual reaction in the process. Not so this time. Her nipples were hard and aching to be touched. She was glad she wore a leather jacket, which concealed her inappropriate response to his alluring body. She was also glad he wasn't a vampire, who would have smelled her arousal.

"I can give you the full version. Maybe over a glass of wine or whiskey?" Wesley added and smiled.

She had to grudgingly admit that he had a certain charm—and he used it to his advantage. But she wasn't stupid. This wasn't personal for him. He'd clearly used the same charm to rope the entire Baltimore compound into whatever scheme he was working on.

"Don't bother. I get what you're up to. It's not working."

"What am I up to?"

"Trying to win me over like you've done with the others." She motioned toward the floor above. "They're still young. Too green to understand all the consequences of their actions. I, on the other hand, am not."

"So, you're an experienced older woman, is that what you're trying to say?"

"I'm old enough to recognize when somebody's full of shit."

His response was unexpected. He chuckled. And damn, if that sound didn't send a shiver of pleasure down her neck and all the way to her nipples, lighting them on fire like Roman candles.

She had to get a grip of herself. Distract herself no matter how.

"You don't like witches much, do you?" he suddenly asked.

"I don't like witches who're able to breach our defenses," she shot back, not missing a beat.

"It was the only way to make contact with your kind."

"Only Stealth Guardians are able to use our portals, no other creature has ever even managed to open one, let alone operate it."

"Guess I'm a genius."

She tilted her head to the side, studying him. "Either that, or you've had help from the demons."

"What?"

"You heard me. The demons are the only other preternatural species who operate portals. If anybody might have a chance at accessing one of ours, it's them." Which was the Stealth Guardians' greatest fear. Because if the demons ever gained access to one portal, they'd have access to all of them and could destroy her race from within.

"I've never met a demon. And nobody helped me. It was a spell I cast."

"What kind of spell?"

"A transformation spell."

"That does what precisely?"

"It made the portal think I was one of you."

He looked smug, and she wanted to wipe that smugness off his face. Or perhaps kiss it away.

Stop it! Not another thought in that direction!

The faster she could get him into the lead cell, the better. So why was she still standing around here, letting him drag her into a conversation?

"Let's move it, witch. Time to lock you up."

He huffed. "Name's Wesley. It's really not that hard to remember."

Only to make him comply, she conceded, "Fine, Wesley."

"See, wasn't that hard, was it?"

Another one of his charming smiles. Did this guy ever give up?

She pointed to the next flight of stairs leading down. "This way."

Wesley followed her command, but instead of walking ahead of her, he walked alongside her. She knew if he tried to go for her dagger, she'd have no trouble overpowering him. After all, the runes that lined the walls, floors, and ceilings of the compound had stripped him of his magic. Only once he was outside again, would he gain his powers back. So why then did his closeness put her on edge? Was it because she felt another power in him? Not witchcraft, no.

The potency of a man.

When they finally arrived at the cell, Virginia was relieved. She unlocked the door and swung it open. She looked into the dark, lead-lined interior. The cell was meant for members of their kind who'd committed crimes or, worse, had been compromised by the demons. It was escape-proof. Stealth Guardians couldn't pass through lead; it stripped them of their ability to make themselves invisible and drained them of their strength. Eventually, if locked up in a lead cell for an extended period, a Stealth Guardian's powers would be extinguished for good and they would become human.

She'd heard of cases where Stealth Guardians had been locked up for a year—punishment for treason—then released into the human world, outcasts to their race. A harsh sentence.

"So, you're really not gonna change your mind, huh?"

At Wesley's words, she met his gaze. His baby-blues locked with hers. For a moment she felt hypnotized. And for a fraction of a second she wondered what would have happened between them had they met under different circumstances.

A soft smile suddenly curled the corners of his mouth upward. "One day you will."

His gait confident, his head held high, he walked into the cell. Once inside, he turned around. "You're an interesting woman, Virginia. I'm looking forward to getting to know you..." He paused, his gaze dropping to her lips. "...more intimately."

Cocky bastard!

As if he knew what effect he had on her! As if he could see right through her.

Trembling—whether with rage or arousal, she wasn't sure—she slammed the heavy door shut and turned the key in the lock.

Her heart pounded, and she leaned against the door, when she heard his voice through it.

"Sweet dreams, Virginia."

A chuckle followed.

This witch would be her downfall if she wasn't careful.

3

———

Impatiently, Zoltan paced in front of the lava pit in his study. Impatiently, because he'd received word a few hours earlier that the two demons he'd sent on a secret mission had made a discovery they had to convey to him in person.

A knock at his door. Finally!

Zoltan pressed against a pebble protruding from the mantel around the lava pit, and a flat stone slid over the fire, covering it entirely.

He sat back behind his desk. "Come!"

The door swung open. The first demon to enter was Vintoq, his right hand, a tall man with thick, dark hair. He'd chosen Vintoq as his main advisor shortly after taking power, because he seemed smarter than his brethren. He wasn't just a follower—he contributed ideas and suggestions, showing initiative.

"Oh Great One, you asked that Ulric and Fletcher be brought to you the moment they returned," Vintoq said, his green eyes like beacons in the darkness. Those eyes, the only outward sign of a demon's nature, were also their Achilles' heel. Because it made them immediately recognizable to the Stealth Guardians.

"Have them come in."

Vintoq looked over his shoulder and motioned toward the dark corridor behind him. Seconds later, two more demons entered. Ulric was on the stouter side with small, beadlike eyes and a full head of blond hair, attesting to his Viking heritage. Fletcher, the other demon who now, like Ulric, bowed his head in greeting, was taller and darker.

Zoltan nodded at Vintoq. "Close the door."

When Vintoq reached for the door, Zoltan added, "From the outside."

Vintoq complied quickly, bowing on his way out. Zoltan would fill him in later after he'd fully formulated his plan. But first he had to find out whether Ulric and Fletcher had returned with actionable intelligence.

"Rise!" he commanded.

The two demons lifted their heads instantly. "Oh Great One," they said in unison.

"Hmm." Zoltan rose from behind his desk. "What do you have for me?"

Ulric stepped forward. "Your hunch proved fruitful. We found the location."

Zoltan's heart pounded with excitement. His efforts had paid off. "You found their stronghold?"

Ulric nodded. "One of their strongholds. We can't be certain of its importance, but it's one of their compounds. If we can penetrate it—"

Zoltan lifted his hand. "I know we can. But first things first. Show me where it is."

Ulric produced a sheet of paper, unfolded it, and walked to the desk, placing it in front of Zoltan. It was a portion of a map. He studied it for a moment, focusing on the cross Ulric had made at one spot.

Zoltan looked up. "How many guardians were present?"

Ulric exchanged a helpless look with Fletcher.

Fletcher gave a shrug. "We were unable to investigate further without risking detection."

Zoltan contemplated his words for a moment. "I want you to take three of your men and return to these coordinates. Make it clear to everybody that this is a reconnaissance mission only. Don't attack. All I want you to do is get the lay of the land. Number of guardians, portals, weapons. I want an overview of the compound, entrances, exits, places to hide. Everything. Don't get caught."

"But how do we get in?" Ulric asked.

"You have the location. You only need a visual to be able to project your vortex." With a vortex, a demon could travel anywhere he wished —as long as he had a clear visual of the destination. Luckily, getting a clear visual was much easier these days with the Internet and Google street view.

"But the compound is hidden, invisible," Ulric said.

"But it's there. Find the outer walls. Touch them," Zoltan advised. "Then project your vortex and concentrate your mind on a spot a few yards behind the wall as your destination."

It was risky, and there was no guarantee that his subjects wouldn't transport directly into a stone wall that would crush them to death. But he was willing to take that risk. It was worth sacrificing a few demons as long as one came back to report on the Stealth Guardians' defenses.

"Yes, oh Great One," Ulric said.

Fletcher added, "It will be done."

"Leave, and send Vintoq in."

The two demons bowed and left. A moment later, Vintoq entered.

"You wanted to see me?"

"We have work to do, Vintoq. Soon we'll be able to destroy the Stealth Guardians for good." He laughed. "And then nobody will be able to prevent my ruling the earth."

He would not only be ruler of the demons, but ruler of all mankind.

Soon, every living creature in this world would bow to him, Zoltan, the Great One.

4

———————

While a night in the cell wasn't exactly what Wesley had planned, he wasn't complaining. The back of his prison housed a rudimentary shower, sink, and toilet, and the cot wasn't quite as hard as he'd expected. He'd woken early and showered, glad that he'd borrowed fresh clothes from Aiden the day before. At least he was clean and presentable.

Funny that that was his biggest concern: to look good for Virginia, even though she'd given him the cold shoulder the night before. But he wasn't easily discouraged.

When he finally heard footsteps coming toward his cell, his heart began to beat excitedly. He combed his fingers through his hair, smoothing it down, and took a deep breath, readying himself for the hot Stealth Guardian woman in her Catwoman outfit. Man, was she sexy! All night he'd had the image in his head, leaving him with a permanent hard-on.

The key turned in the lock.

Wesley's pulse raced; at this rate, it could win the Kentucky Derby.

Finally, the wait was over, and the door swung open. The silhouette wasn't Virginia's. Too tall, too broad.

"You wanted pancakes, didn't you?" Aiden stood at the entrance, a breakfast tray in his hands. "Hope you won't mind if I don't come in, but lead doesn't exactly agree with me. Sucks all the energy right out of me."

Wes tucked that piece of information away for later use and approached the friendly guardian.

"Thanks, really appreciate it. If it were up to Virginia, I'd probably starve." Wesley snatched the cup of coffee from the tray and took a big gulp of the hot liquid, feeling it revive him.

"Careful with her," Aiden cautioned, leaning in and lowering his voice. "She was an enforcer before she joined the council. She could go totally Rambo on you. You wouldn't stand a chance. So be careful what you say to her."

Wes grinned and took a pancake, folded it, and shoved it into his mouth. He'd already gotten a taste of Virginia's attitude. He swallowed. "So, an enforcer, huh? She can enforce me all she wants."

Aiden's eyes widened, and the scar above his eyebrow seemed to twitch. "Are you crazy? Don't play with that woman! She means business."

Wes smirked. "So do I. Don't worry, I know how to handle women like her. She'll be purring like a kitten in no time."

"Totally insane. I should have known it. I should have seen it the minute you showed up here." He shook his head. "Why the fuck would you want to get into her pants? She eats men for breakfast."

Wes chuckled. "Right up my alley, just like I thought."

"Insane. And I even bothered calling my father to put in a good word for you. But you're a lost cause."

Wes chased his second pancake with a gulp of coffee. "Your father? What's he got to do with this?"

"He's *Primus* of the council."

"Primus?"

Aiden huffed impatiently. "Like chairman, you know. He has a lot of influence."

"Cool. Well, thanks for talking to him. I really appreciate it. You're a friend."

"Yeah, a friend who's going to regret really soon that he trusted you," Aiden hissed. "You won't do your case any favors by making a pass at Virginia. She's a council member, and though she's new, she has a vote. She only has to turn four other council members against you, and your fate is sealed."

"What's that supposed to mean? What could they possibly do to me?"

"Execute you for breaching our defenses."

Not exactly a prospect he relished. "Well, in that case, I'd better make sure Virginia takes a liking to me."

Aiden rolled his eyes and pressed the tray into Wesley's hands. "Why am I wasting my breath?" He reached for the door to close it, as another figure appeared in the corridor: Virginia.

Wes shoved the tray back at Aiden, wiped his hands on his pants and took a step into the corridor.

"Lost cause," Aiden murmured even more quietly and turned away.

"Morning, Virginia," Wes greeted his jailor with a smile, and ran his eyes over her.

"What's he doing out of his cell?"

Aiden lifted the tray in his hands by way of explanation. "Man's gotta eat. And I for sure ain't stepping into that cell."

Virginia seemed to accept the excuse, then finally looked at Wesley directly. "The council is ready to hear your case."

So much for having time to influence Virginia's opinion of him. He'd hoped for a little delay. "That was fast."

"They are quite eager to find out how you were able to use the portal," she said to his surprise.

It seemed Virginia was feeling a little more talkative today than the previous night. Could he exploit that fact somehow?

"And I'm just as eager to make their acquaintance," Wes lied.

He would have preferred to spend more time here at the compound, or even better, alone with Virginia, to work his charm on her. He knew she'd eventually give in; he just needed time. Apparently, he was fresh out of time.

"Let's go," Virginia ordered.

"Have a pleasant trip," Aiden said.

Wes met his gaze and saw the warning it carried. *Don't do anything stupid.*

Would I ever? Wes mouthed.

With an exaggerated eyeroll, Aiden pivoted and walked away.

Virginia motioned to a second corridor.

"We're taking the portal, I assume?" Wes asked, recognizing where it led as he walked along, Virginia right next to him.

"It's the fastest and safest way. I don't want to spend endless hours on a plane."

"So, it's far then?" He didn't really care, but he wanted to keep her talking.

"That's not for you to know."

Hmm. Apparently, that had been a bad question. "So, you don't like planes?"

"I have nothing against planes."

"Then why wouldn't you want to fly? Frankly, I found being tossed around like a ragdoll in that portal a little unsettling."

She cast him a sideways look. "Because it would mean spending endless hours with you."

He laughed. "I walked into that one, didn't I?"

He'd seen it coming. He knew playing the hapless fool had its charms and worked on many women—humans and vampires alike. He'd gotten laid plenty of times, because women had found him cute and not at all threatening. Little did they know that under the happy-go-lucky attitude lay the iron will of an alpha male.

Seducing women had always been a pleasurable pastime, a hobby. Seducing Virginia would be nothing of the kind. It would be a critical mission, not because he needed to forge an alliance with her kind, but because the alpha in him wanted her like he wanted his next breath.

"Get in!"

Virginia's order interrupted his musings. They'd reached the portal. The door or whatever they called the entrance was already open. He nodded and walked into the dark, cave-like space. It was no larger than a hotel elevator capable of carrying eight people.

Virginia joined him, and a second later, all went dark. The opening had closed.

He was bracing himself to be tossed around again, when Virginia took his arm. His heart stopped for a brief moment. What the fuck was happening? Was she finally responding to his charm? Was she giving him a sign that she was interested?

Hell, he wouldn't turn down a little fumble in the dark!

"So, you like it in the dark, huh?" he murmured, and put his other arm around her waist, drawing her to him. "I don't mind that at all."

"What the fuck are you doing?" she ground out and yanked his arm off her, keeping a tight grip on his biceps with her other hand.

Totally confused, he stuttered, "But, but you were touching me. I thought..."

"Goddamn it! You thought I—?" She stopped herself. "Hell no! I have to touch you to take you with me. If I didn't, you'd stay right here."

"Oh."

Well, that was a tad embarrassing. But he shrugged it off like he shrugged off any minor setback. It would have been too good to be true. But another opportunity would present itself soon. He wasn't giving up hope yet. After all, it had taken him years to learn his craft as a witch, and he'd had many setbacks on the way. He was used to trying again and again. Particularly when the reward was worth it.

All subsequent thoughts vanished, because in that moment he was tossed into the air like clothes in a dryer. "Ah fuck! I'm not a wet sock!"

"Easy, we're nearly there." Virginia's voice was surprisingly soothing, as was the fact that suddenly both her hands were on him, steadying him.

He concentrated on her touch and nothing else, blocking out the feeling of tumbling in space. Maybe traveling through the portal wasn't so bad after all.

5

———

Virginia let go of Wesley's arms.

They'd arrived at their destination. But she needed a few moments to steady herself—and not because of the ride in the portal. As a Stealth Guardian she didn't experience the disorientation that humans and other creatures seemed prone to when traveling this way. However, touching Wesley, something she'd been forced to do to transport him with her, had sent a tingling feeling from her palms through her entire body. A not at all unpleasant tingling feeling. And that unnerved her.

His muscles had tensed under her touch, and she'd felt their strength. Despite the fact that he wasn't as strong as she, it was clear that this man took care of his body, trained it to gain physical strength that didn't automatically come with being a witch. Stealth guardians, demons, and vampires, yes, their physical strength was part of their nature. But a witch's body wasn't much different from that of a human. Only their knowledge of magic made them dangerous. Of course, within the walls of the Stealth Guardians' compounds, magic couldn't exist.

Then why did she feel as if she was under his spell whenever he looked at her with those baby-blue eyes? Did he have other powers, powers she had no defenses against?

"Something wrong?" Wesley asked all of a sudden.

"We're here." She jerked her thumb behind them, where the portal had already opened.

"Thanks for the ride." He smirked and turned around to leave the portal.

She was glad for it, because his words had conjured up an altogether different kind of *ride*, a ride that involved her straddling a naked witch. And the image made her cheeks blaze with fire. Forcing the thoughts out of her mind, she exited the portal.

Wesley stood in the corridor, waiting for her.

"Funny," he said and shook his head. "No alarm. It went off like gangbusters when I used the portal the first time."

Virginia nodded. "Because you used it alone. The presence of a Stealth Guardian overrides the alarm."

"Interesting."

Hmm. Maybe she shouldn't have told him that. Too late. Not that he would be able to do anything with it. He couldn't very well overpower her or any other member of her species and force that person to operate the portal for him.

"So, where are we?"

"At the council compound."

"And where's that?"

Virginia scoffed. "Do you really think I would tell you? Only the Stealth Guardians know its location. Not even their human mates are privy to that information. So, I'm sure as hell not gonna give it to you."

Wesley shrugged as if it didn't matter to him. "Just making conversation."

She didn't believe that for a second. "Sure." Then she tilted her head toward one of the corridors. "This way."

He turned, but waited until she was next to him, before he started walking. Knowing that any escape attempt would be futile, she didn't insist on having him walk ahead of her. She could watch him just as well from the side. At least this way, she wouldn't have to look at his tight backside, which filled his pants in a way that should be illegal.

The walk was a short one, two corridors, two flights of stairs, and they reached the double doors to the council chambers. In front of it, a warrior was standing sentry. He nodded at her, a sign that he recognized her.

Virginia stopped a few feet away from him. Wesley did the same. "Is the Council of Nine assembled?" she asked.

"Yes, Counselor Robson. They are ready for you." He stretched his hand out. "Any electronic devices, please."

Without hesitating, she pulled her cell phone from her pocket and handed it to the guard. When he looked at Wesley, Virginia shook her head. "The prisoner's phone has already been confiscated. It's still at the compound we came from."

The guard nodded and placed Virginia's device into a niche next to the double doors. The cell phones of the other council members lay there, too. It was a security measure: no recording devices were allowed in the chambers, so the council members could speak freely.

The guard opened the double doors. "Go right in."

Virginia nodded to him, then motioned Wesley to enter with her. The door shut quietly behind them.

When they entered the council chamber, the councilors were talking quietly amongst themselves. Now, all their murmuring ceased, and eight pairs of eyes landed on her and her prisoner.

"Primus," she said. "Fellow council members."

"Virginia, we received your report," Barclay, the head of the Council of Nine replied. "Take your seat, and we'll start."

"Would you like me to give you some background first?" she asked.

Barclay shook his head. "Not necessary. Your report from last night was quite comprehensive." He gestured to the empty seat at the half-moon-shaped table.

Knowing what was expected of her, she took her seat, leaving

Wesley standing, facing the nine members of the Guardians' governing body.

"So, you're the witch," Barclay started.

Wesley smiled. "Name's Wesley Montgomery."

Barclay glanced at the notes in front of him. "Yes, so I hear. Our understanding is that you were able to use one of our portals to invade our Baltimore compound."

Wesley shrugged. "Invade is a harsh word. I visited."

Several council members snorted in displeasure.

"Let's not mince words. I have a detailed report here about what you did on your *visit* to the Baltimore compound. According to this you were of great help to the warriors there. Because of it, I'm giving you the benefit of the doubt."

Virginia snapped her head in Barclay's direction. Her report had said nothing about Wesley being of great help. It could only mean that one of the guardians at the compound had contacted Barclay behind her back. And she had no doubt about who had done so: after all, Aiden was Primus's son.

She gritted her teeth. So Wesley had buttered up Aiden to help him put a good word in with Barclay.

"Now explain to me and my fellow council members how you were able to operate the portal," Barclay demanded.

"Well," Wesley started, shifting his weight to the other foot. "Wish I could explain it myself, but—"

"Spare us your dillydallying, witch!" Geoffrey snapped. "Primus might be in a lenient mood today, but the rest of us are not."

Wesley visibly swallowed. He took on a different tone, and continued, "My apologies, sir. What I meant to say was that I was quite surprised that what I did actually worked. You see, about two weeks ago, I saw one of your kind disappear into a portal in the woods of Sonoma. He saw me, too, so it shouldn't be too hard to verify my story. I did some research, and I found references to your species in some of my old books. The texts described the guardians as a race of warriors dedicated to the protection of the innocent from evil supernatural forces. If that's true, I figured you might be the kind of people who would be interested in an alliance with Scanguards."

"Mmm," Geoffrey murmured, then looked at the other council members. "Do we have any information on Scanguards?"

Barclay tapped his finger on the piece of paper in front of him. "An emissarius has been dispatched. We're waiting for more information." Then he looked at Wesley again. "Continue."

"Anyway, I decided to try to make contact. And since the portal was my only lead, I started there. I've been experimenting with transformation spells."

"Transformation spells?" Norton, another council member asked.

"Yes, it's a spell that puts oneself into a trancelike state during which one can take on the attributes of another species. It's of a very short duration, seconds only, a minute at most, but it was sufficient to make the portal believe that I was a Stealth Guardian, not a witch. It opened for me, but I have no idea how I landed in Baltimore. That's the God's honest truth. I was tumbling around in there without any idea how to steer the thing."

Virginia suppressed the awe she felt at the witch's skills, keeping her stern expression in place. He was powerful, no doubt. And that made him dangerous.

"Interesting," Barclay mused and glanced at the assembled. "Any questions?"

Riona raised her hand and upon Barclay's nod, asked, "The guardian this witch saw, has he been identified yet, so he can corroborate this story?"

Virginia cleared her throat. "The Baltimore compound sent a message to the other compounds inquiring about this incident. It's the reason we were notified in the first place. At least at other compounds, guardians follow the rules—"

"Yes, Virginia," Barclay interrupted. "We're quite aware that rules have been broken. We'll get to that later." He glanced past her at Riona. "To get back to your question, Riona, we believe that a guardian from the Seattle compound will be able to confirm the witch's story—"

"Name's still Wesley," the prisoner piped up.

A collective gasp traveled through the assembled. Nobody interrupted Primus.

Barclay tossed him a glare, then turned his gaze back to the council members. "I've sent for the guardian in question. He'll be arriving shortly. Any further questions before we begin discussions?"

Nobody spoke up.

Barclay pressed a button on the table. A moment later, the door opened and a guard entered.

"Primus?"

"Lock the prisoner up."

The guard approached, but Wesley took several steps toward the table. "But you haven't heard me out yet. I'm here to propose a potential alliance between your kind and Scanguards; you haven't let me explain!"

"There will be time for that later." Barclay looked at the guard again. "Take him to his cell."

"But—"

For a moment, Virginia felt a twinge of regret at seeing Wesley dragged away. Were they being too harsh on him? Or was Barclay right in exercising extreme caution when it came to the witch?

If only she knew whether Wesley's words could be trusted.

Or whether he was putting on the greatest performance the world had ever seen, fooling them all.

6

———

Nearly an hour went by without the council reaching any kind of consensus. The guardian from Seattle had come and gone. He had confirmed that he'd observed Wesley working together with several vampires to put down a group of rogue vampires who'd tried to flood the market with dangerous drugs. Believing that these drugs, which facilitated mind control over a long distance, should not fall into the hands of the demons, the guardian had advised the witch to destroy the drugs and all traces of the vampires' operation. A follow-up visit to the woods of Sonoma had confirmed that Wesley had indeed done so.

That knowledge helped ease the minds of some of the council members, including Virginia.

However, there was another, much bigger concern on everybody's mind. A concern that could put their very existence at risk: how the witch had been able to use the portal.

Nobody could explain how a spell could overcome the portal's fail-safe controls and allow a non-guardian to operate it. Assumptions were raised and then tossed out. Ideas were shared, then rejected. Yet, one thing was clear: they couldn't allow the witch to leave for fear that he might teach others how to penetrate their defenses.

"Then what do we do with him?" Cinead, the oldest and one of the wisest of the council members finally asked.

"The way I see it, we have two choices: lock him up for good, or kill him," Ian proclaimed.

The latter choice sent a cold shiver down Virginia's spine. As much as she didn't trust Wesley, could she really vote to kill him? Never before had she hesitated to execute a prisoner if it was warranted, so why was she hesitating now? Had he somehow wormed his way under her skin, penetrating her defenses, just like he'd penetrated the compound?

"There's a third choice," Barclay said.

Virginia stared at him, as did the other council members. "Yes?"

"We let him go and follow him. See where he leads us."

Immediately, everybody started talking. Virginia remained silent. While Barclay's suggestion was unorthodox and dangerous, it was nevertheless feasible. It was easy for a member of their species to follow anybody—after all, invisibility lent itself to such a task. If anybody could follow a witch without being discovered, it was a Stealth Guardian. Still, the idea was fraught with danger. Too many things could go wrong.

The voices in the chamber grew louder, reaching a fever pitch. Virginia jumped up, trying to get the others' attention.

She didn't succeed.

Because something else caught everybody's attention first. Strobe lights suddenly flashed overhead, followed by a loud shrill sound, which drowned out the conversations in the room.

A computer voice followed. *"Intruder detected. Security breached."*

"Fuck!" Virginia cursed.

The alarm continued. *"Intruder detected. Security breached."*

Everybody jumped up.

"Initiate security protocol!" Barclay ordered.

The double doors flung open and two guards charged in. "Demon attack!"

"Is that confirmed?" Virginia yelled at the guard who'd spoken, running toward him.

"Confirmed."

"How many?"

"We don't know yet," the guard replied, as the second guard issued orders. "Council members, to the portal, now!"

"Quickly!" Barclay yelled.

It was essential that the Council of Nine survive the attack, but Virginia had been a warrior for too long. She couldn't just run. She had to stay and fight.

"You go," she said to Barclay. "I'll make sure the witch pays for this!"

Barclay grabbed her arm. "You don't know that this is his doing."

"Wake up, Primus! Nobody's ever breached our defenses before. And the moment I bring this witch here, the demons attack? That's no coincidence. I'll make him pay, even if it's the last thing I do."

Virginia ripped free of Barclay's hold and charged out of the council chamber. Guards were swarming the corridors, running in one direction. She raced past them, veered off into the next hallway, then barreled down one flight of stairs, toward the cell.

She'd let her feelings—her irrational physical attraction to a damn witch—cloud her judgment like a fogged mirror. She'd been ready to volunteer shadowing him to find out what he was up to. She'd been prepared to give him the benefit of the doubt. But she had no doubts any longer.

Somehow, Wesley Montgomery had led the demons to their stronghold.

And for that he'd pay with his life.

Virginia ran faster, hoping she wasn't too late, hoping the demons hadn't already freed their accomplice from the lead cell.

As she approached, she heard Wesley's voice echoing in the corridor.

"Hey! What's going on there? Somebody get me out of here!" he yelled through the slit in the door. "Can anybody hear me?"

"I can hear you," she murmured to herself. "Don't you worry. I'll take care of you."

With one hand she pulled her dagger from the sheath at her hip, with the other, she unlocked the door and yanked it open.

"Thank God it's—" His voice died mid-sentence, his gaze pinning the dagger in her hand. "What the fuck?" He stumbled backward, farther into the cell.

"You led the demons to us! You're dead, witch!" She lunged at him, following him into the lead cell. A mistake, she realized immediately, but she was armed, and he wasn't, and if she was quick about it...

"Virginia, don't!" Wesley yelled, throwing his arms up in defense, blocking her dagger.

Shit! She should have had no trouble killing him with one well-aimed thrust.

But the lead in the cell was already starting to drain her supernatural powers. No matter. She would still kill him.

Again, she lunged at him.

WESLEY DUCKED SIDEWAYS. Virginia meant business. She really wanted to kill him. The dagger in her hand said as much. And if that wasn't enough, her eyes spewed pure venom.

"Shit, Virginia! I don't wanna hurt you!" Though he had to defend himself.

"But I wanna hurt you!"

He walked backward, and like two fighters in a ring, they started circling each other. Somehow, he had to get her to listen to him. Before she managed to drive that dagger into his flesh.

"Please, Virginia. I've done nothing."

"You led the demons to us. It was you!" she hissed. "It couldn't have been anybody else. I don't know how you did it. But you did."

"No! I would never hurt you or your people. You have to believe me."

"Liar!"

She charged toward him, and he had no choice but to act. He deflected the dagger by raising his arm and pushing against her, driving her back. The move was surprisingly easy, as if she wasn't trying very hard. Why wasn't she using her supernatural powers against him? She could have easily smashed him against the wall and pinned him there, slit him open with her dagger without much effort. What was holding her back?

When she jumped toward him again, he managed to grab her dagger hand, wrapping his hand around her wrist and thus disabling her. She tried to pull free of him, but failed.

That's when it hit him: the lead cell. Aiden hadn't wanted to enter it either. What had he said? Something about the lead draining his energy. Wes realized it then: being inside the cell was weakening Virginia. It meant he had a chance.

"Fuck, Virginia! Stop this. I'm not gonna hurt you." How could he when he wanted nothing more than to kiss her?

"You betrayed us!" She glared at him. "You're a dead man!"

She kneed him in the balls, a move he hadn't seen coming.

"Ugh!"

He doubled over. Clearly, even in her weakened state, she was still a respectable warrior.

He'd lost. Shit!

Maybe he should have heeded his boss's warning. But he'd been cocky, thinking his charm could get him out of any jam. Apparently not. He was about to die at the hands of a woman he lusted after. What irony!

When he heard a sound, he lifted his head to look his killer in the eye. But Virginia was spinning around, looking toward the cell door. A figure darkened it.

"Fuck!" Virginia cursed.

Though Wes couldn't see the guy's face, he saw two green lights flickering where his eyes had to be. An altogether different kind of green than the flecks of emerald in Virginia's eyes. An unnatural green. He'd spent sufficient time with the guardians at the Baltimore compound to know that those were green demon eyes—the only outward sign of a demon.

Virginia was already charging toward the attacker, dagger in hand. The guy was massive. And while Virginia wasn't exactly petite, but tall and clearly a well-trained warrior, she was weaker inside the cell. It was evident. Which meant he had no choice but to help her defeat the demon—or they would both die.

"Crap!" Wes grunted and barreled after her.

In the dim light of the cell, Virginia was exchanging blows with the demon. It was immediately clear that her enemy was stronger. Somehow Wes had to try to divert the demon's attention from her so she could slip past him and draw him outside, where she'd be stronger. He could only hope that once outside the cell, her strength would immediately return, or they'd still be fucked.

"Hey coward, fight somebody your own size," Wes yelled.

The taunt made the demon whirl his head to glare at Wes. With a dismissive huff, he turned his attention back to Virginia. The second's distraction hadn't done anything to improve her situation. She could barely keep her attacker at bay, kicking him, trying to land blows and thrusting with her dagger hand. To no avail. The demon landed punch after punch.

"Shit!"

With a yell akin to an Indian war cry, Wesley jumped and kicked his leg high up where it connected with the demon's forearm, preventing him from thrusting his dagger into Virginia's chest. But instead of losing his grip on the weapon, the animal pivoted and lunged at Wes.

"Ah fuck!" Wes dove to the left, out of the demon's path not a second too soon, tumbling and rolling. He found his footing again a moment later and spun around, arms wide, legs in a fighting stance, but the demon had already lost interest and charged toward Virginia again.

Wes watched the demon fling her against the wall and go after her.

Somewhat dazed, Virginia tried to land on her feet but failed. Her dagger clattered to the stone floor and she lunged for it. The demon got there first, his foot landing on the dagger's hilt.

Virginia lifted her head, staring up at the demon. "Shit."

"Ah fuck it!" Wes grunted and jumped the demon from behind, wrapping his arms around the guy's neck in an attempt to choke him. But the asshole was too strong. Wes could only hold on for dear life while the demon tried to shake him off.

"Get out of the cell, Virginia! Run!" he yelled, just as the demon managed to pry Wesley's arms off him and fling him into a corner.

Immediately, the demon ran straight after Virginia, who was racing into the corridor.

With the door clear of any obstruction now, light from the corridor briefly reflected on something on the floor. Wes snapped his head toward it. The dagger. Virginia hadn't managed to take it. And without a weapon, she wouldn't have a chance against the demon.

Wes staggered to his feet and snatched the dagger, then charged out of the cell.

What he saw nearly stopped his heart. The demon had Virginia pinned to the floor. She was struggling, kicking and punching to save her life, but her attacker's dagger was getting closer and closer to her neck. How much longer could she hold him off?

Wes lunged at the demon, aiming his foot at the demon's head, kicking it like David Beckham. The demon's head snapped to the side, and the momentum flung him sideways, lifting him off Virginia. But Wes knew the guy wasn't defeated yet. He jumped onto him and plunged Virginia's dagger into the demon's heart. Twisted it. Drove it deeper.

"Go to hell!"

Breathing hard, still on top of the demon, who was gurgling

helplessly now, Wes saw green blood spill from the wound. Disgusted, he jumped up before the vile liquid could stain him.

Without taking his eyes off the dying demon, Wes asked, "Are you okay, Virginia?"

He heard her getting to her feet and chanced a look at her. She seemed unhurt.

"Talk to me, Virginia."

She walked toward him, unsteady at first.

"You killed the demon."

Wes stared at the creature. He wasn't moving anymore. No sound. No breath. Just green blood staining the stone floor, the hilt of the dagger sticking out from his chest.

"Yeah, he's dead."

"Why did you kill him?"

Wes tossed her a questioning look. "What the fuck?"

"If this is a ruse to make me trust you..."

"A ruse?"

"Yeah, to save me from a demon so I'll believe you're not working with them."

For an instant, he stood there frozen in stunned disbelief. Then he shook his head and raised his arms in defeat.

"You know what, Virginia? I've had it. I'm at the end of my wits. Go ahead, kill me. Do whatever you want to me, because clearly, no matter what I do—save your hide, risk my life for you, or whatever else—you're never gonna believe me anyway. Just put me out of my misery."

Suddenly she grabbed him and pressed him against the wall, pinning him there.

He met her penetrating gaze, trying to read her intentions. "Virginia?"

"Shut up, witch!"

Her lips were on his a split second later, paralyzing him. For a moment, he couldn't even react, too surprised by her action. But then his instincts kicked in, and he wrapped his arms around her, holding her to him. He kissed her hard. Then he separated his mouth from hers.

"Name's still Wesley."

He didn't give her time to respond. Instead, he slanted his lips over her mouth and took what he'd wanted from the moment he first laid eyes on her. Her lips softened under his demand and parted to accept his invasion.

Virginia was different from what he'd expected. The tough warrior with the will of steel was gone. In its stead was a woman who molded her tantalizing body to his as if her life depended on it. As if she submitted to him without question.

Her lips tasted of hunger, her tongue of need, and her breath of desire. With every slide of his tongue against hers, with every swipe against her teeth, every press of his lips to hers, the fire inside him intensified. He'd kissed a lot of women, slept with more than he cared to remember, but rarely had a woman ignited such need in him. Or roused his cock so rapidly. Because, boy, was he hard.

Wes slid his hand down to Virginia's leather-encased ass and jerked her against his hard-on, needing to show her what she did to him. She moaned into his mouth, a reaction he welcomed. Maybe she was finally accepting that he had no intention of hurting her. That his intentions were of an entirely different nature and involved them being naked and clinched in an altogether different battle: the battle of who would make whom come first.

And why not start with their clothes on? Determined to make this headstrong redhead surrender to him in every way, Wes grabbed her ass with both hands and rubbed his cock against her center. Even through her leather pants he could feel her heat.

Virginia was more passionate than he'd expected, even for a redhead. She was fire personified. Hot to the touch. Sizzling hot. Nothing could stop him now. He didn't care what it took, but to make Virginia climax in his arms was his mission now. It didn't matter that they were in a corridor, with a dead demon lying at their feet, where anybody could come upon them. He couldn't waste this opportunity.

He had to show Virginia that she could trust him. And what better way to do that than by showing her what pleasure he could bestow on her?

Beep-beep-beep.

The high-pitched sound nearly pierced his eardrum.

Beep-beep-beep.

"*Evacuate,*" a computer voice announced from somewhere in the ceiling.

Virginia stopped moving against him and ripped her lips from his. "Shit!"

7
___

Virginia gave Wesley a quick shove, forcing him to release her. She'd been about thirty seconds away from climaxing, and it had taken her nearly two seconds to realize what the beeping sound meant—so dazed had she been.

"What's going on?" Wesley asked, his eyes darting up and down the corridor, then back to her. "Virginia, what is that?"

"Self-destruct. The compound's gonna blow." She grabbed his arm and dragged him with her. "Run!"

"Fuck," he cursed, and raced alongside her down the long corridor.

"We have to make it to the portal," she said, motioning to where the corridor intersected with another. "This way!"

"Evacuate!" the computer voice repeated.

"How long do we have?" Wes asked as they charged into the next corridor.

"I don't know. Maybe thirty seconds." Barely enough time to get out.

Just then, the computer voice announced, *"Fifteen seconds till detonation."*

"Guess it's fifteen seconds," she corrected herself. Even less of a chance to make it.

"And there I was worried we didn't have enough time," Wes responded dryly.

"Down the stairs!" Virginia yelled.

She raced ahead, Wes on her heels. When she reached the landing, she didn't even break her stride and lunged toward the wall only ten feet away.

"Ten seconds till detonation," the computer voice taunted her.

The only thing identifying the portal was an ancient dagger carved into the stone wall.

"Nine," the countdown continued.

She slammed her hand onto the carved dagger and felt heat build beneath her palm.

"Eight."

The portal recognized her, yet everything seemed to take longer than usual.

"Seven."

She looked over her shoulder, seeing with relief that Wes had reached her.

"Six."

Finally, the wall disappeared. The portal was open.

"Five."

Virginia grabbed Wesley's arm and dragged him inside with her.

"Four."

"Whatever you do, hold onto me. Don't let go," she urged him.

"Not a chance."

She willed the portal to close, but for some reason it didn't. "Shit!"

"Three."

She concentrated again, taking a deep breath this time, trying to clear her mind.

"Two."

Suddenly, it was dark around them. She heaved a sigh of relief. The portal had closed.

The next sound was muffled, but even through the closed portal, she could still hear it: *"One."*

She felt Wesley grip her more tightly, one arm around her waist, one holding on to her bicep. Ignoring his presence for a moment, she willed her mind to concentrate on their destination. Away from the demons, away from the compound that had been compromised.

The explosion hit with such power that the walls of the portal shook. She was flung in the air. Wesley's arm around her waist slipped. Panicked she reached for him, slung both arms around him to hold on to him. She felt him do the same, wrapping his arms around her like a vise.

Another explosion rocked the portal. Cracks split the stone walls.

"Shit!" she cursed.

Then the entire portal seemed to be lifted into the air, tossed around like a pebble in a rockslide. All she could do was hold on to Wesley and hope they survived.

Fucking demons! If she could, she'd charge right into the demon's lair and slaughter every single one of them.

"If we're gonna die, just wanted you to know that I've never had a better kiss," Wesley suddenly said.

Tears welled in her eyes and despite their perilous situation, she managed to bury her face in the crook of his neck. "Oh Wes, I—"

The feeling of sudden freefall cut off her words and made a scream burst from her lips.

"Aaaaaahhhh!" Wes yelled.

The impact knocked the wind out of her and ripped her out of Wesley's arms. She'd landed on hard rock, groaning in pain. At least it meant she was alive.

"Wesley?" She lifted her head, searching for him.

He lay only a few feet away from her. He, too, had landed on rocky ground. It was dark, though a glimmer of light shone through a crack in their stone surroundings. Were they still in the rubble of the council compound? Or had they made it out? She tried to get her bearings, but the explosion had clearly destroyed the entire compound and left only a pile of rock.

Wesley suddenly lifted his head. "Did we make it?" He patted his chest and thighs. "Are you hurt?"

She shook her head. "I'm good. Did you break anything?"

He sat up and groaned. "Don't think so. Where are we?" He looked around, then stared in the direction of the light source.

"Not sure yet." She looked closer at the rock formations around them, then let her hand glide over a dark, smooth surface. "Lava rock." To her knowledge the council compound was constructed of limestone. Nobody had ever mentioned anything about lava rock. "That's strange."

"What?" Wesley sounded instantly alarmed.

"Touch the stone."

He shrugged. "What am I supposed to feel?"

"It's lava that's hardened to rock." She was certain of it now. "We're not in the council compound anymore."

"Well, I guess that's good news. We made it out." He leaned closer. "Thanks to you."

"Don't thank me yet." She staggered to her feet, and felt some aches and pains. Nothing that wouldn't heal quickly.

She took a few steps toward the large boulder, when she heard Wes get up and join her. He took her arm. "Wait."

Virginia looked over her shoulder.

"We'll figure out together where we are." He smiled. "You're not getting rid of me that easily."

"I wasn't trying—"

"I know," he interrupted and let go of her arm, only to take her hand and twine his fingers with hers.

For the first time in a long time she was glad not to be alone. She stopped herself short from saying so out loud. Had she hit her head or was it Wesley's kiss that had rendered her all emotional and soft? Goddamn it, she was a warrior, not some damsel in distress! She had to get a hold of herself before she said something she might regret later.

She pointed to the boulder. "Let's check out where that light's coming from." She marched toward it, Wes by her side, while she pretended not to notice that he was still holding her hand.

The rock was taller than herself by about two feet and as wide as a garage door. She slowed her steps, made eye contact with Wesley, and put her index finger over her lips. He nodded.

Careful not to make a sound, she inched around the side and peered past the boulder. A path wound its way through a formation of rocks. She looked up. The ceiling was made of stone, though she couldn't really call it a ceiling. It seemed natural, not man-made. A tunnel of sorts.

The light came from flames that seemed to shoot through cracks in the rock. Behind her, Wesley moved and squeezed his head past her. She felt him inhale audibly, and her own nose itched at the same time.

"Sulfur," he whispered into her ear.

She'd recognized it, too. Worry traveled up her spine. She turned her head to look at Wes and motioned him to follow her. She treaded lightly, careful not to make a sound in the cavernous walkway, her gaze vigilant. She looked for signs that might help her figure out where they were, but there were none. No markings on the walls, no runes, nothing.

The stench of sulfur grew stronger.

Somewhere in the distance she heard a rumbling. She froze instantly. Wes slung his arm around her from behind and pulled her against his chest. Before she could protest, she heard something else: footsteps. More than one person was approaching.

"This way," Wes whispered in her ear and tried to pull her in the opposite direction.

She shook her head, twisted in his arms and pressed him against the wall, then put her hand over his mouth. There was no time to get away. If she could hear footsteps, whoever was approaching would hear theirs. Maybe they already had.

All she could do was stay where she was.

And render Wesley and herself invisible.

Just in time, as it turned out. Because the three men walking toward them weren't human.

In the subdued light of the cavern, their eyes shimmered green. Demon green.

8

Wesley wanted to curse. Two things prevented him from doing so: Virginia's hand pressed over his mouth, and the knowledge that should he utter a sound, they were as good as dead. Because it was now clear as glass where they'd landed: the Underworld.

The few days he'd spent with the guardians at the Baltimore compound had given him a general understanding of the world of the Demons of Fear and what role the Stealth Guardians played in it. The rest he could piece together by himself.

Sulfur—not just the smell of it, but also the thin yellow layer that covered portions of the walls and ground—lava rock, and guys with glaring green eyes. Yep, welcome to Zoltan's Underworld. From the frying pan into the eternal fire. His day had just taken a turn for the worse. He could only hope that Virginia's powers worked down here, and that she was able to cloak them so the demons would just walk by. Surely that was her plan, even though he didn't feel any different, and he could still see her. But there was no time to ask her and get any reassurance. All he could do was stand there like a potted plant and hope for the best.

Not his favorite pastime.

Though he wasn't going to complain about one thing: Virginia's body pressed to his, her soft fingers on his lips. While this was no romantic embrace, at least knowing that she was trying to protect him made him feel somewhat better about the situation.

Holding his breath, Wes watched the three demons approach. They carried daggers in their hands and on their hips, their clothes not dissimilar from that of any guerilla group: brown or dark green cargo pants, shirts with plenty of pockets for knives, weapons, and whatnots, jackets with even more pockets, heavy boots to kick the shit out of anybody or to crush a rodent beneath their soles.

Apart from their eyes, they looked humanoid. Just a bunch of average, everyday human scum. And that's exactly what they had been before turning demon—Aiden had explained it a few days earlier. Committing an evil act in the name of the demons turned a human's soul so dark that the demons could make it theirs, thus turning the human into a demon.

Wes shuddered at the thought.

When the demons were only a few feet away, Wes instinctively put his arm around Virginia's back, drawing her even closer—as if he could protect her that way. He knew he couldn't, but it didn't stop him from holding her tight.

Without even glancing at him and Virginia, the demons marched past them. Wes turned his head to watch them disappear in the other direction, but he didn't dare breathe until finally, after an eternity, he couldn't hear their footsteps anymore.

He looked back at Virginia, and realized only now that she'd taken her hand off his mouth.

She swallowed hard. "We're in the demons' domain."

"No shit," he murmured back, keeping his voice low. "What are we gonna do now?"

"Well, you tell me!" she snapped and freed herself from his embrace. "I didn't do anything to bring us down here. You must have done something when we were in the portal."

"What?" he ground out. "You were driving! So don't put this on me!"

"You must have done something. No member of our kind has ever entered the Underworld." She glared at him in suspicion.

"Well, that's rich! I saved your ass back there in the compound and—"

"So, what was your plan? Deliver me to the demons?"

"My plan?" He grabbed her and pressed her against the stone wall. "My plan was to fuck you, okay? My plan was to strip you naked and sink my cock into you until neither you nor I could move another limb. When will you get that into your pretty little head? I'm a man, and I've got the hots for you. Maybe that's stupid. Maybe it's gonna cost me my life. But, by God, I have no ulterior motive other than getting into your pants!" He released her and pushed back from the wall. "And now I want to get the hell out of here before those fucking demons find us and kill us!"

"So, you really—"

He cut her off with a glare.

Virginia nodded quickly. "Fine, let's find a way out. Maybe you can start pulling your weight by using your witchcraft."

"My witchcraft?" He frowned. "But—" That's when it struck him. He looked around. No runes anywhere he could see. The runes carved into the walls, floors, and ceilings of the compound had bridled his witchcraft, but down here, he saw nothing that prevented him from accessing his powers.

He grinned. "Excellent!" He suddenly noticed how Virginia inched away from him. Scoffing, he rolled his eyes. "One of these days you're going to learn to trust me." He offered his hand, palm up. "Haven't I laid my cards on the table? The only thing you have to fear from me is me trying to kiss you again. Other than that, you're safe." He smirked.

A blush rose to her cheeks, then she placed her hand into his.

"Can you keep us cloaked?"

She nodded. "Yes. I'll have to touch you. I could do it with my mind, but it takes more energy. And I'd rather save it in case we're discovered and need to fight."

He raised an eyebrow, grinning. "I have no problem with you touching me."

Now it was her turn for an eyeroll.

As if she hadn't enjoyed the kiss as much as he had! She'd moaned out her pleasure for everybody to hear, and the way she'd ground her pelvis against him hadn't exactly been chaste either. She'd wanted it. Wanted him. But Wes kept that thought to himself. It was best not to aggravate her any further.

Instead, he said, "Let's go. I need to perform a guiding spell to find the way out."

"Can't you do it right here?"

He shook his head. "I need a water source. A witch's power comes from the elements. Mine comes from water, and in the absence of any of my other tools, it's the only thing that will give me enough power to perform a spell." He glanced down the corridor.

"How are we gonna find a water source down here?"

"We find limestone, we find water. Not all the rock down here is lava. Let's keep our eyes and ears open. There have to be aquifers somewhere, underground rivers or springs. Any water source will do."

Hand in hand, they started walking.

"And you're sure we're invisible, right?" he asked, looking at her.

She nodded.

"It's just, it's kind of strange that I can still see you." He motioned to his own body. "And myself."

"There are different stages of cloaking. Would you like to see?"

Before he could answer, Virginia disappeared in front of his eyes.

"Fuck me!" he let out in surprise. He tugged at her hand to pull her to him, then ran his hands over her.

"What are you doing?" she hissed and pushed against him, freeing herself.

"Just had to check you were still here."

All of a sudden Virginia became visible again, probably only so she could glare at him. "How about you start trusting me, too?"

He smirked. "What makes you think it's a trust issue? What if I was simply taking the opportunity to cop a feel?"

The jab into his ribs that followed wasn't entirely unexpected. The fact that Virginia didn't use her full preternatural strength to hurt him, however, was.

9

—————

In his private rooms, Zoltan breathed through the crippling pain that assaulted his head. The migraine-like attacks were getting worse. He'd been lucky again this time: when the pain had surfaced, he'd already been on his way to his private quarters, and had made it just in time, before he'd collapsed on his bed.

Now, half an hour later, he felt drained and knew he had to go up top, to the human world, to replenish his energy and feed off the fear of a human so none of his subjects realized that something was wrong with their leader. Because once they did, the hyenas would prey on him. A weak leader, no matter whether the weakness was physical or mental, was a dead leader.

Zoltan shrugged into his coat, armed himself with two daggers, one hidden in his inside pocket, one in his boot, and left his quarters. As he walked toward one of the vortex circles, the only places in the Underworld where he could conjure a portal that would carry him into the human world, he contemplated his options.

It was time to prepare for the worst. He needed an escape plan, in case his affliction was ever noticed. One that nobody, not even Vintoq, his closest confidant, knew of. A safe place somewhere in the human world, where he could disappear when things got too hot in the Underworld.

Once he was done feeding off the fear of a human, the fear that would make him strong again, he would go about it immediately.

Before he even reached the vortex circle, a cave where six tunnels met, Zoltan knew something was wrong. Yannick, the demon who oversaw all vortex circles, was arguing with one of his subordinates.

"What is this?" Zoltan thundered.

Both demons spun around to face him, bowing their heads briefly in a show of submission.

Then Yannick said, "Nothing important. There's been a disruption in the force field."

"What kind of disruption?" Zoltan asked.

"Just a flare, the same kind that happens when we conjure our vortexes."

Zoltan made a dismissive hand movement. He wasn't in the mood to hear about problems his underlings should work out themselves. "Then it was probably just that: someone conjuring a vortex."

Zoltan took a step toward the center of the circle, but the other demon stepped in front of him. "With all due respect, oh Great One—"

Zoltan glared at him. "What is your name?"

"Quentin, oh Great One."

He snatched the insolent demon by the collar. "Then get out of my way, Quentin. Or I'll crush you with my bare hands."

"But the force field wasn't centered in one of the vortex circles." The demon's voice trembled.

"What?"

Quentin motioned to Yannick. "I was trying to explain to Yannick that the disturbance came from somewhere else."

Zoltan snapped his head toward Yannick. "Is that true?"

"It can't be," Yannick stated. "It's impossible. No demon can cast a vortex outside of the vortex circles. And I've had all of them checked. The guards were unanimous. Nobody opened a vortex during the timeframe Quentin claims to have felt the disturbance. I keep meticulous records."

Zoltan nodded. Just as he'd asked Yannick to do so he could keep close tabs on the movements of his demons. Which meant something was seriously wrong. He turned back to Quentin.

"Where do you believe the disturbance happened?"

Quentin pointed to one of the tunnels. "It came from there. I'm certain."

"How do you know?"

"There was a sound that accompanied it. And a shock wave." He pointed to a niche. It contained a clipboard with papers. "The paper began to flutter."

Since there was no wind in the tunnels, air could only be stirred up by a few things: a vortex being conjured, a demon running in the tunnels, or an explosion blasting through it.

"Come with me," Zoltan ordered. "Show me where you think it happened." He glanced over his shoulder at Yannick. "You guard the circle in the meantime."

Yannick nodded dutifully, and Zoltan followed the other demon into the tunnel he'd pointed out.

"Have you seen anybody come out of this tunnel today?" Zoltan asked, while he let his gaze wander, searching for anything that looked out of the ordinary.

"I started my shift only an hour ago. But I've seen nobody since I felt the disturbance." He motioned to a cross tunnel a few yards ahead. "If anybody wanted to avoid passing by me, he could have used one of the other tunnels."

"Hmm."

A tunnel intersected with the one Zoltan was using. Quentin passed it and Zoltan continued following him. The flames shooting out of various cracks along the stone walls painted eerie shadows on the walls and ceilings. The smell of sulfur was particularly strong in the tunnels where the scent had no place to escape.

"It must have been somewhere here," Quentin suddenly announced and looked over his shoulder.

"What makes you say that?"

"There's a different smell here."

Zoltan sniffed the air around him. "What is that?"

"I believe it's almonds."

The smell of almonds, it was very distinct now. And stronger to his left. Zoltan turned in the direction his nose was leading him. He noticed a large boulder and a narrow opening next to it. He sniffed again.

While most modern explosives had no distinguishable odor, he knew that there was one that had a distinct smell of almonds: Nobel 808, an explosive nobody in the modern world used anymore. But then, he knew of one species that hadn't exactly gone with the times. A species that still fought with old weapons. What if they were still using an old explosive?

"Go through there and tell me what you see," Zoltan commanded his underling.

Quentin did as he was told and slipped through the opening. A moment later, he called out, "There's nothing, oh Great One. Just some rubble."

"Any sign of explosives?"

"None, oh Great One."

Reassured that it would be safe to enter the hidden cave—one of so many in the Underworld—Zoltan marched through the opening. It was dark there, so he reached into his pocket and pulled a match from it, then drew it along the boulder. It ignited and illuminated the space.

He searched the ground. Footprints. He knelt down. They appeared to be fresh. Two sets of boots at least. Two people.

"Look around, Quentin," Zoltan ordered. "Somebody was here not long ago."

He noticed Quentin strike a match, too, while his own burned down to his finger. He tossed it and lit a new one.

"Oh, Great One, here."

Zoltan pivoted and reached for the item his subject handed him. "A button?" He brought it closer to his eyes and examined it. It was silver, and when he tilted it just right, the light of the match made an engraving visible: a dagger.

A dagger he had no trouble recognizing. He'd been injured by daggers like this one often enough. The daggers of the Stealth Guardians.

Fury charged through him. They were here. They'd entered his domain. How, he didn't know. But he was certain it was them.

"Put everybody on alert."

Quentin stared at him blankly.

"We have intruders." Intruders who could make themselves invisible. Were probably roaming his Underworld right now, scoping out the layout, searching for weak spots, spots which they could attack. But not even their cloaking powers would help them evade the weapon he was about to unleash.

"Get the dogs!"

10

———————

They'd walked through a labyrinth of countless tunnels that all appeared to look the same. Virginia had lost track of which direction they were headed in, they'd turned left and right and turned back at dead ends so many times. For all she knew they were back at the same place where they'd started.

Whenever they'd heard voices or other sounds, Wesley had dragged her in the other direction, clearly wanting to avoid another demon encounter. But what if they were heading too far away? What if the reason they hadn't come upon another demon in the last half hour was because they were walking toward an area that even the demons avoided? And what if there was no water in this direction either? Surely the demons would congregate around the water sources in this hellhole, since they, too, needed water for survival.

"We have to turn around," she said quietly but firmly.

Wesley glanced at her, but continued walking. She tugged at his hand and stopped, forcing him to do the same. With a sigh, he faced her. "What?"

"We'll never find water here. If there's any, it'll be where the demons are. They must have caves they live in. There has to be water there." She motioned to the dark corridor ahead. "There's nothing down there."

"Then what do you suggest?" He ran a hand through his hair. "If we go back there, our chances of being discovered get exponentially higher. Eventually they'll hear us, even if they can't see us. And then what? We have no weapons. Or do you want to throw rocks at them and hope we can take a few out like David took out Goliath?"

She blew a breath through her nostrils. "I wish it was that easy, but only weapons forged in the Dark Days can kill a demon." She pointed to her empty holster. "And I lost mine."

"I know. Listen, I know how you feel."

She raised an eyebrow. How could he know how she felt?

"It's not in your nature to avoid a fight, but we're outnumbered, unarmed, and unprepared," Wesley said, and partially, he was right.

"No other member of my kind has ever entered the Underworld. This is an opportunity I might never get again. This is perhaps the only chance I'll ever have at getting the inside scoop on our archenemy. Maybe find a way to destroy them once and for all."

Wes shook his head vehemently. "We have no idea what we're dealing with down here. Going on a spying expedition is too dangerous. I like a good fight as much as the next guy, but I know when to turn tail and run."

Virginia opened her mouth to protest, but Wesley suddenly pressed his palm on it and nodded his head in the direction they'd been heading in. She froze. Then she heard it, too. Footsteps. Rapidly coming closer. She nodded, signaling her understanding to Wesley and pressed her back flat against the jagged rock formation that formed one side of the tunnel. Wesley did the same next to her, so their bodies were touching. She felt the brittle stone at her back crumble, and small pebbles rolled down to her feet.

Alarmed she looked at them, hoping the sound hadn't alerted the demons that were fast approaching.

Moments later, five of the evil creatures charged by them, not even glancing at the spot where Virginia and Wesley were standing. They were armed to the teeth—as if they were heading into war. If only she had a dagger or two, she would take them out one by one like a shadow they couldn't even see coming. But without a weapon she felt helpless, and she didn't like that feeling. No, she didn't like it at all.

Grudgingly she had to admit that Wesley was right—if only this one time—and that an encounter with the demons could prove fatal.

Virginia didn't breathe until the sound of the demons running had completely vanished. Then she pushed herself off the rocks at her back, making more of the porous stone crumble under the pressure and collect at her feet. Instinctively she bent down and brushed them off her boots. Fine white dust remained.

She pivoted, but Wesley had noticed the same thing and was already inspecting the rock they'd been leaning against.

"Limestone," he said. He knocked against it, and more of it crumbled, as if it were as thin as drywall and just as fragile.

She met his eyes. "Do you think there's water behind it?"

Wes nodded. "It sounds hollow. I need a rock, something to knock through it." He glanced around, took a few steps forward, and bent down. He came back with a piece of granite no larger than a grapefruit. "I hope I'm right."

With the rock in one hand, bracing himself against the wall with the other, Wes pulled back his arm and took aim. The rock connected with the limestone and drove right through it. The momentum pulled Wesley with it, knocking him against the wall.

The impact shattered the wall, creating a large opening. Wesley tumbled through it.

Shock made Virginia's heart race at a million miles an hour. She dipped her head through the hole, and to her surprise, she saw her own face reflected back at her. As if in a mirror. A wet mirror-like surface.

"Found it." Wesley's voice coming from only a foot away jolted her. He was getting up, dusting off his pants. He hadn't fallen more than a couple of feet and had landed right at the edge of a pool of water.

Some light filtered through cracks in the rock and provided

sufficient illumination in the cave that was maybe as large as a tennis court.

Wesley reached for her hand. "Come in."

She lifted her feet over the remainder of the wall that had crumbled and allowed Wesley to help her down, even though she could have jumped the foot or two without effort. But somehow feeling his hands on her hips gave her a sense of safety.

Still in his arms, she lifted her lids and met his gaze. Damn, could those baby-blues actually be sparkling more down here, or had she started hallucinating?

"Let's do the spell," he said, his lips barely moving.

"Yes, yes, the spell," she stammered and eased out of his embrace.

Her hands suddenly trembled, and she blamed the fact that Wesley was about to use magic, a power she was both afraid and in awe of, and not the sexual tension that seemed to crackle between them ever since he'd kissed her.

Witchcraft was something she had no defenses against. Fighting with deadly weapons was one thing, defending oneself against a witch's spell was another altogether. And what if he had in fact already used witchcraft without her knowledge? What if he'd whispered a silent spell to bewitch her so she would trust him, believe in him, desire him? How would she even know?

"You okay?" Wesley suddenly asked, looking deep into her eyes.

"I'm fine. Let's just get this over with." The sooner the better. And she would watch him like a hawk, just in case he tried to pull a fast one.

Stop fretting! He won't betray you. Just remember what he said. He needs you alive, because he wants you in his bed.

And that thought was frightening in itself. Because it meant he'd work his way through her defenses, just like he'd found a way through the limestone wall.

~

VIRGINIA WORE AN APPREHENSIVE LOOK. Was she worried that he wasn't up to the task and not as skillful a witch as he'd told her he was? Maybe twenty years ago she would have had to worry, but he'd mastered his craft, and a guiding spell was the stuff of novices.

"Don't look so doubtful," Wes murmured with a smile. "I can do this in my sleep."

"Has anybody ever told you that you've got a big mouth?"

He chuckled and knelt down in the sand that surrounded the water. "Trust me that's not the only thing that's big." When her chin dropped in stunned silence, he winked at her. "You have to admit, you practically handed me that one."

"Are we gonna chit-chat or do the spell?"

"It's called flirting, and yes, we're doing the spell." He couldn't help himself, rattling Virginia's stern façade was too much fun. Whenever she lost her cool, he could practically see the flames she wanted to torch him with. But he wasn't easily burned. She'd have to get a lot closer for that.

"Okay then." He took a deep breath and looked at the water's surface. It was as smooth as he imagined Virginia's skin to be.

Concentrate!

As smooth as silk. Better.

He looked at his reflection in the glassy surface. "*Egressus,*" he murmured softly and began to chant a Latin incarnation. The words repeated over and over again, until they all seemed to be one. One word, one mission, one goal.

Ripples built on the water's surface, traveling outward toward its shore.

Faster and faster they came and washed over the sand.

"*Egressus,*" Wes repeated the Latin word for exit.

Then the next ripple rose like a serpent and snaked onto the shore. It drew a pattern in the sand, moving as fast as a tornado, yet as gentle as a mother's touch. A corresponding fire scorched his arm, though no flame was visible.

Like a child's crayon the serpent drew a picture in the sand. And then just as quickly, it seeped away in the ground, leaving only a patch of wet sand. The fire on his arm extinguished. He exhaled sharply.

"Oh my God," Virginia said, her voice carrying respect and admiration. "It looks like a map."

"It is." He studied the drawing his spell had created in the sand. "It shows where we are." He pointed to a dot near a small pond. "And where we need to go." He followed an arrow that wound its way through a labyrinth of tunnels and ended in a circle.

Virginia pointed to it. "What do you think this is?"

"Not sure, but it looks like a roundabout, you know, with all these tunnels leading to it. Maybe a stairway or something leading up? I mean, we're gonna have to go up, right? We must be deep down somewhere in the earth's crust." At least it felt like it with all the lava, the sulfur, and the stench that came with it.

"Your guess is as good as mine. The Stealth Guardians have always assumed that the demons must be somewhere below ground, but we've never been able to confirm that." Then she pointed to the map again. "But how will we remember this map once we're back in the tunnels? I don't have a phone to take a picture."

"Then maybe we should use this map," Wes said and unbuttoned his shirt sleeve, then rolled it back to expose the inside of his forearm, where a twin of the map was emblazoned on his skin like a tattoo. He'd felt the temporary burn while the spell had worked its magic, but now the discomfort was gone.

Virginia gasped and ran her finger over his forearm. "How?"

"Pretty neat, huh?" He took her hand and squeezed it. "We won't have much time. The map will vanish from my skin within an hour, or even earlier."

He jumped up and pulled her with him. Moments later, they were hurrying down one of the tunnels, following the map on Wesley's forearm.

11

Virginia heard the dogs before Wesley did.

"Fuck, they've got dogs," she cursed.

Wesley whirled his head to her. "What does that mean?"

"They're using dogs to sniff us out. They know we're here. And they know we're invisible."

"Ah, fuck!"

"We need to run." She pointed to another tunnel.

He shook his head and pointed in the direction the barking of the dogs was coming from. "Our way out is in this direction."

"Not if the dogs rip us to pieces."

"Then we have to make sure they don't smell us."

"They'll smell us. We've gotta get out of here." She turned.

He snatched her arm. "Take off your jacket."

She snapped her gaze to him. "What for?"

"Just do it." Wesley was already unbuttoning his shirt and sliding it off his shoulders, revealing a sculpted chest and muscled abs.

Virginia looked away from the tantalizing sight and took off her leather jacket. "What are you planning?"

"Spit on the jacket."

She looked at him and witnessed how he rubbed his crumbled-up shirt under his armpits, then spit into it, and realized what he was doing: transferring as much of his scent onto the piece of clothing. Quickly, she spit onto her leather jacket.

"Now what?"

Wesley pointed to the tunnel that veered off to their left. "Let's leave the stuff down there."

They started running, until Wesley stopped her. "Stuff your jacket into this crack." He motioned to a large hole in the rock.

Virginia followed his order. "And yours?"

"A little farther up." He ran and she followed him closely, cloaking him with her mind instead of her touch now.

A dozen yards farther, he stopped and shoved his shirt into another crack. Then he turned back and they both ran back toward the tunnel they'd come from.

"They'll still smell us though," Virginia said.

"Not if we cover our scent with something much stronger," Wesley said. "And I think I've got just the thing. Come on."

He was already running back down the tunnel they'd originally come from. She was on his heels. Following her was the barking of the dogs, coming closer with every second. Her heart started to pound. Stealth Guardians weren't exactly fond of dogs, for obvious reasons. She could only hope that Wesley had a plan to disguise their scent so the bloodhounds didn't discover them.

Wesley finally stopped and crouched down. She followed his gaze and noticed a yellow substance he was scraping off the base of the tunnel wall.

"What is that?"

"Sulphur deposits. Rub the stuff over your T-shirt and pants, and your arms, too."

Virginia bent down and reeled as the smell of rotten eggs assaulted her even more violently than before. "Shit," she cursed, but started scraping the vile substance off the wall and smearing it over her T-shirt.

Wesley did the same, though in addition to staining his pants with the stuff, he also rubbed it all over his naked torso. Within seconds, they both reeked of it.

He met her eyes. "Ready?"

She nodded.

"Let's get back to where the other tunnel veers off."

She grabbed his hand, and felt him freeze for a moment, a soft smile forming around his lips. "Just so I don't have to waste energy making you invisible with my mind," she explained.

"Yes, just to save energy."

Careful not to make a sound, though the approaching dogs were loud enough now to drown out their faint footsteps, they hurried back to the intersection of the two tunnels.

In the distance, Virginia could already see them coming. Bloodhounds, Pitbulls, and Dobermans. On long leashes, their snouts moving constantly, sniffing, their muzzles open and drooling with spit, the animals charged in their direction, dragging their demon masters with them.

She knew immediately that the dogs had already caught on to her and Wesley's scent. In a few seconds they would be here, proving their worth to their masters.

Virginia gripped Wesley's hand tighter. In response, he put his other hand over hers and met her eyes. His attempt at reassuring her failed—the dogs had just reached the point where the tunnels intersected, and were only yards away.

The dogs appeared to hesitate, one heading in one direction, two others in the other, while two more dogs seemed indecisive. They sniffed and yowled, tossing doubtful glances back at the demons.

"Find them!" one of the demons yelled.

One of the dogs took off in one direction, dragging his demon owner with him. But a Doberman suddenly made a beeline for the spot where Virginia and Wesley were pressed against the wall.

"What the fuck's wrong with the dogs?" one demon asked the other.

The fellow shrugged. "Give 'em time. They'll pick up the scent again. Won't you, Rex?" he said to the Doberman who had just reached Virginia's feet.

Fuck! Another second and they'd be discovered.

The dog continued sniffing. She could almost feel his snout at her pant leg. She dared not move, didn't even dare look down for fear of making a sound.

Something warm suddenly seeped through her pants and ran down to her ankle. Warm and wet. She glanced down to her feet. The Doberman, his leg lifted, was peeing on her.

Crap!

One of the demons laughed. "Yeah, sure that'll help him find them."

The Doberman's master jerked at the dog's leash. "Stupid dog, let's go."

"Hey, this way!" another demon hollered, his voice coming from the tunnel where Virginia and Wesley had stashed their clothes. "We've got their scent. Hurry!"

The other demons ushered their dogs down the tunnel and raced down it with them.

Virginia breathed a sigh of relief, then shook her leg to rid herself of the dog's piss, but some of it had seeped into her socks and boots. Feeling Wesley's eyes on her, she turned her gaze to him.

"Don't even!" she snapped under her breath, cutting off whatever wisecrack remark was sitting on his lips.

"In that case, let's hurry. They'll discover our ruse soon enough. But we're not far now." He looked at the tattoo on his forearm and took her hand.

They started running down the path from which the demons had come with their dogs. Another turn into a wider tunnel, then Wesley took a fork to the left. There was light at the end of the tunnel, more light than Virginia had noticed in the others.

She instinctively slowed her steps, and Wesley did the same. He motioned to his forearm and pointed to the circle that was still emblazoned on his skin, but had grown fainter. She nodded, understanding what he was trying to convey. The open area they were approaching in about ten yards was the exit the map was indicating.

Slowly they crept closer, until they were at the end of the tunnel where it spilled out into a circular area. Several other tunnels spread out from there, leading in different directions. A demon was leaning against a wall, his expression bored.

Virginia noticed Wesley look up, and she followed his gaze: the ceiling was higher here, but still, there was no way out. No staircase, no opening, no exit.

She stared at Wesley who finally met her gaze. He shrugged, then pulled her back into the tunnel, not too far so they could still see the round cave, but far enough so they could whisper to each other without being overheard by the demon.

"Are you sure that's the exit the map's pointing to?" she asked.

"I'm certain."

"Maybe you got turned around."

He glared at her. "I know how to read maps."

"But there's no exit, nothing that shows us a way out. Just more tunnels."

"But there's a demon."

"So?"

"He's standing sentry."

Wes paused, and suddenly a light switched on in her mind.

"He's guarding something," she murmured.

"Exactly. There must be a door or something. We'll just have to look for it."

Virginia picked up a sound. "We'd better make it quick. I think they just discovered our ruse." Somewhere in the distance, a dog was barking.

"Fuck," Wesley suddenly hissed. "More demons."

She snapped her head back toward the circle. A second demon was coming from another tunnel.

"State your business," the demon who stood sentry suddenly demanded.

"Going up top on Vintoq's orders," the other demon replied.

She exchanged a quick look with Wes. "Up top," she murmured.

They started moving at the same time, hurrying toward the circle.

"Go ahead," the guard said and made a note on a clipboard.

The demon raised a hand and made a swirling motion, and just as Virginia and Wesley reached the edge of the circular cave, a vortex of dark fog and wind opened up and took over the middle of the cave. The noise accompanying it drowned out everything else.

This was it, the way out. That's why the map had pointed to this place. It was like one of the Stealth Guardians' portals, a way of traveling to and from the Underworld that only a demon could access.

Virginia locked eyes with Wes and murmured, "We have to piggyback." She was certain of it now. It was their only chance.

"Piggyback?"

"Trust me!"

Holding on to Wesley's hand, she dragged him toward the vortex. His eyes went wide, and his lips moved, though no words came out. *Fuck me*, he mouthed, but stayed with her.

The moment she saw the demon jump into the vortex, she followed with Wesley. They were still invisible, and the noise of the swirling wind would drown out any other noise she and Wesley made.

Inside the vortex, gray mist engulfed them, but she could see the demon clearly. With her free hand, she reached for him, careful to grab a hold of his coattail only, so he wouldn't be able to feel her. Yet she would still be connected to him. She had to assume that the vortex operated in the same way the portals did: a physical connection between the demon and any passenger was required, or he'd leave them behind.

Just then, Virginia felt herself lifted into the air and knew they were traveling. She didn't care where to, as long as it was the human world. Once there, they'd find their way.

Vintoq's an idiot. It's a stupid idea!

The words pierced Virginia's mind as if somebody had spoken them, though her ears hadn't picked up anything.

She shot a gaze to Wesley, and his eyes were wide as saucers. He too had heard the words. Or rather, *felt* them.

She stared at the demon's back. What she'd heard could only be his thoughts.

Shit! Had the vortex created some sort of telepathic connection between them?

Did that mean the demon could hear her thoughts too?

Before she could even finish the thought, the demon spun around, his green eyes glaring.

Who the fuck?

His thoughts again.

Then several things happened all at once.

The vortex stopped spinning. Virginia let go of the demon's coattail. Wes let go of her and pushed her to the side. As she tried to keep her balance, she watched in horror as the demon reached for his dagger. But Wesley's knee was already connecting with the demon's balls. He kicked the bastard backward, lunging after him, falling. Their torsos disappeared outside the vortex.

Virginia jumped outside, afraid the vortex would close and drag her back into the Underworld. It was dark around her. She landed on dirt. Next to her, Wesley was holding the demon at bay. But just barely.

The demon's dagger was still in its sheath. She lunged for it, pulled it out.

"Wes! Off him, now!"

With a grunt, Wesley rolled off the demon. Before the demon could rear up, Virginia plunged the dagger into the vile creature's heart. This time, there was no gurgling sound, no last labored breath, no attempt at fighting back. Just death. And green demon blood staining the demon's coat.

Virginia let herself fall back on her ass, breathing heavily. She cast a look back over her shoulder. The vortex was gone, vanished.

Panting, Wes sat a few feet across from her, the dead demon between them. He had a look of admiration in his eyes.

"Don't take this the wrong way, but I've never seen anything sexier in my whole life than you stabbing a demon to death."

She scoffed and shook her head. "You're a very strange witch, Wesley."

"Strange good or strange bad?"

"I haven't decided that yet."

Though currently she was leaning toward *strange good*. Oh yeah, strange *very* good.

12

Wes tore his eyes from Virginia's flushed face and glanced back at the dead demon. This time she'd saved him. But then, who was keeping score?

"What are we gonna do with him?" He pointed at the dead demon.

"Normally I'd say, we burn him, but"—She patted her torso and legs—"I don't have any of my usual gear with me." She looked around and peered into the dark. "Maybe we can just hide his body. Come back for it later?"

"Works for me."

When she made a motion to get up, Wes jumped up to help her up, but she was faster. She looked around. "Where do you think we are?"

He let his eyes wander. There were streetlights in the distance, maybe a small town. He heard the sound of cars passing by. He looked in the other direction. "That looks like an overpass. We could be near a freeway." He squinted and was able to make out a large green sign. "Definitely a freeway."

She nodded. "Good. If that's the case, we can find shelter in a motel."

"A shower wouldn't go amiss either," he added.

"But first, let's hide the demon." She pointed to the overpass. "Underneath there."

Together they dragged the dead creature about twenty yards to a pile of illegally dumped trash and stashed him behind it, covering him as best they could. It would hide the body once the sun came up.

Then they made their way up toward the embankment. It wasn't busy on the freeway, a sign that it was either very late at night, or this was a remote area, or both.

"There are signs for motels in that direction," Wes pointed out.

"Let's go then."

They started walking. For a moment, there was silence between them, then Wes said, "That was risky, jumping into the demon's portal."

"It's called a vortex, and it worked."

"Did you know it would?"

"I suspected it. We've always assumed that the demon's vortexes worked similarly to our portals. It was a calculated risk."

"What about hearing his thoughts? Did you know about that too?"

She cast him a sideways look. "I didn't at the time."

"What's that supposed to mean?"

"What I said. But now that you mention it, I recall a report I read last year that mentioned one of our guardians accidentally stepping into a demon's vortex during a rescue mission. He'd also heard the demon's thoughts. Though his report didn't mention whether he believed the demon could read his thoughts too. That's probably how he figured he wasn't alone."

Wes chuckled. "Yeah, that, or our stench."

"You do reek."

"You smell a little past your sell-by date too."

"Is that a dig at my age?"

The fact that Virginia was bantering with him made the tension roll off him. They'd just escaped from the Underworld and cheated certain death. If that wasn't a little stressful, he didn't know what was.

He smiled at her. "Did I mention I like older women?"

Virginia rolled her eyes and looked at the lights ahead.

Though Wes had no idea how old she was, he had to assume that she was older than the guardians at the Baltimore compound, most of whom were around two-hundred. And that definitely made her older than him. And possibly more experienced. And that part he didn't mind at all.

It took another ten minutes until they reached an area with a motel, a gas station, several fast food places, and a large store that could have rivaled a Walmart or a Target Superstore in size, though it appeared closed.

"I'll make us invisible again," Virginia suddenly said and took his hand.

"Works for me." Feeling Virginia touch him was always a welcome feeling. "I assume we don't have any money or credit cards, do we?"

"No, we don't."

Knowing instinctively what she was trying to do, he motioned to a door toward the end of the motel, away from the office, where a middle-aged man was watching TV.

"That room looks empty."

"Let's try it."

When they arrived at the door, Virginia put her finger on her lips, then dipped her head through the door so her entire torso disappeared from his view.

Freaky!

But definitely a handy skill.

He suddenly felt her release his hand and disappear entirely. Nervously he looked over his shoulder, but the man in the office had his eyes glued to the TV monitor, and there was nobody else around. And for all he knew, Virginia was probably still cloaking him with her mind.

Suddenly there was a click, and the door opened.

"Quickly!" Virginia said. She pulled him inside and eased the door shut quietly.

Only then she flipped the light switch. Wes looked around. Two beds. Two chairs and a table, a TV, a microwave and a small refrigerator. A few coat hangers on a rack, and a door into a bathroom.

After spending the last hours in the Underworld, this felt like a palace.

"Okay, you stay here, while I go and get us some supplies. What's your shoe size?"

He gave her a surprised look. "Why?"

She pointed to his boots. "Because they look and smell like shit."

Glancing at them, Wesley had to admit they looked a little worse for wear. "I'll come with you."

"You can't. The store is closed. I'll need to pass through the door, and I can't take you with me."

"Then do what you did just now. Go in first, and then open up for me."

"And set off the alarm?"

Damn! He hadn't thought of that. He felt like a fool. "Sorry. I wasn't thinking."

She shrugged. "You've been through a lot today. Can't blame you." She sighed. "Get out of those clothes and put them in the trash. I'll toss everything when I get back so we don't spread the stench in here. Take a shower. I'll be back in a few minutes." She was already turning toward the door, when she looked over her shoulder. "Shoe size?"

"Twelve. Thanks."

He watched her pass through the door and disappear. He wasn't used to a woman doing something for him. But Virginia was a special woman.

Glad to be able to get rid of his dirty clothes, Wes unbuttoned his pants, then lowered the zipper. His gaze fell on the beds. Just his damn luck that he'd unwittingly picked a room with two beds and not just one. There would be no reason for Virginia to share his bed tonight.

Unless she decided that after the danger they'd been in, she needed a little relaxation—relaxation he was more than willing to provide.

THE WARM SPRAY of the surprisingly large shower felt good on Wesley's skin. Twice he'd already soaped up with the cheap soap the motel provided, and twice he'd rinsed the residue of the dirt of the Underworld off. Now he stood beneath the showerhead and simply enjoyed the water caressing his skin. His tense shoulders relaxed, and he started to feel normal again.

The last eighteen hours had been a supernatural rollercoaster with more twists and turns than the Underworld labyrinth they'd narrowly escaped.

Wes turned his face into the water raining down on him, reluctant to get out of the shower.

A sound drifted to him. Was Virginia back? He hadn't heard the door, but then she wouldn't use the door, given that she didn't have a key to it. She would just pass through it. What a cool skill that was!

"Virginia?" he called out.

He'd left the bathroom door ajar. Just so he would hear if anybody entered the room.

Liar.

He sighed. So what if he'd left it open because he was hoping Virginia would take the hint and join him in the shower? Was that maybe the reason why he was still standing here, even though he could have dried off much earlier?

Well, clearly it wasn't happening.

Another sound made him whirl around. But it was just his active imagination that made him imagine the faint footsteps. Disappointed he turned back and reached for the faucet.

"Don't turn it off yet."

Virginia's voice jolted him, and he spun around. And stared at nothing.

But he heard her. She was stepping into the shower, and he saw that her feet displaced the water that had collected in the shower pan. For an instant he just stood there, then he grinned.

"I hadn't pegged you for the shy kind." Or why else would she be invisible?

"Who says I'm shy?"

An invisible hand suddenly touched his chest. His heartbeat accelerated. Instinctively he followed her hand, running his fingers up to her shoulder, touching her naked skin.

"If I were shy, I wouldn't let you wash me," she murmured.

He took the hint and pulled her closer, stepping out of the spray to make space for her.

"Well, I guess I've got a job to do then." A job that didn't feel like a job, more like a reward.

He turned to reach for the soap. When he turned back, he saw with surprise that Virginia wasn't entirely invisible anymore. The water pearling off her created a silhouette that looked almost ghostly. Mystical. And sexy as hell.

Her curves were delectable, her legs long and shapely, her hips round, her breasts firm and the perfect size for her tall stature.

"You're looking at me," she said.

He lifted his lids to gaze into her face. "Did you ever see the movie *The Invisible Man*?"

Her head bobbed up and down.

"He was outside in the rain, and suddenly you could see him, see his outline." Wes lifted his hand and traced her shoulder down to her arm. "That's what I see right now." He brought his hand to her waist and slowly ran it up along her torso. "You're more beautiful than I imagined."

"And you weren't lying about being big."

Her hand moved, and he could see the direction it was taking: to his cock that had already started rising. He stopped her before she reached his groin, wrapping his hand around her wrist.

"Not so fast, baby, I want to savor this." He pulled her hand back to her side and released it. "Now be a good girl and let this big bad witch wash the sulfur off you."

He soaped his hands so the suds covered his palms, then reached for Virginia. He started at her shoulders, then soaped up her right arm and thoroughly cleansed her from shoulder blade to fingertips, then did the same with the other arm. The soap made her body stand out even more.

Turning her into the spray, he watched the water sluice off the suds and wash away the grime of the Underworld.

"Spread your legs a bit wider," he ordered and crouched down to her feet.

He lifted one foot on his knee and worked the soap over her foot and leg, sliding upward to her thigh in long strokes. God, it felt good touching her, exploring her body. He did the same with the other leg, before he rinsed the soap off her thoroughly.

"Turn around," he murmured. "I'll do your back."

He watched her silhouette turn and began to run his soapy hands over her back, under her arms, and then followed the curves of her body down to the soft swells of her ass.

Fuck, was the water getting hotter?

His cock sprang to full height.

He ran both hands down her ass, more caressing than washing her. A sigh came from her and he brought his face next to hers.

"You know what I want, don't you?"

"You were pretty open about that." There was a husky undertone in her voice he hadn't heard previously.

"Just want to make sure you don't get any bad surprises." He turned her so her back was under the showerhead, raining down on her. "Now to the best parts."

He reached for the soap again, foaming up his hands once more.

He slid his palms over her breasts, the foam giving him a better view of their shape. An involuntary groan left his lips. Virginia's nipples were hard.

"I never imagined that touching you like this, without really seeing you, would be so hot." He'd always been a visual guy, had always had the lights on during sex so he could look his fill. But this, seeing Virginia's body only as an outline, as a mere sketch, fired up his imagination and made him hornier than he'd ever been.

"I like the way you touch me," she replied and placed her hands onto his. "But you're not quite done." Slowly she pushed his hands down to slide off her breasts, over her torso and her stomach.

"You're right, I've got a job to finish, haven't I?"

He let one hand glide over her triangle of curls, then delve between her legs. He rubbed his soap-covered fingers over her sex, gently and slowly, washing her there too.

She gripped his biceps then, holding on to him, a moan tumbling from her lips. "Oh."

"Yes, let's get the soap off you, and then I'll take care of you." Because he'd used up all his patience. What he needed now was to get inside of Virginia.

Reluctantly, he took his hand from her, then used both hands to scoop clean water over her to rinse her breasts and sex.

He turned off the showerhead, then pivoted to reach for the towel that hung just outside the shower. He wasn't fast enough. Virginia pressed him against the tile wall and dropped down to her knees. Her outline was barely visible now that she was free of soap, and most of the water had pearled off her. Still, he couldn't take his eyes off the little he could see.

One hand she braced on his thigh, with the other she reached for his cock. He felt her soft fingers wrap around his root, and he sucked in a trembling breath. Every thought in his brain vanished, except for one: Virginia was about to blow him.

13

———

Virginia had only wanted to tease Wesley for a little bit when she'd joined him, invisible, in the shower. But when she'd realized that it apparently turned him on, she'd decided to remain invisible.

And she wasn't teasing anymore. No, she was seducing now.

Wesley was a formidable specimen of manhood. She'd noticed it already in the Underworld, when he'd taken off his shirt. He was tan and sculpted. And that was just his chest. His thighs were muscular and toned, but what lay between his legs was what really drew her interest.

Surrounded by dark hair, his cock stood there like a flagpole—firm, long, and rigid.

She could feel just how firm, how hard he was. Her fingers barely reached around his root. His long shaft seemed to pulse in her hand, and she hadn't done anything yet. And there was so much she wanted to do. And in her invisible form, she felt powerful.

Today she'd seen how powerful this witch was. How skilled. But now she had to prove to herself that she could still bring him to his knees, despite the powerful witchcraft he possessed.

Because she had power, too. The power a woman wielded over a man. The power for which women had been vilified for centuries. For millennia. The power of sex.

This was a battle she was determined to win. Just so Wesley would know his place. So that he would never underestimate her. And so that he would regret it if he played her.

"Are you just gonna stare at my cock, or are you actually gonna take what you want?"

His voice pulled her out of her reveries. "Impatient much?"

He chuckled softly, a sound that sent a shiver down her back. "It's just, if you're not gonna suck me, then I suggest we move this show to the bedroom so you can spread your legs for me and let *me* suck *you*."

His offer made vivid pictures explode in her mind. God help her if he went down on her. She'd lose all control. And she couldn't let that happen. She had to remain in control. Always. So she wouldn't make the wrong decision. So history didn't repeat itself.

"Thanks, but I'd rather suck you," she said and licked her tongue over the swollen head of his cock.

A sharply exhaled breath came from Wesley and she felt his cock press against her mouth. Obliging him, she wrapped her lips around him and slid down on him, taking him inside her mouth as far as she could.

"Fuck!"

His enthusiastic yelp made her smile and she pulled her head back, letting his hard-on slip from her mouth. She blew a cool breath against his skin, before capturing him again and sucking gently.

His hips began to move and she steadied him, pressing him back against the wall of the shower. She was in control now. And she loved being in control. Particularly when the man in question tasted so good. She loved feeling his erection in her mouth, loved his hands on the back of her head, cradling her, loved the way he fought against her hands pinning him against the wall.

"Babe, that's good. So good."

His words trickled over her body like hot drops of water, scorching her skin. But she kept going, kept sucking his beautiful cock, licking her tongue along its underside, squeezing him at the root, withdrawing and descending in ever increasing tempo.

She could feel how close he was. And she knew how to send him over the edge. Releasing his thigh, she brought her hand to his balls, cradling them. The sac containing the precious stones tightened under her touch, and she couldn't resist gently sliding her fingernails over it.

"Fuck!"

Wesley suddenly pushed her back and freed himself from her mouth. In the next instant, he pulled her up and gripped her wrists, immobilizing her. "Not so fast!"

His eyes were dark and shimmered with unbridled lust. His chest heaved as if he'd run a marathon. "I'm gonna come when I'm inside your pussy. And not any earlier."

Before she could protest, he found her lips and captured her mouth. Then she felt herself lifted up and carried out of the shower. She barely felt the towel he used to haphazardly dry her off, his passionate kiss distracting her and making everything else melt into the background.

Maybe this witch was more powerful than he let on. Maybe he was, right at this moment, bewitching her. And she had no defenses against it. And what was worse: she didn't want to fight it any longer.

She wanted to surrender. To give into what her body craved. To be taken by a man stronger than her, more powerful, more dominant. Maybe that's what she needed. Just this once.

All of a sudden, she felt a mattress beneath her back, and Wesley pressing her into it.

She sucked in a breath of air and realized that he'd released her lips.

"Now it's my turn," he murmured, kissing his way down her neck.

He lapped at her nipple a moment later, drawing the hard bud into his mouth. She shivered at the sensual onslaught and arched her back. But Wesley didn't stay there for long. Already, he was moving farther south.

Strong hands pushed her thighs apart, and she watched him dip his head in the space he'd made.

"Oh God," she whispered to herself.

He briefly lifted his head and smirked. "Name's Wesley. Feel free to scream it."

Before she could slap him, he dropped his face to her sex and licked his hot tongue over her slit, making her all too aware how wet she'd become. And with every lap of his tongue, every touch of his lips to her aroused flesh, she felt more wetness pool at her center.

Wesley pressed her thighs apart farther, and she allowed it, opening up for him in a way she'd never done for any other man. Allowed him to explore her, to caress her with his fingers and his tongue. Allowed him to tease more and more moans from her chest, more and more sighs from her lips, and more and more tension to release from her tightly-wound body.

She let go of it all, of the need to control, the need to lead, the need to be in charge.

"That's it, babe." His murmur sent ripples through her body.

Her clit tingled, and Wesley seemed to know exactly what she needed. He pressed his tongue onto her center of pleasure and rubbed it up and down, left to right. With each swipe he added more pressure and increased his tempo.

Her breath hitched. "Wesley! Yes!"

A deep grunt accompanied his next movement: he slid one long finger into her channel, while continuing to lick her clit. It was too much. Like a vat of gunpowder, she exploded, and the smoldering ripples traveled through her body, burning down the wall she'd built to protect herself.

"Wes!"

～

IN THE MIDDLE of her orgasm, an orgasm that made her muscles squeeze his finger as if in a vise, Virginia turned visible in front of Wesley's eyes.

He lifted his head from her sex, drinking in the sight. She was even more beautiful than he'd glimpsed in the shower. Her skin was rosy and flawless, her pussy guarded by curly red hair that glowed like fire, her soft petals pink, swollen, and wet—and ready for his cock.

When he lifted his eyes to take in the rest of her, he met her gaze. Her green irises seemed to glow, not like a demon's eyes, no, but like a deep pool of water he wanted to drown in. Her red hair was curling from the moisture.

"You can see me," she murmured.

"Guess you lost your concentration." He chuckled and rolled over her. "Now you're finally ready for me."

For a moment she seemed to want to protest, but then he nudged his cock at her warm and wet pussy, and her eyelids fluttered.

"Now that you're all relaxed, we'll take our time." Because that's how he liked his loving: slow and deep and drawn-out. Like a lazy Sunday afternoon. Not like a race to the finish.

Virginia put her hand on his nape and pulled him to her. "You're a strange witch, Wesley."

He smiled. "Yes, but strange good." To underscore his statement, he drove his cock into her, slowly and steadily, until he could go no farther.

Virginia's lips parted on a sigh, but her eyes remained locked with his. He brushed her hair back from her face and brought his lips to hers. Then he began to move. Slowly he eased from her welcoming sheath, then just as slowly, he inched back inside, relishing in the feeling of her muscles imprisoning him on his descent.

Virginia's breath ghosted over his face and her hips tilted upward, pressing against him.

"I'm not gonna rush this, babe. I've waited too long for it."

"You only met me last night," she protested.

"As I said, it was a long wait."

A soft laugh rolled over her lips. "I should have made you wait longer."

He drew his hips back and thrust harder on his next descent into Virginia's heavenly cave. "Maybe I should have made *you* wait longer."

Though he was only teasing her. No way could he have waited another minute to have her, to be inside her. He knew he was already losing the battle with himself. It wouldn't take much and he'd lose control just like she had earlier when he'd had his mouth on her—something he promised himself he'd do again soon. It seemed to be a surefire way of making her surrender. And nothing felt better than having this headstrong warrior surrender to him. Even if he had to surrender to her at the same time.

Knowing he couldn't hold back much longer, Wes increased his tempo and drove in and out of her with more force. He wanted to make sure she got what she needed. For all he knew her previous lovers had all been strong preternaturals, warriors that gave her a frantic fucking. And under no circumstances did he want to fall short of her expectations.

He looked at her eyes, watched how her breathing changed, how her hips moved. He read her signs, the accelerated heartbeat, the rapidly pulsing vein at her neck, the parted lips.

"Yeah, you like it a little harder, huh? Tell me," he encouraged her.

A breathless moan tumbled over her lips, while she tightened her legs behind his butt, urging him deeper. He got the hint and plunged harder into her. When her eyes rolled back and she pressed her head harder in the mattress, arching her back, he felt his hips working harder and faster.

"I'll fuck you any which way you want. You just tell me."

Her gaze flew to him, pinning him. She seemed to hesitate. Then she opened her mouth to speak. "Take me hard. Take me like you mean it."

Nothing easier than that. Unleashing that part of him that was all man, all alpha, he wrapped his hands around Virginia's wrists and pinned her arms to either side of her head. With her red hair like a halo around her head, her eyes wide now, her mouth open, she looked like a captive. For a second, he stared at her and saw the excitement that had taken hold of her written all over her face. He understood then. She needed him to take her hard so she could let go.

He pulled out of her. Disappointment spread over her features. But he flipped her onto her stomach and gripped her hips, pulling her ass to the edge of the bed. Her face landed in the mattress, her gasp muffled by it. He stood behind her and plowed into her, seating himself to the hilt.

He felt her entire body tremble, but knew it wasn't out of fear. Thrust for thrust he delivered, plunging deep and hard into her drenched pussy, not giving her a chance to even pull herself up and brace herself on her elbows. No, he was fucking her as if he didn't care about her pleasure, when in truth, it was all he cared about: to give this woman what she needed. So she would grant him what he needed: her surrender.

Every time he plunged deep, his balls slapped against her flesh, making them burn as if they'd landed in hellfire. But for Virginia's sake, and for his own, he held onto his control with an iron fist.

From his standing position, he was able to deliver each thrust with more force. And he was able to watch his cock enter her and see her vulnerable flesh quiver with each movement.

"Your pussy is gorgeous. So fucking gorgeous."

He let go of one hip, but continued to thrust. His hand free, he reached around her and brought it to her front. A moment later he found her clit, the little organ swollen and throbbing.

"Now come for your lover," he demanded and pinched her clit, while he thrust hard from behind.

Virginia screamed into the mattress, and her interior muscles spasmed around his cock. Relieved, he let himself go and shot his seed deep into her. He continued to thrust, unable to stop, the added lubrication making every descent even more irresistible. It took a long while until he slowed and eased out of her. But he didn't want to lose the connection to her and dropped back onto the bed, pulled her to his chest, her sweet ass lining up with his groin, and drove back into her, still hard, still wanting.

Sighing, he pressed a kiss to her neck and wrapped his arm around her.

He could get used to this. To her in his bed. To *her*.

14

They'd eaten the food Virginia had appropriated from the store across the road and then gone to sleep. Wesley had tucked her against his big body, wrapped his arm around her, and held her like that all night. She hadn't protested, though she knew what she was doing was wrong. Technically Wesley was still her prisoner, and the council hadn't made a determination yet on what to do with him. But right now, even she had to admit that in order for them to survive she had to bend the rules and trust the witch. He'd saved her life more than once. For that she owed him.

The next morning, after taking a shower and eating breakfast—coffee she'd heated in the microwave and donuts from the supermarket—she sat down at the small table in the motel room and emptied a second bag. She was wearing the clothes she'd stolen last night: black jeans and a black knit sweater over a matching bra and panties set, with black boots that laced up her calves.

Wesley, freshly showered and dressed in the black cargo pants and gray long-sleeved T-shirt she'd gotten for him, joined her at the table. He reached for a donut and bit into it, then pointed to the items she'd spread out on the table: a local map, a calculator, a notepad and pen, and a brand-new pre-paid cell phone and sim card.

"What's all that for?"

"We need to figure out where the closest portal is so we can get back," she explained without looking up. She was already sliding the sim card into the phone and powering it up.

"Good idea. Let's go back to the compound in Baltimore."

She raised her head and looked at him. "I have to make contact with the council."

"But that place blew up."

"There's an emergency safehouse for situations like this."

Wesley grimaced, clearly not happy about going back to the council. "Does that mean you're planning to have me locked up again?"

She hesitated. If she brought Wesley back to the council, they would want to take every precaution against a second attack. Not even her testimony of how he'd helped her escape the demons' Underworld would sway her fellow council members, particularly since it wasn't clear why they'd landed in the Underworld in the first place. They would insist on Wesley being locked up until they could determine whether he was a risk or not.

"Don't bother answering," Wesley said.

"Wes, I'm s—"

"Don't say you're sorry when you're not."

She sought his eyes, but he looked away. "I have to follow the rules. If I don't, I'm putting my people at risk. I can't—"

"Were you following the rules last night? Or is sleeping with a prisoner not against the rules?"

"That's not fair."

"Isn't it?"

She tore her gaze from him and busied herself with the phone so he wouldn't notice that his words had hurt her, when they shouldn't have even dented her armor.

Wes rose and walked to the microwave, opened it, and popped another mug of instant coffee into it.

Blocking out Wesley's presence, Virginia connected to the motel's

Wi-Fi network, then opened the phone's browser. She couldn't risk making a phone call to central command to get information on the closest portal, but there was another, safer way to get the same information.

She navigated to a site and typed in her access code, a string of sixteen random letters, numbers, and symbols. A window popped up, asking whether the site was allowed to access her phone's GPS system. She tapped *allow* and waited. Within a few seconds, several strings of numbers appeared. She noted them down on her pad, then disconnected from the website, shut down the Wi-Fi access, and shut off the phone. The entire process had taken less than twenty seconds. Not enough time for anybody to trace her movements, even if anybody had been monitoring the motel's Wi-Fi system. Which was unlikely in itself.

But even if somebody had been able to note down the same strings of numbers she'd scribbled down, they would need a degree from MIT to figure out what they were looking at.

She started her calculations, using the calculator she'd taken from the big box store. The formula was complicated and the variables she had to use in order to get the correct outcome known only to the Stealth Guardians. They'd developed this method of finding the coordinates of the closest portal only a short while ago, after it had become clear that not all portals were located in a guardian compound.

The *lost* portals, as they were called, could be anywhere. A special task force had been established to locate all lost portals and catalogue them. She could only hope that this part of the country was already in the catalogue.

"What's all this?" Wesley asked over her shoulder.

"Trying to find the coordinates of the closest portal." She continued scribbling figures on her pad.

"Looks like math to me."

She glanced up. "Scared of smart women?"

"Not of smart women, but smart-*ass* women," he retorted and leaned down to her, giving her a kiss on the cheek. "You're a piece of work." Then he winked. "But you do have a really cute ass."

Shaking her head, she chuckled, then asked, "So you're not mad at me anymore?"

"I didn't say that. But if you want to appease me, I can tell you how." He slid his hands over her shoulders, extending his fingers down her front, slowly dropping lower. "You got out of bed so quickly this morning."

"Do you ever think about anything other than sex?" Though she had to admit, she was thinking of it, too. She was having to call on decades of discipline to help her push those thoughts into the background.

His mouth was at her ear, and his palms were on her breasts now. "I also think of the sounds you make when you come." He gently massaged her boobs. "And the way you reacted when I woke you in the middle of the night."

"Mmm." At first, she'd thought it was a dream when he started whispering naughty things to her, but his hands had shown her that it was real. And his cock had felt even better when he'd taken her the second time. She closed her eyes and took a deep breath. "You have to stop this." She grabbed hold of his hands and lifted them off her breasts.

"Later then," he murmured into her ear and stepped back.

She felt his eyes on her back, but continued with her calculations. A few minutes later, she was done. She opened the map and spread it out on the table, then plotted the coordinates.

"There," she said triumphantly.

Wes bent over the map. He pointed to another spot on the map. "And we're here?"

She nodded. "Shouldn't be more than an hour's walk." She folded up the map and rose. "Let's pack up the trash and toss it in the dumpster behind the building. And then we need to burn the demon's body."

"How're we gonna do that?"

She opened another shopping bag. "Lighter fuel and matches."

Wesley grinned. "I've never liked going shopping with women, but somehow I feel like I wouldn't mind shopping with you."

15

———————

It was easy to find the spot where they'd jumped out of the demon's vortex the night before. It was just as easy to find the trash and debris behind which they'd hidden the dead demon's body. Unfortunately, it wasn't at all easy to find the body itself: it had vanished.

"That's impossible!" Virginia ground out.

Wesley scratched his head. Maybe the wound Virginia had delivered hadn't been fatal and the demon had only been unconscious, not dead. "What if he was still alive?"

Virginia spun her head to him. "When I kill a demon, he's fucking dead."

He put a hand on her forearm. "Hey, easy. Nothing personal, okay? I saw you kill him. And he looked dead to me. I just wonder whether he could have played dead in the hopes that he'd get a chance to escape later."

She slanted him an assessing look. "That might make sense for any creature other than a demon. But a demon doesn't plan ahead that far, not in a situation of life and death. If there'd been any life left in him, he would have continued fighting. It's an instinct. I've fought enough demons to know that. I hacked a demon's arm off at the shoulder once, and he was staggering, losing blood faster than an open faucet, and he grabbed a dagger with his other hand and lunged for me. He didn't have a prayer, but he tried with his last breath." She met his gaze. "That demon was dead."

Wesley let her words sink in. Admiration for the warrior in her collided with the fear that one day Virginia would come across a demon she couldn't defeat. He didn't voice either thought. Instead, another concern pushed to the forefront. "Then I think we have a problem. Somebody disposed of the demon's body. And if it wasn't you or me, or any of your colleagues, then it must have been another demon. If a human had found him, this place would be swarming with police."

Virginia sucked in a visible breath. "Which could mean one of two things. And I don't like either."

Wes lifted his chin. "Meaning?"

"Either another demon knew where he was heading and came looking for him, or somebody followed us."

"I don't see how the second scenario is possible. How could they have tailed us? And if they had, why not follow us to the motel and kill us in our sleep?" After all, he and Virginia had been rather distracted while in bed. Anybody could have snuck up on them. He made a mental note to surround them with a guarding spell next time—though in his defense, he didn't have his tools on him. They were probably still in the Baltimore compound, since Virginia hadn't brought them along to the council meeting.

"Do you remember back in the Underworld when the guard at the vortex asked our friend to state his business?" Wes asked, suddenly remembering something.

Virginia's eyes widened as the memory came back to her.

"He said he was going up top on somebody's orders," Wes added, though he couldn't remember the name the demon had mentioned.

Virginia nodded. "On Vintoq's orders."

"Exactly. So, whoever this Vintoq is, he knew where our dead demon was heading. And when he didn't return, he must have sent somebody after him, or maybe even come himself."

Virginia let her gaze roam. There were trees and bushes in the vicinity, an old shack maybe a quarter mile away, and a water tower in the distance. When she turned her gaze back to him, she leaned in.

"What if they're still here watching us?"

"What for?"

"So they can follow us."

"Why would they even suspect that we'd come back here? To the scene of the crime, so to speak." Only an idiot criminal would do that —and he and Virginia, apparently.

"They'd expect us to return to dispose of the demon's body because we can't afford to let humans know what we're dealing with. It would cause widespread panic."

"But wouldn't they assume that you'd remain invisible?"

She shook her head, and her red hair picked up the sunlight and shimmered like it was on fire. "Not necessarily. Cloaking takes a lot of energy. Even the demons know we can't keep it up all the time. And out here, without any human around to witness us burning a body..." She shrugged. "They'd know there's a good chance we wouldn't cloak ourselves."

"I see." And considering what they'd gone through in the Underworld—and later—he was certain that Virginia was exhausted. "We should leave now."

She nodded. "We have to be prepared that they might follow us."

"That's why I think it's a bad idea to return to the council now."

Virginia slanted him a suspicious look.

He sighed. "And, no, it's not because I don't want to land in that lead cell again."

"Uh-huh." She gave him a no-shit-Sherlock look.

"If they really are following us, then the last thing we should do is have any contact with the council. You said yourself that they're the leaders of your race. I'm taking a wild guess here, but when was the last time any of the council members went hand-to-hand with a demon?"

When she hummed in agreement, he continued, "The best thing we can do is to transport to a compound where all they do, day in, day out, is fight demons."

"Let me guess. You want me to transport us to the Baltimore compound."

"Glad you agree."

"You do know that the guardians at that compound have been breaking every rule in the book, right?"

Wes grinned broadly. "Anybody can follow the rules. But these guys can improvise. They're perfect. And I trust them."

"Fine, but if something goes wrong, I'll have your hide," she warned.

He drew her into his arms and pressed a quick kiss to her lips. "You can have my hide anytime you want. I'm not opposed to being tied up and ridden like a bull if the woman riding me lets me admire her gorgeous naked body while she does so."

"You're impossible."

"Impossibly sexy?"

"Impossibly annoying," she shot back.

Wes slid his hand into her mane and pulled her head to him. Her flushed cheeks were too tempting, and if there wasn't the chance that some demon was lurking in the shadows, he would take her right here. But he was smart enough to know when his desire for her had to take a backseat.

"You'll get used to it, babe. Now let's get out of here."

VIRGINIA HAD to grudgingly admit that Wesley was right. They couldn't go meet the other council members. Most had been sitting on the council for many decades, some even for centuries. They weren't warriors anymore, and while they had all learned how to wield a sword and a dagger in their youths, they were out of practice. They had other obligations and left the fighting to the young guardians, the men and women who lived in compounds all around the world, eager and prepared to do battle any day of the week. Willing to fight to the death. That was what they'd all signed up for.

She'd done the same back then. Trained and fought as a guardian in a compound. Protected humans worth protecting. Fought demons. Killed a lot them. But she'd made mistakes. Mistakes that had cost her compound dearly. Because she'd broken the rules, trusted the wrong person.

To repent she'd punished herself by vowing never to mate, and instead had signed up with the enforcers, an elite troupe of exceptional fighters who enforced their race's rules. She'd undergone the most gruesome training and bowed to their stringent rules. And she'd managed to excel. All because she'd expelled emotion from her life.

Successfully.

Until now.

As they hiked toward the lost portal, Virginia cast Wesley a sideways look. He was everything she'd avoided for so many decades: a man who lived by his intuition, skirted the rules whenever it suited him, and didn't seem to have a serious bone in his body. On top of that, he was driven by his desires—which turned out to be insatiable— and took every opportunity to rattle her, as if he found pleasure in seeing her lose her composure.

Any other man she would have beaten to a pulp by now. But there were other sides to Wesley that she had a hard time resisting: the man who risked his own life to save hers, the lover who made her body hum with pleasure, the witch whose skill both fascinated and frightened her.

And then there was the way he called her *babe*. And the way he looked at her with his baby-blues.

"Could that be it?" Wesley asked and pointed to a church that stood on a small hill, surrounded by tall grass that clearly nobody had mowed in months, if not years.

Virginia looked back at her map. "Seems so. It's the only structure I can see. The portal needs something to anchor itself to, like a rock face or the side of a building, a wall, something with structure. It can't be in the ground."

"The portal I used in Sonoma was in a rickety old shack that was leaning against a boulder," Wesley volunteered.

"One of the lost portals. The portals are centuries old. So the material they're anchored to has to be old. In many cases it's rock."

"You said lost. What does that mean?"

"Until about a year ago we weren't aware that there were any portals in places other than our compounds. But we were wrong. We've since found hundreds spread out all over the world. Not tied to any compound."

"How do you think they came into existence?"

"We're not sure."

"Mmm." Wesley ran a hand through his hair. "You said they have to be anchored to something like rock?"

She nodded. "Yes, or some other material that's been around a long time."

"Interesting. You think a portal could be moved?"

"Moved?" That thought had never occurred to her. "Like how?"

"Let's say some company excavated a bunch of rock from a plot of land to clear it, and somewhere in all that rock was the entrance to a portal, and then somebody used it to build"—He pointed to the church—"a church or something. Would that stone still be the access point to the portal?"

She stopped walking. "Oh my God." Wesley's idea made sense. How could a witch who knew very little about their kind have come to that conclusion? But it was logical, and it would explain the existence of the lost portals. It would explain so much.

"What?" he asked.

"How did you figure that out?"

He chuckled. "I'm good for more than just sex, you know."

She smiled and shook her head. "Let's go inside and find the portal."

Inside the church it was musty. Nobody had let any fresh air inside in a long time. The windows were dirty, most of the pews had been ripped out. There was no artwork left, just one large wooden cross hanging behind a stone altar. To one side was an old confessional, but the doors had been removed, and the seats had been stripped of their upholstery, leaving small metal tacks sticking out from the wood.

Virginia headed straight for the altar, Wesley followed her. She examined the heavy stone, ran her palms over the rough surface to find the sign that indicated that this was the portal. Every inch of its surface she touched, but there was nothing. She looked up, meeting Wesley's gaze.

"I don't understand it. It must be here," she said.

"Let's check the rest of the place," Wesley suggested, his voice calm as if he wanted to soothe her.

She nodded and examined every square foot of the church's walls, every stone under her feet, while Wesley started at the other end of the building. With every minute that passed, she grew more nervous. Had she made an error in her calculation? One mathematical error, and her coordinates could be hundreds of miles off.

"Found it!"

Wesley's triumphant voice made her spin around and practically sprint to where he stood: at the confessional. When she reached him, he pointed inside the area where the priest would sit. She followed his finger and saw it, too. The ancient dagger their kind used to identify a portal was carved into the wall.

Quickly she pressed her palm against it and felt heat build beneath it. Moments later the portal opened behind the priest's pew.

She looked over her shoulder, and Wesley nodded at her, indicating that she go first. Virginia stepped over the seat and jumped into the darkness, then turned and reached her hand out to Wesley.

As soon as Wesley was inside the portal, he put his arm around her waist.

"Drive carefully, will you? I get a little motion sick," he said with a wink.

"It'll be over before you know it," she promised and concentrated on their destination.

Within seconds, they arrived. Virginia eased out of Wesley's arms and adjusted her clothing. Now that they were back in the compound, where in a few moments they'd be around other Stealth Guardians, it was paramount that nobody found out what had happened between her and Wesley. If they did, it would undermine her position. Fraternizing with a prisoner—because technically Wesley was still her captive and his fate hadn't been determined yet—was equivalent to treason.

Virginia stepped out of the portal and looked over her shoulder, watching as Wesley did the same. She met his eyes and took a breath, about to explain to him that any physical contact or familiarity between them had to cease. But she didn't get a chance to speak.

A loud beeping suddenly sounded. She froze.

"What is that?" Wes asked, panic in his voice and eyes.

A high-pitched scream came from somewhere in the building, then a loud thud echoed through the corridor.

"Shit!" Virginia cursed.

"Demons?" Wes was already heading toward the stairs. "We have to help them."

She gripped his forearm, jerking him back. "We need weapons." She pivoted, away from the stairs and toward another corridor. "The arsenal is this way. Hurry!"

She charged ahead, her heart beating into her throat.

Had the demons managed to attack not just the council compound, but also the other compounds around the world? If they had, then she wasn't sure all the weapons in the arsenal would be enough to defeat them.

16

The hell pit was a crater filled with bubbling tar that consumed anything unfortunate enough to fall into it. There was no surviving it; it was a slow, torturous death. Every leader of the Demons of Fear before Zoltan had used it to punish traitors among their kind, and it had become a useful deterrent. Which was the reason why Zoltan liked to assemble his demons around its edges—to remind them what would happen if they didn't execute his orders. If they didn't succeed in fulfilling their duties.

And they hadn't succeeded.

Not this time.

They had failed miserably.

"You had bloodhounds, and still, you couldn't find the intruders!" Zoltan bellowed now, his voice thundering in the cavernous space.

A few hundred of his demons stood in front of him, their heads bowed, their eyes averted. His other followers, the thousands dwelling in the many caves of the Underworld, would soon hear of this assembly and count themselves lucky that they hadn't been among those tasked with sniffing out the Stealth Guardians who'd intruded into their world.

"Who was in charge of the dogs? Step forward!"

There was a movement in the crowd. Zoltan focused on it and watched as a demon with strawberry blond hair made his way through the assembled. Everybody seemed eager to get out of his way. It took a few moments before the demon who supervised the kennels and trained the dogs separated from his brethren and stopped a few yards away from Zoltan.

He bowed. "I am Klaus, oh Great One."

"What have you got to say in your defense?"

"We did everything we could. The dogs picked up a scent, but it turned out to be a diversion. The guardians must have disguised their smell. We couldn't anticipate that."

Wrong answer. Zoltan grabbed Klaus by the throat and pushed him back to the edge of the pit. There, he snarled at him. "Excuses! I don't want to hear excuses. Do you understand that?"

"Yes, oh Great One," the demon groveled.

"Now try again. Why did you fail?"

"It was m-m-my fault. Entirely mine."

Zoltan chuckled. "Better." He tossed a sideways glance at his subjects who were watching the exchange with fear and trepidation. "And what do we do with men who fail me?"

"Kill him," the crowd said in unison.

Satisfied that his underlings still towed the line, Zoltan looked back at his captive. "Did you hear what your brethren demand I do?"

Klaus was trembling now, knowing that his fate was sealed. Zoltan felt satisfaction roll over him. He felt the other demon's fear, loved the way it wrapped around the man like a cocoon. But this wasn't the kind of cocoon that protected. This was the kind that destroyed from within. Because fear weakened. Fear undermined. Fear debilitated. That's why he loved it so much: it turned his enemies into whimpering fools unable to fight back.

Just like this shivering coward wasn't fighting back.

All Zoltan had to do was release him and he would tumble backward into the hell pit to be swallowed up by the liquid tar, suffering an agonizing death. But his death wouldn't be for nothing: it would be an example to his brethren, teaching them that failure was unacceptable.

Zoltan pushed Klaus farther back so his upper body was hanging over the pit, his legs still anchored to the ground, but off balance. Then he started to loosen his grip.

"Oh Great One!"

Zoltan glanced over his shoulder and saw Yannick hurrying into the cave.

"Can't you see I'm busy? What is it?"

Yannick made a perfunctory bow, then quickly said, "The men you sent on the mission, one of them is back."

Zoltan knew immediately what mission Yannick was referring to. He pulled Klaus back so he stood on his own again. "Only one?"

"Yes, oh Great One." He motioned to the tunnel he'd come from. "This way."

Nodding, Zoltan released his grip on his captive's neck, and turned to join Yannick, when he heard Klaus sigh in relief. He spun on his heel and glared at the demon.

"Bad move."

With one hand, Zoltan shoved Klaus backward, sending him over the edge.

A desperate scream dislodged from the demon's throat as he fell into the hell pit. More screams followed. Screams of horrific pain and despair. But Zoltan was already marching out of the cave. As much as he wanted to watch his subject suffer, he had more important things to do.

Ulric was waiting for them in the throne room, the largest cavern in the Underworld. Red flames flickered through the cracks of the uneven stone walls, gas burned from sconces along it, and a massive stone throne sat on a rock platform, stairs leading down to the large area where his subjects assembled to hear the Great One speak. Today the great hall was empty.

"You may leave, Yannick," Zoltan said without looking at him. He waited until the footsteps grew fainter and then vanished completely.

Then he looked at Ulric. He appeared worse for wear, his clothes torn and green blood oozing from various wounds.

"You're alone?"

Ulric nodded.

"Where are the others?"

"Dead, oh Great One."

"Why?"

"I'm not sure. We transported into the Stealth Guardians' compound and spread out to do our reconnaissance, when I heard an alarm go off, and sounds of men fighting. I can only assume that my men were discovered."

Zoltan narrowed his eyes in suspicion. "Yet you escaped. How fortunate."

"I tried to help them. I did what I could. There was much confusion. Too many Stealth Guardians running around, heading for their portal. I waited for them to leave in the hope of accessing their portal after them."

"Hmm." At least that seemed like a smart idea. The best Ulric had probably had in his entire life. "And?"

"They initiated a self-destruct sequence."

Zoltan sucked in a breath. "They willingly destroyed their own compound?"

Ulric nodded eagerly. "They did. There was nothing left of the portal. I was lucky to get out alive."

"What took you so long to get back? I sent you there over twenty-four hours ago."

"The explosion. It knocked me unconscious. I hurried back as soon as I came to."

Hurried footsteps echoed from one of the tunnels leading to the throne room. Zoltan snapped his head in its direction and saw Vintoq running toward them.

"I came as quickly as I heard, oh Great One," Vintoq said. "Yannick informed me that your reconnaissance team attacked the compound."

Zoltan spun his head back to Ulric, glaring at him. "You didn't say your team attacked first."

Ulric's lips trembled and his eyes darted to Vintoq, then back to Zoltan. "We didn't attack. I told my men to be stealthy. I cautioned them to hide, not to use their weapons. They knew it was a reconnaissance mission first and foremost. I never gave an order to attack."

"Hmm." Zoltan contemplated his words. Was Ulric lying to save his hide?

Vintoq sidled up to Zoltan. "Oh Great One, that's not what Yannick overheard Ulric mumbling when he stepped out of the vortex on his arrival back here."

"No!" Ulric protested and searched Zoltan's eyes. "You must believe me. I did nothing wrong. I followed your instructions to the letter."

"He's lying. Punish him!" Vintoq demanded and reached for Ulric's throat. Ulric pushed back.

"There's something else," Ulric said, his gaze swinging back to Zoltan, panic evident. "In my pocket. I found something just before the place blew up. Just outside what looked like a conference chamber."

"Lies!" Vintoq hissed and squeezed Ulric's throat, causing him to choke.

Zoltan stepped in and reached into Ulric's pocket. He pulled a shiny device from it. A cell phone covered in a silver casing.

"Vintoq, stand down. Release him!"

Vintoq shot a look at Zoltan, defiance spewing from his eyes. "But, oh Great One. He's a failure. He didn't follow your orders."

Ulric fought for air, clawing at Vintoq in desperation.

"Let him go!" Zoltan repeated. "Or you'll suffer his fate instead."

Immediately, Vintoq released his victim. Ulric coughed and breathed hard, sucking deep breaths of air into his lungs.

Zoltan lifted the cell phone, showing it to Vintoq. "This will more than make up for the botched mission." He woke the cellphone and scrolled through its contact list. Dozens of names and numbers. A veritable goldmine.

He lifted his head and looked at Ulric. "Despite your team's failure, you've done well." Because this phone was better than a blueprint of the Stealth Guardians' compound.

"Congratulations. You get to live."

For now.

17

───────

Armed with two daggers, Wes raced after Virginia, who'd already reached the door to the kitchen from which loud sounds of banging and voices originated. She looked over her shoulder, nodding at him. She was equally armed, and judging by the fierce expression on her face, ready to fight to the death.

Virginia put her hand on the door handle, but Wes stopped her and whispered, "Smoke." He put his palm on the door to feel if it was hot, but to his relief it wasn't. "It's cold." At least they wouldn't be hit with a backdraft, though there was no way of knowing what would greet them.

"I'll take the left, you take the right," Virginia instructed.

Wes nodded, then Virginia ripped the door open and charged inside. He barreled after her into the room, smoke making his eyes tear up immediately. Still, he was ready to fight, even if he had a hard time keeping his eyes open.

"Ugh!" Somebody coughed.

The sound was high-pitched, coming from a woman, he was certain.

"Virginia?"

Another sound, this time a whooshing sound, then some clanging and the sound of an exhaust.

Then a thud and the sounds of two people fighting in hand-to-hand combat.

"Fuck!"

This time, Wesley recognized the female voice. "Enya?"

He charged toward the melee, able to see the outlines of the two people fighting. "Shit, Virginia! Let go of her. It's Enya." The smoke was dissipating now, being sucked out through the powerful exhaust over the stove.

He reached Virginia and Enya just as Virginia let go of her fellow Stealth Guardian.

Enya stumbled backward. "What the fuck was that for?" She glared at Virginia, her eyes mirrors of fury.

From the open door, Wes perceived the sound of rapidly approaching footsteps.

"The alarm," Wes quickly explained, whirling toward the door, his daggers ready. "You're under attack by the demons."

"What?" Enya choked out.

Two men charged in: Logan and Manus.

"What's going on here?" Logan yelled.

Virginia, breathing hard, rushed to Wesley's side. "We heard the alarm and assumed the compound was being attacked."

Manus stopped and laughed. "That was just one of Enya's attempts at cooking."

"Shit, that was the fire alarm?" Wes asked, turning his head to Virginia, who stared at the two men, her mouth agape.

"There's no need to laugh, you ass," Enya griped from behind them. "Not my fault that the pancakes burned. I was just trying to keep them warm."

Logan walked to the stove. On top of the burners sat a tray with pancakes that resembled the lava stones of the Underworld in color, though not in temperature: they were still smoldering. Logan chuckled and pointed to the controls of the oven, the door of which still stood open. "You do know what broil means, Enya, don't you?" He turned the knob to the off position and turned his back to the oven.

Enya grunted something unintelligible. "Well, it's still no reason to charge in here and attack me. I was dealing with it." She pointed to the fire extinguisher that lay on the floor.

Virginia braced her hands on her hips and glared at Enya. "Well, excuse me for wanting to save your compound from a demon attack!"

"Why don't we all calm down, huh?" The advice came from Aiden, who'd just appeared in the door. "We've got bigger fish to fry than Enya's inedible pancakes." He turned his gaze to Wesley. "You're alive." And as if he only now noticed Virginia, he quickly motioned toward her and added, "You, too, Counselor."

Wes nodded. "It's been quite a trip."

"We got word of the attack on the council compound. Nobody had word of either of you. We didn't think you'd made it out."

"Yeah, and I can tell how broken up you all were about that," Virginia said in an icy voice.

Aiden cast her a sideways glance. "No offense, Counselor, that we weren't all sitting around crying, but we've been busy shoring up our defenses to protect our own compound. Every compound in the world is on lockdown; we're all running on emergency protocol."

Virginia nodded and took a visible breath. "Fine. What of the rest of the council? Did they all make it to their safe houses?"

Aiden nodded. "I was in contact with my father not an hour ago. There are no losses to report. But nobody is leaving the security of the compounds for a while."

"And here?" Wes asked. "Is everybody accounted for?"

"Hamish is bringing Tessa back from City Hall as we speak. There was an important meeting she couldn't miss. Jay and Sean have brought their charges to a safe house and will remain there with them until this blows over. Pearce is in the command center, monitoring all messages coming in from the other compounds."

"And Leila?" Wes asked, surprised that Aiden hadn't mentioned his wife yet.

"She's been feeling sick this morning. She's in our quarters, resting." He motioned to Enya, grinning. "That's why Enya volunteered to cook, with catastrophic results, if I may add."

"Can we stop talking about my cooking skills?" Enya snapped and glared at her colleagues. "And if Counselor Robson hadn't taken Wesley away, I wouldn't have had to cook, now would I?"

"I'm right here," Virginia ground out from between clenched teeth. "And I won't tolerate your insubordination."

"Well, then maybe I should file a complaint about you attacking me out of the blue when you could clearly see it was me! How would that look on your spotless record, huh, Counselor?" Enya narrowed her eyes, daring Virginia to respond.

And from what Wesley could see, Virginia was going to respond, which would only escalate the situation. "Maybe you can cut your counselor some slack, considering that she just took a trip to the Underworld and barely got out alive."

That shut everybody up.

Logan whistled through his teeth.

"Are you fucking serious?" Aiden asked, his gaze bouncing between Wesley and Virginia like a ping-pong ball in a confined space.

"That's impossible," Manus croaked.

"How?" Enya asked. "Nobody's ever been to their world."

"We'll happily give you a full update and—" Wes said.

"Get everybody together in the command room, I'll brief you," Virginia interrupted him.

The four Stealth Guardians were already marching toward the door and into the corridor, when Virginia grabbed Wesley's arm and held him back.

"You're not gonna exclude me, are you?" he asked. So much for having saved her life.

"I'm not. But you have to understand one thing: you're not in charge here. This is my domain."

Wes raised an eyebrow. "You're worried. Something I should know about?"

"Just don't forget that you're still a prisoner, even though I'm not locking you up."

He was about to reply, when Aiden called out, "Are you coming?"

"Yes!" Wes replied and hurried into the hallway, catching up with the others.

Logan was on the phone. "Meet us in the command center. Yes, ten minutes." He disconnected the call. "Hamish will be back in a few minutes."

"Good, then we won't have to tell the story twice," Wes said.

"Can't wait to hear about it," Aiden said, slapping Wesley on the back. "I'm really glad you made it. Gave us all a bit of a scare when the council told us that you were missing. They suspected you had something to do with the demons' attack and that you might have killed Virginia."

"Hope you didn't believe that."

Aiden shrugged. "The part about you helping the demons, maybe. But when my dad said that Virginia was believed to be dead and that you might have killed her, I knew he was wrong." He leaned in and lowered his voice. "You wouldn't kill the woman whose pants you want to get into, right?"

"Right." Even though right now he was a tad pissed at the woman whose pants he'd already *been* in, because she was treating him like he meant nothing to her. But that was none of Aiden's business. He'd deal with that later.

Hamish showed up as promised and joined them in the command center only ten minutes later—without Tessa. He'd taken her to check on Leila in case she needed anything. Pearce sat at the console, keeping an eye on the messages that popped up on various screens. Aiden had pulled several chairs around the console for everyone to sit, but Wes hopped on a desk and sat there instead, while Virginia leaned against it, keeping her distance from him as if she didn't want to get too close.

"Okay, let me give you the basics," Virginia started and launched into a retelling of their ordeal in the Underworld, including how they'd escaped, but excluding what had happened later at the motel.

Once or twice a guardian interrupted her to clarify some part of the story, but for the most part all of them listened intently, soaking up every single word. After a lot of head shaking, exclamations of admiration, and a considerable amount of cursing, Virginia had the other guardians up to speed on the events that took place in the demons' lair.

For a moment there was silence. Then Aiden said, "I remember hearing Zoltan's thoughts in the vortex when we were rescuing Leila. It's exactly how you described it."

"I read the report a while ago," Virginia said, "but I didn't realize that was you."

"Not that this knowledge has helped us in any way," Aiden replied. "I think what Wes figured out is much more valuable."

Wesley lifted his chin. "You mean my theory of how the lost portals came to be?"

Hamish pushed away from the console he'd been leaning against. "I found the first of the lost portals over a year ago. I've been trying to figure out ever since how they could have come into existence." He looked at Virginia. "Counselor Robson, I'm sure you remember the stories from the Dark Days when many of our compounds were destroyed by not only demons, but also by human wars and natural disasters. I suspect that the old rocks that disguised the entrances to our portals were later reused by humans to build other structures: bridges, monuments, churches, warehouses."

"That makes sense," Wes said, "after all, quarried rock was hard to come by. People would have reused whatever they could, especially after a war."

"We'll have to inform the council members of this," Virginia added.

"Doing it right now," Pearce confirmed, punching away at his keyboard.

"Good. Now to something else: does the council have any suspicions as to how the demons were able to find and enter the compound?" Virginia asked.

"You mean other than that they believe Wesley led them there?" Manus shot back.

Logan jabbed him in the ribs and mouthed something unintelligible to him. "Sorry, we're just all a bit on edge."

"The council has no leads as of yet," Pearce said, pointing to the computer screen. "But the other compounds have come up with plenty of theories."

"Let me hear them," Virginia demanded.

Pearce looked at the screen and started. "Betrayal by a council member."

Virginia grunted.

"Been done, you know," Aiden said.

Virginia motioned to Pearce. "Go on, what else?"

"A human mate being blackmailed by a demon. Torture of an emissarius. Betrayal by a guardian turned demon. Carelessness by a guardian traveling to the compound. Coincidence."

"Coincidence?" Wes repeated, frowning.

Pearce shrugged. "A blind man may perchance hit the mark—if he takes aim often enough. Law of probability. The demons have been on our asses long enough."

"Unrealistic," Virginia said dismissively. "Any other theories?"

"What's an emissarius?" Wes asked, recalling the word Pearce had thrown out earlier.

"A human who works for us, spies for us, keeps us abreast of anything important," Aiden explained. "They know who we are, and they are loyal to us. But they wouldn't be able to betray our compounds."

"Why?"

"Because they don't know where they're located," Virginia answered in Aiden's stead.

Wes gave her a sideways glance. "Then how do they get in contact with you when they have news for you?"

"They're given a phone number to call, and we get in contact with them when it's safe."

"And the number," Wes mused, "can it be traced?"

"No," Pearce said firmly. "Not a chance."

That didn't leave very many theories that were viable. "Virginia, you said the mate of a guardian wouldn't know where the council compound is located, right?" Wes didn't look at her, but turned to the others, all of whom, to his surprise, were suddenly staring at him as if he'd just committed the greatest faux pas. He quickly glanced at Virginia, who was glaring at him sternly.

"*Counselor Robson* is right," Aiden said, putting emphasis on the first two words.

That was when Wesley realized why everybody was looking at him as if he'd grown horns. He'd called Virginia by her first name.

"Oh, for fuck's sake, people," Wes cursed. "What are we standing on ceremony for? We could all be dead by tomorrow for all we know. So, let's not get bent out of shape because I called Counselor Robson by her first name. I think after saving her ass from the demons, I've earned it."

For a second everybody seemed to hold their breath, then Virginia looked at the guardians and said, "I suppose it makes things easier for everybody. Forget about calling me counselor." When everybody nodded, she addressed Wesley again. "You were saying?"

"The human mates of your guardians. Though they don't know the location of the council compound they would know the location of the compound they lived at with their mate, right?"

Both Aiden and Hamish squared their shoulders.

"What are you insinuating?" Hamish hissed.

"Our women are beyond reproach," Aiden grunted.

Wes lifted his hands in a defensive motion. He had no intention of alienating Aiden and Hamish. "I didn't mean to suggest that your wives would do anything to hurt you or your kind. But I'm sure you're not the only guardians who have human mates. Any of them could be a weak link that the demons could exploit."

"Hmm." Hamish crossed his arms over his chest.

Aiden did the same.

Wes sighed. So much for voicing his opinion.

Manus now rose from his chair. "Don't worry about those two. They're just protective of their women. But since I'm objective, I can follow your logic."

Hamish scoffed at Manus's comment. "That'd be a first."

Manus tossed him a shut-the-fuck-up look, then said, "So, Wes, what I think you're saying is that it's possible that the demons got to one of the human mates, maybe even without her knowing it, possibly by simply following her."

"Exactly. She might not have even been aware she was being tailed. She might have inadvertently led a demon to one of the compounds, where the demon found the portal and accessed the council compound from there. Isn't that possible? I mean can they access a portal with their powers?"

"We're not sure. In any case, there was no alarm," Virginia said.

"What if the demons were able to eliminate the alarm?"

"Hmm. But they'd have to have had a Stealth Guardian with them in the portal to operate it."

Wes thought about Virginia's assertion. She'd said as much when she had transported him to the council compound. "Is there any other way into the compounds? This sounds like a dumb question, but did you check the front door? Is there a front door?"

The guardians hesitated, then their glances turned to Virginia—looking for approval.

Finally, Hamish answered, "There are doors, simply because we can't get humans or other creatures, witches for example, through the walls. So should we arrive at the compound in any way other than via a portal, we have to use one of the normal entrances to bring the human in. It doesn't happen often, because humans aren't allowed in the compounds."

"Other than human mates," Virginia clarified.

"Yes," Hamish consented. "Our human mates do occasionally have to use the doors. But that doesn't mean the demons would be able to find them."

"Why not?" Wes asked.

"Because the compounds are invisible."

Wesley's chin dropped. "You mean this entire building"—he made an all-encompassing movement with his hands—"is invisible?"

Hamish nodded. "The old runes you see everywhere, plus our *virta*, our life force, keeps it hidden. The demons can't see it. Neither can humans. Or witches."

"But it's there, right? You can still feel it. You can run into it."

"There's a warding spell on the entire building that prevents anybody from wanting to come closer. They wouldn't even be aware of avoiding it. They'd just turn around and go the other way."

"Pretty nifty," Wes had to admit. "And you know for a fact that this spell works on demons?" The guardians exchanged apprehensive looks. "You don't? Then it's possible the demons could be immune to this spell and could have gotten close enough to the compound to find a way in."

"That's pure speculation," Hamish said.

"So is everything else," Logan said calmly. "I say we go about it systematically. We all take one theory and work through it. Betrayal by a guardian turned demon, a guardian's mate being followed, a rogue council member, a compromised emissarius, and a careless guardian. Work for everybody?"

When nobody protested, Logan turned to Pearce. "Run us lists of all emissarii in our zone, all human mates worldwide, and all council members, past and present, if still alive."

"Also, all the guards who've ever served at the council compound," Virginia added.

Logan nodded. "Good idea. And send out word to the other compounds to compile a report on which of their guardians had meetings with emissarii in the last, let's say, seven days."

"You've got it," Pearce replied. "The list of the emissarii in our zone will be the quickest. You'll have that in two minutes. You can get started on that while I work on the other lists."

Wesley jumped off the desk. He loved the way the guys here came together when push came to shove. They reminded him of his friends at Scanguards—and the fact that he hadn't called them yet to let them know that he was alive.

"And another thing," Virginia suddenly added. "Don't tell anybody that Wesley and I are alive. Not even the council members. If we truly have a traitor that high up, it's best if they believe the witch and I are dead."

Wes met Virginia's eyes. Smart thinking.

When everybody nodded in agreement and then huddled around the computer console, he leaned toward Virginia and murmured, "Name's still Wesley, or have you forgotten?"

"I haven't forgotten anything."

18

Virginia couldn't help but be impressed. Within hours after her and Wesley's arrival at the Baltimore compound, everybody was deeply entrenched in the investigation into the attack on the council compound. They'd spread out in the command center, working the computers and phones, and monitoring messages that came in from around the world.

Virginia was working on the list of council members past and present, when the door to the command center suddenly opened. Two women entered: Leila and Tessa. They carried trays with food. The aroma drifted to her, and she realized how hungry she was.

"Time for lunch, everybody," Leila announced.

The guardians rose from their chairs and walked to the table along the wall, where Leila and Tessa were placing the dishes, and started grabbing plates and heaving food onto them.

Virginia welcomed the break. She looked around for Wesley and saw him waiting his turn for the food. He hadn't talked to her since reprimanding her for not using his name and calling him witch. It had been an attempt at making the other guardians believe that nothing had happened between her and Wesley.

She'd wanted to explain the ground rules to Wesley earlier so that he would understand why she had to give him the cold shoulder in front of the others, but they'd been interrupted by Aiden, and there hadn't been a good time since.

Virginia walked to the table and stopped behind Wesley. Reaching for a plate, she leaned in and whispered, "We need to talk later."

He glanced over his shoulder. "About what?"

Clearly, he wasn't going to make this easy. Fair enough. She couldn't really blame him for his icy response.

"About how things have to be from now on," she said.

"And who decides that?"

She opened her mouth, but hesitated, not sure how to respond. The answer should have been simple: she was the one in charge. But in Wesley's presence she didn't feel like she was in control. She felt... insecure. He made her question her actions, her beliefs, her goals. Nobody had ever done that, and now this man, this witch, who wasn't even as strong as her, stood up to her like nobody before him.

"Hey, guys, you've gotta see this," Pearce called out from the command console where he sat chowing down on his food.

Virginia turned and marched toward him, while several of the others did the same. She stopped behind Pearce's chair.

"It's about Faldo." He blew up a window on one of the screens.

"Faldo?" Virginia asked.

"An emissarius here in Baltimore."

He turned up the volume, and Virginia concentrated on the screen. A reporter stood outside a house. Policemen swarmed the property, and two men were rolling out a gurney: it carried a black body bag.

"Shit!" Hamish hissed next to her.

"Approximately one hour ago," the female reporter on the screen started, *"the police were called to this mansion behind me, belonging to Anton Faldo, a businessman with reported ties to organized crime. Mr. Faldo was found dead by his housekeeper earlier today. Reports indicate that he was found lying in a pool of blood in his study, and the house had been ransacked. The time of death is still unclear, but a statement from*

his housekeeper, who has been on vacation for the past week, asserts that the victim lived alone. It's therefore possible that Mr. Faldo was killed several days ago. As for the cause of death, the police haven't released any details yet. However, early indications are that this was a mob hit."

Behind her on the screen, an elderly white woman exited the house, her face tearstained. Communicating with her producer off-camera, the reporter mouthed something, then looked over her shoulder, catching sight of the woman.

"And here is the housekeeper, Mrs. uh...Jefferson." She turned and stepped in the woman's path. *"Are you Mrs. Jefferson, Mr. Faldo's housekeeper?"*

Startled, the woman stopped, whipped her head in the direction of the camera, then back to the reporter. Somewhat shyly she nodded. *"Carol Jefferson, yes."* She pulled a tissue from her coat pocket and dabbed at her eyes.

"Can you tell us anything about what might have happened to your employer?"

Her lips trembled, but she answered, *"I wasn't here. He gave me the week off. You know."* A sob tore from her chest. *"Because he was supposed to be gone. This should never have happened. He wasn't even supposed to be at home."*

Clearly distraught, the housekeeper blew her nose into the tissue.

The reporter looked back at the camera. *"As you can see, Mr. Faldo's death has come as a shock to everybody. We'll stay on this story—"*

Pearce muted the volume.

Curses bounced off the walls. Hamish exhaled sharply. "Faldo was the one who alerted us to Tessa's needing protection." He put his arm around his wife, who sidled up to him, tears brimming in her eyes.

"I feel so bad," Tessa murmured. "For so long I thought he was just another mobster taking advantage of this city and its inhabitants, but he was better than that. He looked out for me, for us."

Hamish pressed a kiss to the top of her head. "I know. That's why we'll find out what happened. I promise you." Then he looked straight at Virginia. "Unfortunately, there's a good chance the demons were able to connect him to us. They had a person close to Tessa who knew Faldo was the one who brokered the deal for her protection. By the time we found out who it was, it was too late. Faldo's name could have easily been passed on to the demons." He cursed. "It's my fault. I should have had him relocated immediately."

Virginia made a dismissive hand movement. "Let's not waste any time on what could have been." She pointed to the screen. "We need to find out what the demons were looking for at his house. The reporter didn't mention anything about Faldo being tortured."

"We can figure that out pretty easily," Hamish said, then pointed to Logan. "Can you go down to the morgue, and have a look at the body?"

"I can do that," Logan said.

"I'm going to his house," Hamish stated.

"Not alone, you're not," Virginia interrupted. "Take two guardians with you. It'll be faster and safer."

"Fine. Enya, Manus, you're with me."

Pearce swiveled in his chair. "I'll check the logs to see which guardians Faldo has been in contact with over the last few days." He was already typing away on his keyboard.

"I can go with Hamish," Wes suddenly said.

Virginia stared at him. "You're not leaving this—"

"Hear me out on this," he interrupted. "If I go with them, I can use witchcraft to maybe find traces of whoever did this. And perhaps even what they were looking for."

Virginia hesitated. Allowing a prisoner to roam freely within the compound was one thing, allowing him outside with his bag of tricks was breaking the rules at a level that was unprecedented.

"He kept his word last time," Aiden interjected. "And he's good. His magic works."

She knew that, had seen it with her own eyes. But could she risk letting him loose? What if something went wrong? What if he got hurt?

Her own thoughts surprised her. Was she worried about Wesley?

"Come on, Virginia, after all we've been through, I think you owe me a little trust."

He stared at her with his baby-blues, and she knew what he was referring to. Not just that he'd saved her life, but also that she'd surrendered to him in bed, and that he hadn't taken advantage of her vulnerability. She'd been safe with him.

Slowly, she nodded. "But I'm coming with you."

"No!"

The protest didn't come from Wesley, but from Pearce.

"Excuse me?"

"We need you here," Pearce claimed and pointed to the screen.

"What is it?" Virginia asked, instantly alarmed.

"Faldo's last contact with our kind was a council member."

Shit!

"We need to access the details on whom he met and what was discussed."

Virginia took a shaky breath. "You think a council member could have anything to do with this?"

"I'm not making any accusations," Pearce said carefully. "But it's a lead we have to follow up on. Like it or not. The situation is delicate. It's best that you, as a fellow council member, handle this."

"You're right." She looked at Wesley. "You'll go with Hamish, Enya, and Manus. Be careful." Then she connected her gaze with Hamish's. "And you make sure nothing happens to Wesley. He's valuable."

In more ways than one.

19

This was officially Wesley's fifth trip in the Stealth Guardians' portal, and he was getting more and more used to it. Maybe this wasn't such a bad way to travel after all. Or maybe the fact that he was clutching his backpack, which contained all his tools of witchcraft, made the trip bearable.

After transporting to a warehouse somewhere in Baltimore, Hamish led them to a car parked close by, and together with Manus and Enya, they drove off.

Anton Faldo lived in a fancy suburb of Baltimore, among large mansions with manicured front lawns and mature trees giving shade.

Hamish stopped a block away from the house and turned off the engine. Several police and forensics vehicles were still parked outside, but it appeared that they were packing up. The coroner's van had left already.

"We'll wait here, until they're gone," Hamish said. "Shouldn't be long now."

Wesley sat in the passenger seat and turned sideways now, so he could look at all three Stealth Guardians. "So, I take it Anton Faldo is human?"

Hamish nodded. "*Was* human."

"And an emissarius, a spy."

"He worked for us, yes," Hamish said.

"And he knew what you are?" Wes asked.

"Faldo did," Hamish replied.

"But not all of them do," Enya said. "There are some whom we've entrusted with our secrets, mainly because they've stumbled on them one way or another. Others know nothing about who we are or what we do. And we try to keep it that way."

Wesley nodded. "A bit like how we operate at Scanguards then. There are humans who know about the vampires. But we also have people working for us in our human divisions who're unaware of who they really work for."

Hamish turned toward him. "So how many are there at Scanguards?"

"How many vampires?"

"Yeah."

"In San Francisco there are quite a few, plus hybrids, humans, and of course, me, a witch. But we have offices in several major US cities, though San Francisco is our main hub. It used to be New York, but since Samson, the boss, lives in San Francisco with his family, things shifted."

"Family?" Manus piped up from the back seat. "You mean he's married or whatever the vampires call it?"

"Blood-bonded, yes, to a human actually. Three kids, all adults now."

Manus exchanged a look with his two colleagues. "I thought vampires couldn't procreate."

"They can if they bond with a human. But even between two vampires it's possible now. Long story, but—"

"I'm afraid you'll have to tell us some other time," Hamish interrupted and pointed through the windshield. "Faldo's place is clear. We'd better get going." He motioned to Enya and Manus. "I want you two to cloak yourselves and head for the house. Wesley and I will exit the car normally, and once I'm sure nobody is watching, I'll make us invisible. We'll meet you at the back of Faldo's house."

"Got it," Manus said.

An instant later, both he and Enya were cloaked and ready to go. Wesley heard them shift in their seats. A few seconds later, there was silence. They'd left the car without opening the doors, simply passing through them.

"That's a freaky skill." Wes said. "Suppose that can't be taught, can it?"

Hamish chuckled and shook his head. "Nope. It's just for us. And it's come in handy once or twice."

"I bet more than once or twice."

Hamish shrugged. "Let's go. See that high hedge and that tree on the sidewalk? We'll head that way and I'll cloak us once we're in between the hedge and the tree. It should give us enough cover."

"Sounds good."

They both exited the car. It was late afternoon and the sun stood low over the horizon, throwing long shadows over the neighborhood. Wes glanced around, trying to be as inconspicuous as he could. None of the neighbors seemed to be outside.

Everything worked just as Hamish had promised. Invisibly, they reached the back of Faldo's house. The lush yard was large and private. Double doors led from the house out onto a large wooden deck. As they approached, Enya opened them from the inside and ushered them in.

The Colonial style house was decorated in a style that could only be described as mafia-chic: gold tassels on the heavy brocade curtains and all the furnishings, gold-rimmed mirrors, pictures, and coffee tables mixed with bold color choices and eighties-style opulence.

"Whoa. This is... uh... different." Wes exchanged a look with the three guardians.

Manus shrugged. "Just because he worked for us doesn't mean he had good taste."

"What did this guy do for a living?" Wes asked and followed Hamish, who was heading toward the hallway.

"Something in construction."

"Or waste management," Enya added. "Who cares?"

Wes couldn't help but wonder whether that was code for organized crime. "So, he had enemies."

"Everybody has enemies," Hamish said, looking over his shoulder, then pointing to a door. "He was found in his study." He ripped off the tape the police had put over the door and opened it.

Wes followed the others into the room. More mafia-chic décor. More gold tassels. And blood on the oriental rug. Perfect. Wes had been hoping there'd be blood. He needed it for his spell.

He knelt down next to the large spot where Faldo had bled out and opened his backpack, taking out a few crystals. When he looked up, he found the three guardians looking at him with wary expressions.

"I could use some help here. Somebody find a bathroom and bring me some Q-tips or cotton wool to soak up some of the blood. And find the spice rack in the kitchen. I need rosemary, thyme, and verbena. If there's no verbena, lemongrass will do."

"What are you doing, making tea?" Hamish asked.

"You wanted to know whether any demons were here, right? I don't question your methods, you don't question mine."

After a moment, Hamish nodded. "Manus, bathroom. Enya, kitchen."

"Somebody should check all windows and doors, too," Wes said. "The police didn't say anything about how the killer got in."

While Manus and Enya were already leaving the study, Hamish seemed to hesitate.

Wes rolled his eyes. "You can leave me here on my own. It's not like I'm gonna go anywhere."

"Better not." Hamish turned on his heel and disappeared into the hallway.

Meanwhile Wesley spread out a black cloth with a pentagram stitched in the middle with white thread. He weighed each point of the pentagram down with a crystal. By the time he was done, Manus was back.

"Here, found some cotton wool."

Wes took it and dabbed the dark blood stain with it, soaking the white cotton wool full with Faldo's blood. He did the same with a second and then a third cotton ball, then placed all three in the middle of the pentagram.

"We're really hoping this isn't a spell for conjuring demons," Manus said dryly.

Wes smirked, though he knew that was impossible. "Very unlikely. But in case it is, I hope you're all armed."

Manus put his hand on the dagger sitting on his hip. "Always ready to kill me some demon."

"Leave me some too," Enya said, entering the study. She was carrying several small glass containers with herbs in them. "Didn't find any verbena, but he had lemongrass."

Wes nodded. "Great, put it all down here next to the cloth."

One by one he took the containers and emptied a generous amount over the center of the pentagram, covering the bloody cotton balls. He had just completed his preparations when he heard footsteps in the hallway. A moment later, Hamish re-entered the study.

"That looks creepy," Hamish said and pointed to the pentagram.

Wes shrugged. "Did you find out how the killer got in?"

Hamish shook his head. "No sign of forced entry." He exchanged a look with his colleagues. "And as we know, demons aren't exactly delicate when it comes to breaking in. They don't care what they break. It's possible that Faldo let his killer in, or he had a key."

"Or the killer got in the way you guys do. By walking through the walls." That comment earned him a scolding look from all three guardians. "Just saying. Anyway, we'll figure it out shortly." Wes rose and walked to the massive mahogany desk. It was in disarray, but he found what he was looking for: an ornamental cigarette lighter.

"What are you doing?" Enya asked, eyeing him suspiciously.

He winked at her. "Part of the spell. It needs a little heat to reveal what I need to know."

"Mmm."

"Wanna maybe give us a small heads-up on what we're about to see?" Hamish asked, tossing a circumspect look at the soon-to-be little bonfire.

The lighter in his hand, Wes crouched down again. "Once I light it and the various herbs mix with Faldo's blood, there might be just a tiny little explosion."

"An explosion?" Manus hissed. "How tiny?"

"Just a little poof. Nothing to worry about. But the color of the resulting smoke will determine what kind of creature killed Faldo. Preternatural or human."

"We're preternatural too. And so are you. So, it only eliminates humans?" Hamish asked.

"Basically. But if it does show that a preternatural creature was involved in Faldo's death, there's a way to eliminate you guys, and my own kind as well."

"How?" Enya asked.

"By adding DNA of your kind and of mine."

Enya narrowed her eyes. "You mean you want our blood?"

"Spit will do." Before she could say anything else, he continued, "If the smoke turns red, it means a preternatural was involved. If that's the case, spit into the fire while it's still burning. If it turns black, one of your kind is involved. If it remains red, I will spit and watch for the same reaction. If it still continues to burn red, then neither Stealth Guardians nor witches were involved in his death. That would leave the demons as the most likely culprits. Got that?" He looked at all three guardians.

They nodded.

"Let's do it," Hamish said.

"Stand back a little," Wes cautioned and knelt before the pentagram. Then he concentrated on the small pile of herbs and bloody cotton balls and inhaled. He'd never done this particular spell before. It had better work, or he would look really dumb.

He lit the herbs with the ornate lighter and watched as the small flame consumed the kindling. So far, so good. The flame reflected in the crystals on the cloth. Then suddenly, and without warning, the flame shot up in the air, higher and larger than Wes had expected.

A few gasps sounded around him, but Wes didn't take his eyes off the fire.

Something sizzled loudly, and the crystals seemed to hiss in response.

The flame touched the blood-soaked cotton balls, sending them shooting up in the air like little firecrackers. The crystals hissed, and smoke rose. White smoke. Pure white smoke.

Wesley relaxed and sat back on his heels, then lifted his eyes to the guardians. "No demon activity. In fact, no preternatural activity at all. The killer has to be human."

Hamish cursed. "That's not exactly what I expected. Are you sure?"

"One hundred percent."

Hamish exchanged a look with Manus and Enya.

Manus grimaced. "Doesn't mean the demons weren't involved. What if they had a human do their dirty work?"

"It's possible," Hamish said slowly. "Let's go through the house and see whether we can find any other clues. Figure out if anything seems to be missing."

Wes collected his crystals and the cloth. The cloth with the pentagram hadn't burned, because it had been protected by the crystals. He shoved everything back into his backpack.

He heard footsteps; the guardians were leaving the study to search the rest of the house.

When Wes placed the cigarette lighter back on the desk, he noticed an indentation on the leather mat on the desk. He rubbed over it with his palm.

"Paperweight," he murmured to himself.

"What?" Enya said from behind him.

He pivoted. "There used to be a paperweight there on the desk. Heavy. Probably glass or metal, not sure."

"So?"

"Considering the amount of blood on the carpet, Faldo could have been bludgeoned."

"You think the killer used a paperweight?"

Wes nodded. "That's why it's not here. The police would have taken the suspected murder weapon with them as evidence."

"Well, mystery solved," Enya said and turned to the door.

"Tell me something, Enya," Wes said calmly, "if you were planning to kill somebody, wouldn't you bring your own murder weapon, rather than relying on finding a suitable one at your victim's house?"

She turned back to him and contemplated his words. "Pretty smart for a witch. I'll call Logan to listen in on the police detectives, once he's checked out Faldo's body in the morgue."

Enya pulled out her phone and scrolled through her contacts, and Wes marched into the hallway to help the others with their investigation.

20

———

"Here. I've found the person who last spoke with Faldo."

Virginia looked over Pearce's shoulder. "Who was it?"

"Councilmember Cinead."

A man she respected tremendously. A man beyond reproach. "What was discussed?"

A frown appeared on Pearce's face. "That's just it. There's no note in the log. And Cinead knows better."

Pearce pointed to an entry on the screen, and she read it. Apart from the time of the communication it said nothing. Only that Cinead had made a call to Faldo.

Pearce shrugged. "I mean, it's possible that because of the attack on the compound the log hasn't been updated yet."

As much as Virginia wanted to believe that, she couldn't. "He spoke to Faldo several days before that. Cinead would have had plenty of time to add his notes to the log." She tapped Pearce on the shoulder. "Log out and let me log in. If he entered a confidential note, I should be able to see it with my security clearance."

Pearce followed her instructions, then let her take his seat. A moment later, she looked at the same screen again. There was one short note. "Settle D," she read.

"Do you know what that means?"

She looked at Pearce. "No. But I'm going to find out." She jumped up. "By now all council members should be back in their private compounds. I'll pay Cinead a visit."

"You should take Aiden," Pearce suggested. "I'll call him back from his perimeter watch."

"No," she said. "I'm going alone. I don't think Cinead will tell me what this is all about if I bring a guardian who isn't even supposed to know about this confidential note."

Pearce seemed to hesitate for a moment, but then he said, "You're the boss."

"I'll be back soon." She marched out of the command center, a dagger in the sheath at her hip, another one hidden in her boot.

The members of the council still hadn't been informed that she and Wesley were alive, and she knew that by visiting Cinead this fact wouldn't stay a secret for much longer, but it was more important right now to get the truth from the elder council member.

Fifteen minutes later, Virginia entered Cinead's private home on the foggy coast of Northern California, in a small town called Half Moon Bay. Upon her arrival, a guard ushered her into the library.

While she waited in the large room that was both warm and inviting, with a comfortable sitting area in front of a fireplace, and thousands of volumes of books, she reminded herself that she wasn't an enforcer anymore. She needed to be careful how she handled Cinead. He was a fine man, a staunch defender of their laws, and he'd experienced much hardship in his life: losing his only son as an infant, and his beloved wife decades later. Virginia glanced at the paintings that graced the mantel, memories of a happier life.

At the sound of footsteps, she tore her gaze from the painting of Cinead's infant son, and turned to greet her fellow council member.

"Virginia! You're alive!" He rushed to her and embraced her for a short moment. "When the guard said it was you, I almost didn't believe him."

She nodded. "Wesley and I got out just before the compound blew. Much has happened since we—"

"Wesley? The witch? Where is he now?"

"A safe place." And she wasn't going to reveal where.

Cinead cast her an assessing look. "I thought you went after him to kill him, because you believed that he was the one who led the demons to us."

"I did, but then a demon attacked me when I went after him in the lead cell. The witch risked his own life to save mine. Stupidly, I might add." Because jumping on the demon's back, knowing how much stronger their enemy had been, had been foolish on Wesley's part. Foolish—and brave. "I had a change of mind after that." And that was all Cinead would get out of her when it came to the subject of Wesley.

"So now you believe that he's innocent?"

"Of leading the demons to us, yes. And that's why I came to see you. I've started an investigation into how the demons could have found the compound."

"Alone?"

She shook her head. But she had no intention of telling him who was helping her. Not until she knew for certain that Cinead had no part in the demon's scheme.

"But you're not going to tell me who you're working with, are you?"

"You were an enforcer once, too. You know the rules."

"I do. That's why I won't press you. Now ask whatever you came here to ask me."

"You contacted one of our emissarii several days ago, Anton Faldo. Why?"

Cinead suddenly stiffened visibly. "It's of no importance, I assure you."

"I respectfully disagree. Faldo is dead."

Cinead's breath hitched, and his eyes widened. It was a surprise to him. "Dead? How? When?"

"Killed in his home. He was found in a pool of blood. My people are currently investigating how he was killed and whether a demon was involved. So, whatever you talked to Faldo about when you last saw him, I need to know. It could be important in solving his murder."

"I had given him an assignment and decided at the last minute to withdraw it and take care of it myself. He wasn't involved in any business for us in the last few days. So, my dealings with him won't help you solve this case."

Virginia crossed her arms over her chest. "Let me be the judge of that. The confidential log said *Settle D*, and I don't know what it means. You know as well as I do that as a council member I have the right to know what you were discussing with Faldo before his death. So, you can either tell me now and, should it have nothing to do with Faldo's death, it will remain between us, or I can drag you before the council for an inquiry. Your choice."

Cinead gave her a long look, apparently contemplating her words. He didn't look angry or worried. Rather, he appeared sad. As if what he had to say was difficult. After a few moments of silence, he motioned to the couch. "Take a seat, Virginia."

He slumped down into an armchair. Virginia took a seat on the couch and waited.

Cinead took a long breath, blew it out and started, "As you know, one of the vacant seats on the council was that of a council member who was punished for betraying her race."

Virginia nodded. "Deirdre's seat."

"Yes, and while she had no contact with the demons and thought she was doing the right thing, she went against a council decision, and tried to take matters into her own hands by eliminating a human we had chosen to protect." Cinead lifted his eyes to meet hers.

Virginia nodded. She'd heard the story and agreed with the council's punishment.

"Deirdre was released from her lead cell a few days ago after spending a year in it."

"To strip her of her powers," Virginia said quietly, almost to herself.

"Yes, to make her human and send her into exile. She will have no further contact with any of us." He sighed. "The council's decision was unanimous. We knew it had to be done. But you see..." He hesitated.

Virginia simply waited, not wanting to interrupt his thought process.

"I had assigned Faldo to get her settled in the human world."

"*Settle D*. Settle Deirdre," she murmured.

"Yes, but I couldn't let him do it. I wanted to see her one more time." He smiled a sad smile. "You see, Deirdre is my half-sister. She's all the family I have left."

She hadn't known that, maybe because they didn't share the same surname.

"You spoke to Faldo and relieved him of his assignment, because you planned to do it yourself."

Cinead nodded. "And I did, three days before the compound was compromised. I brought Deirdre to Portland, Oregon, helped her get settled in a small house in a quiet neighborhood, and then I said my goodbyes."

"Was she angry?"

He made a sudden jerky movement. "Angry?"

"For being exiled."

"Oh no. Deirdre has made peace with us and herself. She knows she was wrong."

"Are you sure?"

"Of course, I'm sure. I know my half-sister. She might have been misguided, but she's a good person."

Virginia took a deep inhalation. What she had to say wasn't easy, but she had to say it. "I want you to hear me out, Cinead. This is not going to be easy."

He raised his eyebrows.

"Deirdre knew where the council compound was located. In fact, she knows where every single one of our compounds is located. She knows everything about our defenses, our rules, our habits. If she's seeking revenge for being exiled, helping the demons—"

"No!" Cinead jumped to his feet. "You're wrong. Deirdre would never betray us to the demons."

Virginia rose slowly. "She betrayed the council once. And she paid dearly for it. Anybody would be angry and would want to strike back. Wouldn't you?"

"How dare you make such an accusation?"

"I dare because my concern is for my kind. I dare because it's my duty to keep them safe. And we're not safe, not if the demons know how to find us and how to enter our strongholds."

Cinead narrowed his eyes. "I would be very careful, *counselor*, whom you accuse. I vouch for Deirdre."

"I'm afraid that's not enough. And I'm not accusing anybody. But there's a possibility that you can't see what Deirdre's true feelings are because you care for her. I don't blame you. But I have to follow up on her. Her being released into the human world and the demons attacking us happened too close together."

Cinead continued shaking his head. But Virginia pressed on. "And even if she's not involved, there's still the possibility that you and her were spotted together, and that somehow the demons were able to get to her. Maybe torture her to tell them all she knows."

"Are you accusing me now of being careless?" Cinead barked.

"I'm doing no such thing. But even the most careful of us makes a mistake once in a while." She certainly had made a few, some of which didn't lie that far in the past. "Even if you were careful, if a demon spotted you while you were helping her get settled, he would be curious as to what she means to you. Do you really want me to do nothing? I thought you cared for her. If you do, don't you want to make sure she's safe?"

Cinead snorted. "You have an interesting way of manipulating people."

"You would know, wouldn't you? You've had the same training as I."

"Yes. And that's the only reason I'm not tossing you out on your ass right now."

She nodded. "I will need to know where to find Deirdre."

"Do you have a pen to take down the address?"

Virginia shook her head. "I'll memorize it."

"Good."

21

Following the guardians into the command center, Wes tossed his backpack on the floor next to the door and looked around the room. Pearce and Aiden were both working on computers on the console. Logan lounged on a chair nearby. Now all three turned their heads.

"Hey, you're back," Aiden said. "How did it go?"

"Where's Virginia?" Wes asked.

"She left the compound a while ago," Pearce said.

"Alone?"

Pearce shrugged. "Yeah."

"Where to?" Was his heart beating a little bit faster at the thought that Virginia had left the security of the compound without taking anybody for protection?

Pearce jabbed Aiden in the side, grinning. "Looks like our friend here is a little concerned about the new council member."

"Don't worry, Wes," Aiden said calmly. "She can take care of herself."

"With all that's happening, you let her leave on her own?" Wes wanted to punch somebody for that stupidity.

"It's not like she would have listened to us anyway," Pearce threw in. "Besides, she transported directly to another compound. The demons have no way of tracing her."

"Hmm," Wesley grunted with displeasure, though that knowledge was reassuring.

A beep from the computer made Pearce turn back to the monitor. "She's back."

Logan rose. "What was that?"

"The beep?" Pearce asked.

"Yeah."

"I installed a motion detector near the portal as an extra level of security," Pearce said. "Just in case another witch is even cleverer than Wesley and figures out how to travel through our portal without triggering the intruder alarm. This way, we'll get alerted to any motion down there, even if it's one of us."

"Good idea," Logan said. "Let's wait till she gets here and I'll update everybody on what I found out at the morgue and the police station."

Everybody nodded. A minute later, the command center's door opened, and Virginia stepped in. Wes felt a breath leave his chest, relieved that nothing had happened to her. Damn, why was he so concerned about her wellbeing? He knew she was infinitely stronger than him and therefore shouldn't have to worry that she couldn't take care of herself. But he'd also seen how strong the demons were, and Virginia's powers weren't limitless, particularly not if she was trapped in a lead cell.

"Hey," Virginia said. Her gaze traveled over the assembled guardians and then landed on Wes. She said nothing to him directly, but the fact that she did lock eyes with him for a brief second made him feel better instantly.

"Good, you're back," Logan said. "I was just about to fill everybody in."

"We have news, too," Hamish said.

"Same here," Virginia said, then addressed Logan. "You were at the morgue? What did you find?"

"I looked at Faldo's body in the morgue," Logan started. "He was bludgeoned to death. There's no evidence of him having been tortured before his death. He was hit with a heavy object. Which is consistent with the evidence the police picked up from the house."

"Which is?" Hamish asked.

"A bloody paperweight. Looks like the killer grabbed it from the desk in his study."

Wes nodded to himself. "So, the killer didn't bring a weapon to kill Faldo."

Logan met his gaze. "Looks like it. So maybe this wasn't premeditated. Maybe something went wrong. An argument got heated. Things got out of hand."

"That would make sense, since we didn't find any sign of a break-in," Wes said and motioned to Hamish, Manus, and Enya. "We checked everywhere. He might have let his killer in."

"What else did you find?" Logan asked.

Hamish shifted his weight from one foot to the other. "Wesley did a little spell to determine if there was any demon activity."

"And?" Virginia asked eagerly.

"None. Nor any other preternatural activity. Which means, our kind is off the hook too, as are the witches."

"Are you saying the killer was human?" Virginia followed up.

"Looks like it," Hamish said.

"So, we're back to square one," Logan said.

"Not necessarily," Virginia hedged, drawing everybody's eyes on her.

"Meaning what?" Hamish asked.

"I just came from seeing Cinead."

Hamish raised an eyebrow. "I thought you didn't want anybody from the council knowing that you're still alive."

"I had no choice. Pearce found that Cinead was the last to have contact with Faldo. And since he didn't note his reason for meeting the emissarius in the log, I had to find out for myself." She let out a breath.

"Bad news?" Wes asked.

"I'm not sure. But I know of a human who would have reason to want to hurt us. And this human knew about Faldo, was in fact supposed to meet Faldo, but then Cinead intervened and canceled Faldo's assignment."

"Okay," Aiden said, "how about being a bit less cryptic? Who's the human?"

Wes suppressed a chuckle. Aiden had balls to address Virginia like that.

"Deirdre."

Silence followed Virginia's one-word answer, and it felt like an ice age had suddenly descended on the room. Wesley looked at the guardians, but they all stood there, stone-faced.

"Who's Deirdre?" he finally asked.

"A woman who once tried to kill Leila," Aiden grunted.

Well, that explained why Aiden looked like he'd just swallowed a rotten oyster.

"Oh." Wes refrained from saying anything else, since he was sure the otherwise friendly guardian would change his attitude and bite his head off.

"Cinead confirmed that Deirdre was released a few days ago," Virginia explained. "She served her sentence in the lead cell. Faldo was tasked with settling her in the human world, but Cinead decided last minute to do it himself. So he called Faldo's trip off."

"So that's why the housekeeper said that he shouldn't even have been home," Wes murmured to himself.

Next to him, Manus asked, "What?"

Wes jerked his thumb at the monitor. "Remember when that reporter interviewed the housekeeper? She was babbling that Faldo wasn't supposed to be there. She was distraught. She didn't know that his trip had been canceled."

Manus shrugged. "Whatever."

Pearce swiveled in his chair and typed something on the keyboard.

In the meantime, Virginia continued, "I think we need to consider the possibility that Deirdre might feel resentment toward the Stealth Guardians and want revenge. As a former council member, she knows everything there is to know about our kind. If she's in the demon's camp…"

More silence. Wesley leaned toward Manus again. "Former council member? A human?"

"I'll explain later."

"Explain it to him now," Virginia said. "I want everybody on the same page. That includes Wesley."

"Let me," Aiden said, his voice icy. He turned his face toward Wesley. "All you need to know is that Deirdre once sat on the Council of Nine, our ruling body. But about a year ago, she went against the council's decision and tried to kill my wife, though she wasn't my wife then. Deirdre was sentenced to one year in a lead cell. As you may already have figured out, lead drains our powers temporarily. But long-term exposure will actually make the damage irreversible. After a year in a lead cell, a Stealth Guardian will have lost all supernatural powers and be entirely human. That's what happened to Deirdre."

Wes nodded, letting the information sink in. "That's a harsh punishment."

"That's a matter of opinion," Aiden replied.

"In any case," Virginia interrupted, "she's human, and since you didn't find any preternatural activity at the scene of the crime, everything points to her."

"Not everything, actually," Pearce said from the console.

Wes turned to Pearce, as did everybody else.

The IT geek pointed to the screen. "I just reviewed the interview with the housekeeper. See, she's all teary-eyed and broken up about Faldo's death."

Virginia approached and looked over Pearce's shoulder. "So? She's probably worked for him for a few years. Of course, she's upset about his death. Wouldn't you be, in her situation?"

Wes tapped on Pearce's shoulder. "Run it again, without the sound."

"Sure."

The video started running from the beginning again. Wes concentrated on the housekeeper, not even looking at the reporter now. The absence of sound made it easier to only see the woman's facial expressions.

He pointed to the screen. "See how she avoids eye contact with the reporter?"

Virginia leaned in. "Yes?"

"And how she fidgets. She's nervous. Pearce, now run it with the sound, starting where she speaks."

Pearce turned the microphone up.

"Carol Jefferson, yes."

"Can you tell us anything about what might have happened to your employer?" the reporter asked.

"I wasn't here. He gave me the week off. You know." A sob. *"Because he was supposed to be gone. This should never have happened. He wasn't even supposed to be at home."*

"Stop it here, Pearce."

Silence descended over the room and Wesley turned around to look at the others. "She feels guilty. As if it was her fault. Did you hear how she said that Faldo shouldn't have been at home?"

The others nodded, and Virginia said, "Because he was supposed to be on a mission for Cinead. But then Cinead canceled it."

Wesley gave her a sideways glance. "What if Faldo forgot to tell her that his trip was canceled, and she had plans for the time he was supposed to be gone?"

Hamish and Aiden exchanged a look and nodded to each other.

"I'll check her out," Aiden offered. "I need to get some fresh air anyway." He was already heading toward the exit.

Nobody stopped him.

After the door fell shut behind him, Wes asked, "And what about this Deirdre? What are we going to do about her?"

"Put a tail on her for now," Virginia said. "We need to know where she goes, whom she meets."

"I can do that," Pearce said. "Where does she live now?"

"I have an address in Portland for her. What are you planning to do?"

"I'll put a few bugs into her apartment, some in her shoes and her handbag, so that when she leaves, we'll know where she goes. Shouldn't be too hard. It's not like she can sense me when I'm invisible."

"Good. Do it."

Pearce looked at his watch. "I'll transport to Portland right after dinner." Then he looked at Manus. "Can you get me a few things from the supply room in the meantime?"

"Sure," Manus said and joined Pearce who was already scribbling a list.

Wesley stepped away and approached Virginia. "I guess that means there's not much we can do until Aiden is back with news for us."

She nodded. "Yeah, we might as well all have dinner."

"I'm sure Leila is already cooking something," Logan said and marched toward the door. "Enya, you coming? Let's give her and Tessa a hand."

"Hamish," Virginia said. "I'll be taking the room I slept in the other night. But we need to find a guestroom for Wesley. Is anything made up?"

Hamish approached. "Don't worry, I'll find him something comfortable."

Wes tried to catch Virginia's eye, but she avoided looking at him. At least she wasn't making him sleep in the lead cell again. It was an improvement.

"Let me know where he's gonna be sleeping, so I can keep an eye on him," she said in a firm voice.

Keep an eye on him? Was she still treating him like a prisoner even though she wasn't locking him up in the cell?

It was time to have a word about it with her. The sooner, the better.

When Hamish nodded and headed for the door, Wes finally

connected with Virginia's gaze. Her cheeks appeared a little flushed, though the command room was cooler than the rest of the building.

No reason for Virginia to feel hot. Or look so conspicuously inconspicuous. Unless...

He suppressed the chuckle that was building in his chest.

Virginia had lied to Hamish.

And Wes had an inkling of why.

22

———

After dinner Wesley withdrew to the room Hamish had chosen for him. Aiden hadn't returned to the compound yet, and Leila had looked a little pale, but had claimed she was fine. Apparently, the mention of the woman who'd tried to kill her had stirred up painful memories. Pearce was getting ready to transport to Portland to bug Deirdre, and everybody else was trying to get some rest while they waited for more news.

Wes took a shower to let the water sluice away the tension that had been building up all day. He was just drying off, when he heard a sound in the bedroom. He wrapped a towel around his waist and walked out of the ensuite bathroom.

He wasn't surprised to see his visitor, though he was surprised that she hadn't slipped into something more comfortable. While Virginia seemed to have changed into a different set of clothes, her hair still damp at the tips, she was dressed as if she was ready for battle.

He noticed her running a look over his body.

"Virginia."

She raised her gaze to meet his. "We have to talk."

"I figured that much from your attitude today."

She took in a breath. "My attitude?"

"Giving me the cold shoulder, calling me witch, you know, that kind of attitude. As if what happened in the motel never happened."

"Well, you can't exactly expect me to behave like some love-struck groupie in front of the others. They are my subordinates. I have to maintain a, a—"

"—stuck-up attitude?" he helped and took a step closer.

She narrowed her eyes at him. "Well, if you think that I'm such a stuck-up bitch, why did you sleep with me?"

"I never said you were a bitch. And you were the one who blew me in the shower."

"I didn't notice you resisting my advances."

He crossed the remaining distance between them with one step. "It's hard resisting a woman who's so full of fire." He ran his eyes over her heated face and slid his fingers through her hair, then rested his palm at her nape. "A woman who can turn me on with just one searing look. Damn it, Virginia, I was going to tell you that I don't appreciate you treating me like a stranger in front of your colleagues, but I'll settle for it, as long as you continue to share my bed." He leaned in.

"I can't do that."

He pulled back a few inches. "What?"

"It's never gonna work. We're too different."

"Different is good."

"It's against all the rules."

"Yeah, so? Have you never broken any rules?"

An expression of horror flashed over her face, there one second, gone the next.

"I have to maintain my integrity," she claimed.

"And by sleeping with me, you think you can't? That's a lot of bullshit. Why don't you tell me what's really wrong, huh?"

Her eyes shifted to the side, avoiding him.

"Damn it, Virginia, don't I deserve an answer? We saved each others' lives. We escaped the demons. We made love last night. Does that count for nothing?" He wrapped one arm around her and pulled her closer, so her breasts connected with his chest. "Babe, we're good together. It feels so right." He caressed her nape and noticed her eyelids flutter. Yes, she still responded to his touch, was still susceptible to it.

Virginia finally met his gaze. "But what if—"

"Shh. No what ifs." Wes slanted his mouth over hers. "I want you. And you want me, too, or you wouldn't have snuck into my room."

Virginia sighed, but a moment later, her lips parted.

"That's my girl," he murmured.

A gasp behind him made him spin around. Enya stood in the room, holding his backpack. Her chin had dropped, and her eyes were wide as saucers.

"You left your backpack in the command center," she said almost robotically, but she wasn't looking at him. She was staring at Virginia, and slowly her expression changed from one of shock to one of glee.

"Uh, thanks, Enya," Wes said. "Virginia was just making sure I had everything I needed for the night."

"Yeah, I can see that," Enya said.

Virginia rubbed her palms over her thighs as if straightening out her clothes. "Yes, uh, well, seeing that you're settled in, I'll, uh, leave you to get some rest."

Virginia's attempt at looking professional was a major fail on all fronts. Her cheeks were as red as a tomato, her voice lacked strength and conviction, and her body language screamed of embarrassment.

"Virginia," Enya said slowly and deliberately.

Virginia hesitated.

"I don't think Wesley has everything he needs yet." Enya tossed a deliberate glance at the towel around Wesley's waist. "Why don't you take care of that first, otherwise I doubt he'll get much rest tonight."

Enya had clearly noticed the bulge beneath the towel, and was enjoying watching Virginia squirm. They'd been avoiding each other since Virginia had attacked Enya in the kitchen. Apparently, Enya was still a little bit miffed about that incident.

With a triumphant grin, Enya turned on her heel, tossed the backpack on a nearby chair and marched out through the door without opening it.

"Guess the cat's out of the bag," Wes said, shrugging and turning back to Virginia.

"Oh God, I should have never come to your room."

She looked absolutely terrified and ready to bolt. But he wasn't having any of it. Before she could flee, he grabbed her by the shoulders.

"Listen to me. This isn't exactly how I wanted the others to find out about it, but what happened, happened. At least now we don't have to hide it. So, let's not blow this thing out of proportion."

"Blow this thing out of proportion?" She yanked herself free of his grip. "Wesley, you don't understand. I've broken the rules. People die when I break the rules."

"Don't you think that's a little over-dramatic?"

She looked into his eyes, and he suddenly noticed the wet sheen on her irises. "People *have* died, because I broke the rules and trusted the wrong person."

At her admission, his heart stopped for a moment. He now recognized the pain and anguish that was in plain sight. He understood now that Virginia not trusting him had nothing to do with him, but everything to do with something that had happened in her past. For the first time since meeting her, he saw the vulnerable creature that hid behind a façade of rules and regulations, behind a wall of steel and determination. And he wanted nothing more than to protect her.

Without a word, he pulled Virginia back into his arms and gently rubbed his hands over her back.

WESLEY's gentle touch was soothing. Virginia rested her head against his chest and allowed herself to soak up his strength. But she knew she didn't deserve it. Taking a shaky breath, she lifted her head and inched backward, but Wesley's gaze held her back.

"Don't," he murmured. "Don't shut me out. I can see you're hurting. And that hurts me too." He put his fingers under her chin and lifted it. "Help me understand why you can't trust me. Tell me what happened."

"Nobody knows. Nobody but my father. All the others are dead." Dead, because of her mistake. She should be dead, too. She should have paid the highest price for her mistake.

"Come, talk to me," he said and led her to the seating area in front of the fake fireplace.

She sank into the corner of the sofa, and Wes sat down next to her, his body half turned, one hand clutching hers. He lifted her hand to his mouth and pressed a kiss on the back of it.

Virginia forced a smile. Why did Wesley have to be so sweet, so nice to her? Why did he have to be so understanding? Or was it all an act? Like Jonathan's affection toward her had been an act in the end.

"In the 1960s I was assigned to a compound in San Francisco. We were one big happy family, wiping out demons left and right, protecting humans. Then the Summer of Love happened. Flower Power and all that." She let out a mirthless laugh. "I don't know why, but I caught the bug, too. It was infectious, all that free love in the city. I couldn't stay away, because suddenly the future looked so much brighter. There was hope everywhere."

"I wasn't even born yet," Wes said with a gentle smile and combed his hand through her hair, a gesture she increasingly craved. "You've seen so much of history."

"Too much I wish I'd never seen." And even more things she wished she'd done differently. "I met a man that summer. A human. I fell in love with him, though looking back, I think I was more in love with the idea of being in love than with him. But he represented everything that I thought love would be. And to a degree I can also blame *rasen* for how I acted, though I'm not making excuses. It was all my fault."

"Rasen?" Wesley asked.

"The mating call we all experience around the time we turn two-hundred, some a little earlier, some a little later. It hit me too early. I wasn't prepared, I guess." She stopped herself and searched Wesley's eyes. "But I have no excuse for what I did."

He squeezed her hand and nodded in silence.

"I spent more and more time with Jonathan. I started to trust him. He seemed so innocent. Without guile. All he talked about was peace and love and hope. And how this world would be one day. How everybody would live in harmony. He seemed to be without a care in the world. My shoulders, on the other hand, felt weighted down by my duty to my kind. By my promise to defend my race."

"It's a lot to deal with. The demons, the constant battles," Wes said, his eyes gleaming with understanding.

"Yes, but I was trained for it. Yet, when I was with Jonathan, I longed for an easier life. He told me he loved me and urged me to go away with him to some commune somewhere. That's when I confessed to him what I was, that my duty wouldn't let me leave. That I had obligations. I'm not sure he really understood fully what it meant. But he said he'd support me."

She sighed.

"Back then, the drugs of choice were marijuana and LSD. I didn't realize it at first, but LSD seemed to make it easier for demons to influence humans. I made Jonathan swear that he'd never take LSD. But even as he swore it, he'd already taken it. And he continued taking it whenever I wasn't around. I don't know when they got to him, but they did. The demons figured out very quickly that Jonathan and I were an item. They saw us together. And my aura gave me away. They influenced him. One day Jonathan said he wanted to see where I lived. And though it was against the rules, I took Jonathan to the compound. I broke the one rule I should have never broken, because I thought he was finally ready to embrace all of me, not just the fun-loving girl, but also the warrior, the woman who had responsibilities."

A tear rolled down her cheek and she wiped it away.

"We were followed. That's how the demons found our location. They attacked us a few hours later. The compound was unprepared. Every single one of my compound mates died in the attack. I should have died, too. But life isn't fair, and I survived in the rubble of my compound."

"And Jonathan?"

She shook her head. "Nobody ever saw him again. There was no body. Maybe the demons took his body with them. Maybe it burned in the explosion. I don't know."

Wesley sighed. "I'm so sorry, Virginia. I'm so sorry you had to go through this."

"That's not all." Virginia sniffled. "I wanted to confess that it was my fault. That I was responsible for all those deaths. So, I went to see my father. I told him everything. He was disappointed. And angry. I fully expected him to drag me in front of the Council of Nine himself to be punished and exiled, if not executed, but he didn't. He told me that whatever I did, I could never tell anybody. It would not only disgrace my family, it would kill my mother. He didn't care what I did to alleviate my guilt. I couldn't hurt my family, my mother in particular. I'd already hurt so many people, so many families. So, I did the only thing I could: I swore never to trust again, never to love again, and I signed up with the enforcers to undergo the most brutal training a warrior can survive. I made it my mission to enforce our rules. So that nobody else would die." She swallowed and looked into Wesley's baby-blue eyes. "And now I'm breaking the same rules I've sworn to enforce."

A sob tore from her chest. And this time she couldn't hold it in.

Wesley's arms were around her a moment later. He lifted her into his lap and cradled her to his chest, and she let it happen.

23

Wesley felt Virginia's body shake under the force of her sobs, while he held her in his arms to comfort her. The strongest woman he'd ever met was cracking under pressure, and all he wanted to do was soothe her pain.

So much was clear to him now. She wasn't the hard-nosed disciplinarian that the others at the compound would rather see the back of. She was a woman whose guilt was wearing her down, a guilt for which she'd been trying to atone for decades. And by her own admission, she'd never confided in anybody after telling her father, who by the sounds of it, hadn't given her any comfort.

Wesley stroked his hand over her long hair, trying to calm her with his touch.

"You must have saved so many lives since," he murmured softly.

"It's not enough," Virginia choked out.

"You've protected your kind ever since. You've done so much good. Don't you think it's time to forgive yourself?"

He put his fingers under her chin and lifted her head so he could look into her face. The skin around her eyes was red and puffy, her eyes still full of tears. Her lips quivered.

"You couldn't know. We all make mistakes," he said, grasping for anything that he hoped would make her feel better.

"But my mistake cost people's lives."

"How can you be sure of that?" He sighed. "The demons seeing you with Jonathan wasn't your fault. Who knows how many demons are roaming out there, trying to ferret out a way to destroy your kind? It could have happened to anybody."

"But it happened to me."

"And it will happen again, to somebody else. You're never safe from detection. Your aura identifies you as a preternatural. Demons can only be identified by their green eyes. What if they wear sunglasses? And it's not like you can smell them. You're at a disadvantage unless you're invisible. And you said yourself that takes a lot of energy." He rubbed his fingers over her cheeks to wipe away her remaining tears. "What I'm trying to say is, don't let this guilt destroy you. You're better than that. You're strong, and you're good."

"But I have to be punished for this."

"You've punished yourself enough. You continuing to beat yourself up isn't going to bring your friends back. It isn't going to help anybody. Put it out of your mind, and think of all the good you've done, the lives you've saved, the future you have ahead of you."

She sniffled. "But what if I make the same mistake again? What if I've already repeated it?" Virginia met his gaze then, and he read the question in it. The question that had been there since the moment they'd met.

"I can't force you to trust me. All I can do is tell you that I'll never hurt you or your kind. But I understand that it's hard for you to trust a stranger after what you've been through. Just know this: I won't give up on you. I'll do anything to prove to you that I'm worth your trust. No matter how long it takes. Because you're worth it. And because I want you."

She raised her hand and cupped his cheek. Wes turned his face to press a kiss into her palm. "Why are you so understanding? Why don't you condemn me like my father did?"

"He should have never condemned you. He should have been there to help you through this. But I'm here now. I will remind you every single day if necessary that you don't have to feel guilty anymore. You've atoned a hundred times over since then. You deserve to be happy. And if I can help you find a little happiness, then that's what I'm gonna do."

For the first time since Virginia had come to his room, a small smile formed on her lips. "You're so good to me."

He chuckled. "I can be even better, that is, if you want me to."

She tilted her head to the side. "Are you trying to come on to me?"

"Is it working?"

"I don't know, what do you think?" Virginia put her hand on his chest and ran her soft fingers over his skin, making it tingle with anticipation.

"Maybe I should work a little harder on my powers of seduction." He winked at her.

"Really?" She shifted on his lap and slid her hand to his groin, where his cock was starting to lift the towel. "Harder than that?"

"Oh, yeah, much harder than that."

Virginia untucked the towel and peeled it away so she could stroke her hand over his erection. Wes groaned, and felt his cock jerk and pump full of even more blood.

"Babe, you'd better be careful with that."

She slid off his lap and put her hands on his knees, spreading them apart. "Oh, yeah? Maybe in that case I should use something more gentle, like my mouth." She dropped to her knees in front of him.

"Wait!" He took her head into his hands and stopped her.

"I thought every man liked that."

"Oh, I love it." He grinned. "But would you do me a favor and get naked for me first? I want to look at your sexy body while you suck me."

She smiled up at him and rose. Then she peeled out of her clothes, shedding one item after the other, until she was down to her black bra and panties.

"Stop," he demanded. "Like that is perfect. Absolutely perfect." He reached for her hand and pulled her down between his legs. His pulse was racing now, and his cock was hard and heavy, curving against his stomach. Ready to explode.

He looked at Virginia in her skimpy lingerie, looking innocent and seductive all at once. He drew her head to him and pressed a long kiss on her red lips, before releasing her and looking deep into her hazel eyes. The green flecks in them seemed to shimmer.

"Suck me, babe, do what you want with me, but don't let me come. 'Cause I want to come inside your beautiful pussy when you're ready for me. Can you promise me that?"

"I can't promise anything," Virginia murmured with a seductive smile. "Only that you'll enjoy it."

"I've never doubted that."

And then the red-haired vixen lowered her head to his groin and licked over the tip of his cock, while her long hair caressed his thighs.

"Fuck!" He clutched the sofa cushions to his left and right, preparing for the sensual onslaught.

"Mmm." She wrapped her lips around his erection and slowly slid down on him, until he was deep inside her wet and warm mouth.

Needing to touch her, he combed his hands through her hair, cupping her head gently, careful not to take over the lead. He wanted Virginia to take charge, to decide how hard and how fast she would suck him. He wanted to be at her mercy.

Virginia started to move up and down on him, first slowly and with very little pressure, lubricating him with her moist tongue. It felt like sinking into a hole filled with warm cream. Every slide was better than the next. He couldn't remember any woman ever having bestowed such tenderness on him, and he hadn't expected it from Virginia.

"That's beautiful, babe. I love it." He clenched his jaw, warding off the need to let himself go and give in to the desire to thrust hard and deep into her mouth. Instead, he looked straight ahead to the glass cover of the fake fireplace, where the reflection of Virginia on her knees was tantalizing him.

Her G-string-clad ass was moving back and forth with every move of her head. It hid nothing from his view, and made him even hornier. The need to touch her became unbearable, and he reached down the front of her torso to where her breasts were held in by her bra. He ran his fingers over them and found her nipples hard. He pinched them, and Virginia moaned and suddenly sucked him harder.

"You like that, huh? You like your beautiful tits played with."

He didn't need her to answer. Instead, he did it again, this time slipping his fingers underneath the fabric.

"You're made for sex," he praised her, and slid his hands to her back to find the clasp of her bra. He opened it, then brought his hands to her front again and peeled the fabric from her boobs, letting them fall free. He cupped them with both hands, and squeezed. "Fuck, I love your tits."

His gaze drifted back to the reflection in the glass. "And your ass." But since he couldn't reach her beautiful ass, he kept playing with her breasts, squeezing them, pinching her nipples, teasing more moans from Virginia's lips to bounce against his aching cock. Spurring her on.

And Virginia kept going, kept sucking him as if it were an Olympic sport and she was bent on winning a medal. But with every second, the battle to ward off his impending orgasm became more unwinnable.

"Babe," he groaned, "babe, you've gotta stop, I beg you."

She sucked him deep into her mouth, then slowly released him with an audible plop and lifted her face to look up. "I'm surprised you held out this long," she said with a chuckle.

"It was pure torture," he said and pulled her up.

Virginia shrugged out of the bra, then hooked her thumbs into her panties and shimmied out of them.

Wes swallowed hard at the sight. He'd always dreamed of a woman like Virginia, but never dared believe that his dream would come true. Apparently, he was one lucky son of a bitch.

"Tell me what you want," she murmured, her eyelashes almost hitting her eyebrows.

"Ride me," he said without hesitation. "So I can suck your tits and bury my face in them."

Virginia put her hand on his shoulder and pushed him to lean back against the backrest of the couch, then straddled him, bracing herself on her knees. "Like that?"

"You tease, as if you didn't know."

She leaned her torso closer, so her boobs were only an inch away from his face. He inched forward and pressed his face into her cleavage. The soft flesh of her breasts embraced him, caressing his cheeks, cradling him. He inhaled her scent and licked a path down the middle, while he lifted his hands and pressed against the outside of her breasts to squeeze them together.

Then he lifted his lids and saw how she was looking at him, her lips parted, her eyes shining brightly, lust brimming in them.

"You really do want me. You have no ulterior motive, do you?" she murmured as if she hadn't believed it until now.

"I'm a simple man, Virginia. All I want is to get inside of you, and to stay there for as long as you'll have me." And that desire even overshadowed his duty to Scanguards, and his hope that they could forge an alliance with the Stealth Guardians.

"Wes," she whispered and lowered herself onto his cock, bearing down on him in one continuous stroke. Her muscles tightened around him.

Her move pulled him away from her breasts and brought Virginia's face level with his.

"I want you, Wesley."

"You've got me, babe." Body and soul. Though he couldn't tell her that. She wasn't ready to hear it. Instead, he slanted his lips over hers and took her mouth to kiss her. She received him with the same passion with which she took his cock into her body, and he gave himself over to her.

The pleasure of feeling her ride him, of her hips rising and falling, her breasts bouncing with every move, made the fire in his body burn even hotter. Virginia's hair caressed his skin, while her hands were on his chest, stroking him softly. Her movements were rhythmic and measured. Gentle and slow. But right now he wanted something else. He was already teetering on the edge. How long was she going to torture him with her slow and gentle movements, when he'd already felt how strong she was, and how hard she could ride him?

He ripped his mouth from hers. "Goddamn it, Virginia, don't tease me! Fuck me! Or do I need to toss you on your back?"

A light seemed to ignite in her eyes, and she pressed him hard into the backrest. "Suck my tits, and maybe I'll ride you harder."

"Now you're talking." He took her breasts with both hands, then captured one nipple between his lips and sucked on it.

Virginia threw her head back and moaned. "Yeah, like that."

Her encouragement made him suck harder and lick over the nipple to soothe it, before he did the same to her other breast. This time he scraped his teeth over her skin, and felt her shiver in response. For an instant he wished he were a vampire so he could bite her and feel that kind of connection, the deep bond vampires had. But short of that, he had to content himself with sucking her nipple deep into his mouth and squeezing her breasts until she, finally, increased her tempo and rode him faster. Took him deeper.

Still licking her breasts, he dropped his hands to her hips to slam her down even harder, while he jerked his hips upward to double the impact. The result was explosive. His cock was on fire, ready to release its seed into her, ready to fill her with everything he had.

He reached between their bodies, and slid his fingers through the damp hair that guarded her pussy, finding her clit. The little organ was swollen. Perfect. He rubbed over it.

Virginia cried out and pressed her groin against his fingers. He continued rubbing her sensitive button, continued licking her tits, continued thrusting his cock deep into her welcoming cave. Several more thrusts, and Virginia suddenly gasped. At the same time her interior muscles began to spasm and clamp around his cock. He came instantly, shooting his semen deep into her, and his entire body trembled from his orgasm.

Virginia sagged against him, and he pulled her head to him, kissing her lips, her cheeks, her eyelids. For a few moments, he couldn't even speak, could only breathe and fill his lungs. He wrapped his arms around her, pressing her to him, her hard nipples tickling his chest.

"Oh, babe," he murmured and kissed her neck. "That was…" He had no words for how amazing their lovemaking had been. He took her head into his hands and looked into her eyes. "This was the most amazing experience I've ever had. Nothing has ever felt so good."

"I know you're a flirt, Wesley, but please don't say things just because you think I want to hear them." It wasn't a scolding, more like a sober statement.

He sighed. "You're right, I'm a flirt. Always been. But you should know something else about me. I might flatter a woman to get her *into* bed, but once I'm *in* bed with her, I only tell the truth. I only say what I feel. If I don't feel it, I keep my mouth shut and pretend I'm asleep." He grinned. "And as you can see, I'm not asleep right now. In fact, I have no intention of sleeping."

A smile built on Virginia's lips. "You mean that?"

"That I have no intention of sleeping?"

She rolled her eyes. "That's obvious. No, that you don't lie in bed."

"Yes."

"Then maybe we should go to bed," she suggested and pointed to the king-sized bed in the other part of the large room.

"I think that's a brilliant idea." He pressed a kiss to her lips. "I assume you'll use the occasion to interrogate me."

She smirked. "Don't give me any ideas."

He lifted her up and rose with her in his arms, carrying her to the bed. He dropped her to her feet and pulled the duvet back. Virginia slipped underneath the light cover, and Wes followed her, drawing her against the curve of his body.

"Can you promise me one thing?" he asked.

She turned her head to look at him. "Mmm?"

"Stay here the whole night. Wake up with me. When I woke up in the motel, you'd already gotten up."

"Is that all?" She smiled.

"Actually, since you're asking." He nudged his semi-hard cock against her buttocks. "I might get a little randy during the night, since you're naked and so damn hot. I hope you're okay with me waking you to make love to you."

"A little randy?" Virginia chuckled. "Wes, you've been randy from the moment I met you."

"So, that's a *yes* then?"

When Virginia started to laugh, he silenced her with a kiss.

24

———

Wes had indeed woken her—twice—to make love to her. The third time, Virginia had awoken at daybreak with Wesley's cock inside her, gently sliding back and forth, while he'd caressed her breasts tenderly and pressed sweet kisses to her nape and shoulders. She had surrendered to his demands, basking in the affection he showered her with. She could get used to being woken like that every day.

In the shower they'd washed each other just as tenderly, and she would have liked to hide out in Wesley's room much longer, but she knew she couldn't avoid the other guardians forever.

"It's gonna be fine," Wesley murmured as they walked to the door.

She turned her head to look at him. "How—?"

"You're an open book, Virginia." He brushed a few strands of her hair behind her shoulder and caressed her cheek with his thumb. "Nobody is going to think any worse of you just because you're sleeping with me. You could do worse, you know."

He winked at her, and she smiled involuntarily. "You don't take yourself too seriously, do you?"

"What's the point? Life is serious enough." He reached for her hand. "Now, let's have breakfast. I'm starving. I burned a few calories last night. And I need to recharge, or you'll toss me out on my ass when I can't perform tonight."

Virginia shook her head. "Oh my God, you really do think about sex all the time."

Wes leaned in. "Only because you're so damn tempting."

At the door she hesitated. "About what I told you last night—"

"That's only between you and me. Nobody will ever know."

She saw the truth in his eyes and nodded. "Thank you... for everything."

The smile that she'd come to love appeared on his face, and he leaned in and brushed his lips over hers. Automatically, she parted her lips and accepted his tender kiss, because whenever Wesley kissed her, her worries seemed to shrink, and hope that everything would turn out well spread.

Wes lifted his lips from hers and leaned his forehead to hers. "Hmm. You're turning me into an insatiable creature."

"I have the feeling you've always been insatiable."

"Maybe, but nobody's ever indulged me like you."

She chuckled. "I can't quite believe that. I've sure you've had plenty of women catering to your every whim." After all, one look into his baby-blues, and what woman with a pulse wouldn't be drooling?

"I'm taking the fifth on that question."

"It wasn't a question. It was a statement."

"So, you think you know me, huh?"

She tilted her head back and looked into his eyes. "Better than a few days ago, my sexy witch."

He laughed. "Now, see? You calling me witch suddenly doesn't sound like a swear word anymore."

She rubbed herself against him, being deliberately provocative. "What does it sound like now, witch?"

Wesley dropped his hands to her ass and pressed her to him. "Right now, it sounds like you want to jump this witch's bones."

"And it seems like this witch is all ready for it, too." She eased out of his embrace and slid her palm over the hard bulge in his pants. She loved how quickly Wesley could get excited, because it confirmed that she had power over him. The same kind of power he had over her.

He dropped his gaze to her hand and smirked. "You keep that up, *counselor*, and we'll never make it to breakfast."

She smiled and turned to the door, then walked straight through it into the corridor. A moment later, the door opened behind her and Wesley stepped out.

"Very funny," he said dryly.

Side by side, they walked to the kitchen. Virginia could already hear the voices of the other Stealth Guardians behind the closed door. She took a deep breath and entered, Wesley behind her.

Everybody turned their eyes to her, interrupting what they were doing. It was clear that Enya hadn't wasted any time telling her colleagues what she'd witnessed in Wesley's room. Virginia hadn't expected any different.

"Morning," she forced herself to say. Then she looked toward the counter. "Oh good, you guys made coffee." At least she could busy herself with something, and steady her trembling hands by holding on to a hot mug of coffee.

A few "good mornings" came in response, while Virginia poured herself a cup.

"Hey guys," Wesley said cheerfully, "is there no food?"

"We were waiting for you to make us pancakes," Enya said, tossing a sideways glance at Virginia. "Since my last attempt didn't go so well."

Hamish chuckled. "Yeah, we're not letting Enya near the stove ever again."

Enya stuck her tongue out at him. "Like you're any better at cooking."

"I'll do it," Wes said quickly and walked to the fridge. While he took out a few ingredients, he said, "I don't see Leila. She not joining us?"

Aiden shook his head. "She's not feeling well this morning."

Grabbing a bowl and a whisk, Wesley turned toward the island.

"Don't worry, when my sister-in-law was pregnant, her morning sickness only lasted about a month. It'll pass."

Virginia snapped her head to Wesley, then to Aiden, whose chin had dropped.

"How the…" Aiden murmured.

Logan slapped his friend on the shoulder. "Why didn't you tell us?"

"Leila is pregnant?" Manus asked, eyes wide.

Hamish and Tessa exchanged a look. Virginia could see it immediately, though there were no outward signs other than the love in their gazes: the two were indeed bonded. Virginia's earlier suspicion that Tessa had lied to save Hamish from punishment for allowing her to stay at the compound was unfounded.

"I didn't want to say anything," Aiden said, "it's still early, and Leila wanted to wait until she was over the three-month hurdle." He motioned to Wes who was now whipping up the pancake batter. "How did you know?"

Wes grinned. "All the runes around this place might prevent me from casting spells, but I can still sense certain things."

Aiden shook his head, chuckling. "Son of a gun."

"Well, congratulations," Virginia said. "I hope everything goes well." And she actually meant it.

"Thank you."

Hamish patted his friend on the shoulder. "I'm happy for you guys."

"Appreciate it," Aiden said. "But I don't want to detract from everything else that's happening. We've got things to deal with."

Virginia took a seat at the island. "Do you have any news about the housekeeper?"

Aiden nodded. "Logan, can you call Pearce in here? I don't want to go over it twice."

Logan hopped off his barstool and walked to the intercom system next to the door. He pressed a button. "Pearce. You're needed in the kitchen."

A static crackle on the loudspeaker, then, "Be there soon."

"Now," Logan insisted, then added, "Wes is making pancakes."

"Why didn't you say so immediately?"

Logan took his seat again. Moments later, Pearce entered the kitchen, a tablet in his hand.

"Morning everybody." He propped the tablet up on the island, so he could see what was happening on the screen, and took a seat. "Sorry, gotta monitor communications, in case we get any urgent messages." Then he motioned to Wes, who was now standing at the stove, heating oil in a pan. "Hey, Wesley, I'll have three, please."

Manus jabbed Pearce in the side. "Get in line."

Wesley looked over his shoulder. "There's enough for everybody." Then he gestured to Aiden. "Come on, don't keep us on tenterhooks. What happened with the housekeeper? Did she kill Faldo?"

"No," Aiden said immediately. "But I know who did."

Virginia looked up with interest. Finally, a lead.

"I checked out Mrs. Jefferson. She's widowed and lives in a small house in West Baltimore. Not exactly the best area. She keeps a neat house, and there was nothing that seemed out of place. Her kids are out of the house; the son lives in Philadelphia, and the daughter just had a baby and moved in with her boyfriend. Mrs. Jefferson was at home, crying herself to sleep, genuinely distressed about Faldo's death. I guess he was good to her. Paid her well, too, from what I could see from her bank statements. Now she's out of a job. That must hit her hard."

Virginia sighed. "You said you know who killed him."

"I'm getting to that. She has two nephews. I found their address in her papers, so I paid them a visit. They're renting a small apartment together. It's full of stolen merchandise. Everything from cell phones to watches to computers."

"Anything from Faldo's house?" Logan asked, looking up from the pancakes Wes had served him in the meantime.

"I couldn't tell," Aiden said, "but what I did find was blood. On a pair of sneakers."

"Did you take a sample?" Manus asked. "I could run it through the system."

"No. I did something even better. I called the police and gave them an anonymous tip."

Hamish whistled through his teeth. "Nice one. Were they arrested?"

"I waited until the police came and took them away. With the stolen goods in their apartment there's enough evidence to keep them for a while. In the meantime, I'm sure forensics is going to tie them to Faldo's murder. It all makes sense."

Wesley placed another plate heaped with pancakes on the island for everybody to help themselves. "There was no sign of a break-in. Are you thinking that they got their aunt's key?"

Aiden nodded. "That's my guess. She probably mentioned that Faldo was going to be gone for a week, so they figured it would be easy to get in and rob the place."

Manus grunted. "Faldo must have surprised them, so they grabbed whatever weapon they could and killed him."

"The paperweight from the desk," Wes suggested.

Logan nodded. "Exactly. The police took it as evidence. It would have been covered in Faldo's blood and possibly had their fingerprints on it, unless they wore gloves."

"How can we know for sure it was them?" Virginia asked.

Aiden turned to her. "We'll have to wait for the police to release that information. I'm sure it won't take long." He jerked his thumb over his shoulder, and Virginia glanced in the direction he'd indicated: a large TV mounted on the wall in the living area, muted and turned to a local channel. "I'm guessing it'll be on the news soon."

"Guess we'll have to wait then. In the meantime," Virginia said and shifted her gaze to Pearce. "What happened last night with Deirdre?"

"Everything went well. I bugged her place while she was asleep. We'll know who she speaks to, and who visits her. And I put some trackers into several of her shoes and her handbag. We'll know where she is at all times. We're covered."

Virginia nodded. "Good job. Did you notice anything strange about her?"

Pearce shrugged. "Given that she was asleep, there wasn't anything I could detect. But everything in her place looked normal. The place is sparsely furnished, but that's to be expected if she's only been there for a few days."

"Hmm." Virginia contemplated his words. "What if she's not planning to stay there for long? She's still my top suspect. She knows where the compounds are."

"So do a lot of people," Hamish interrupted.

"But she has motive," Virginia said. "And who else is there? We can't exactly pin it on Finlay, he's dead."

"Who's Finlay?" Wesley asked.

Hamish put his fork aside, glanced at Aiden, then said, "He was a traitor. A member of the Council of Nine. A little over a year ago, he made a pact with the demons. He was going to deliver Leila to them in exchange for taking over leadership of the demons."

"Why?" Wes looked at Aiden. "No offense, Aiden, I know you love your wife, but why would the demons want her?"

"Because she's a brilliant scientist," Aiden said. "She was developing an Alzheimer's drug, a vaccine in fact, that, had it been allowed to go to market, would have made mankind so vulnerable to the demons' influence that they would have taken over the world within months. There would have been nothing we could do except stand by helplessly."

"Oh."

Hamish nodded. "Yeah. But luckily, we discovered Finlay's plan and were able to stop him."

"What happened?"

"Finlay kidnapped Leila and took her to meet with the demons," Hamish continued.

"You forgot to mention that he first cut my Achilles tendon and locked me in a lead cell so I couldn't follow him," Pearce interrupted.

"Fuck," Wes cursed, looking at Pearce. "Must've hurt."

"Yeah, he sliced right through it with his dagger." Then he shrugged. "Luckily, we heal fast."

"In any case," Hamish said, "we found them just in time. Finlay was killed, by Zoltan actually, who's now the Great One, the ruler of the demons. He never had any intention of holding up his end of the bargain."

"So, you guys saw Finlay die?" Wes asked.

Every member of the Baltimore compound nodded.

"He was dead as a doornail," Aiden grunted. "Deservedly so."

"And the body? What happened to it?" Wes asked.

"Where are you going with this?" Virginia interjected.

Wes looked at her, then back at Aiden. "What if he had something on him that could have fallen into the demon's hands, like his cell phone?"

Pearce shook his head. "Sorry, impossible."

"But—"

"We recovered Finlay's cell phone after his death. Not a bad idea, but that's a dead end."

Wes sighed. "Hmm, then I don't know either." He heaved a couple of pancakes onto his plate and started eating.

For a few moments nobody spoke, and only the clatter of cutlery clinking against porcelain could be heard while everybody chowed down on their breakfast.

The sound of the door opening made Virginia look over her shoulder. Leila entered, and Virginia froze.

At the other end of the island, Wes let out a gasp. "Oh my God! Leila?"

25

Wesley had to do a double-take. The woman entering the kitchen definitely looked like Leila, but at the same time, it couldn't be her. Because the Leila he knew didn't have golden skin. Not golden in a *Goldfinger* kind of way, but glowing as if a million grains of light were sparkling under her rosy complexion.

He slid off his barstool and walked to her, while the others wished her a good morning as if they didn't even notice her appearance. Stopping a few feet away from her, Wes caught her gaze.

"Are you all right, Leila?"

"Thanks for asking, I'm fine. I smelled the pancakes, and it made me hungry."

He nodded automatically, still unable to tear his gaze away from her face, neck, and bare arms. He quickly cast a look at the guardians closest to him at the island, Manus and Logan, but they were talking to each other as if nothing had happened.

Hamish was whispering something to Tessa, and Enya was shoveling more food into her mouth, while Pearce stared at the tablet and swiped over it with his finger.

"Stop staring," Virginia suddenly whispered behind him.

Wes whirled around. He hadn't noticed that Virginia had jumped off her barstool and approached him.

"But something is obviously wrong with her. Why is nobody doing anything?" he said, trying to be as quiet as Virginia, but the worry he felt lifted his voice. "Maybe it's the pregnancy."

A gasp from Leila made him pivot toward her.

Leila looked at Aiden accusingly. "You told him?"

Aiden stood up and walked toward his wife. "I didn't. Wesley guessed it."

"Oh." Then she smiled and shrugged. "I suppose it was time for people to find out."

As soon as she said it, all the others started talking over each other, congratulating Leila on her pregnancy, expressing their best wishes and their surprise. Tessa and Enya even hugged their compound mate's wife. Yet nobody made a single remark about her golden skin.

For a moment, Wesley just stood there in silence. Was it possible that he was the only one who could see the golden glow? Could it mean that he was sensing that something was wrong with Leila? That she was maybe sick?

He reached for Aiden, gripping his forearm, drawing his gaze onto him.

Wesley leaned in. "Something is wrong with your wife."

Aiden's eyes widened. "What?"

"Listen, I don't know what it is, and obviously none of you can see it, so it must be my witch senses, but I think your wife is sick."

A heavy hand landed on Wesley's shoulder. He spun his head around as Hamish sidled up to them.

Hamish grinned. "You wouldn't by any chance be referring to the fact that Leila is glowing golden?"

Wesley's chin dropped. "You can see it, too?"

Hamish smirked, then exchanged a look with Aiden. "Do you want to explain to Wes here what you did to your wife?"

"None of his business," Aiden said curtly, his cheeks reddening.

"What the fuck is going on?" Wes cursed. "Will somebody please explain to me what this is? Because whatever it is, it's not normal."

"Yeah, well, vampires biting their mates isn't normal for us either," Hamish said dryly. "We have our own sexual practices that might seem a little weird to you." Then he leaned in and lowered his voice to a whisper. "And who knows, maybe you'll find out firsthand someday."

"Oh." Understanding dawned on him. Hamish knew about him and Virginia, and was insinuating that Virginia would introduce him to whatever sexual practice he was referring to.

The question in Wesley's mind, however, was why hadn't she already done so?

Wes turned to where Virginia stood at the kitchen island. She was looking at them. She'd watched them. Slowly, he ripped his eyes from her and looked back at Aiden and Hamish. This was neither the time nor the place to discuss this with Virginia. It was best to divert everybody's attention away from the two of them.

"But Leila is human. Are you sure she's all right?" he asked instead.

Aiden smiled. "I'm touched that you care so much about my wife's wellbeing, but I assure you, she's more than all right." He looked away, and Wesley followed his gaze and saw Leila smiling back at them.

"Do you mind if I congratulate her?"

"Go ahead."

Wes made his way through the well-wishers. Leila looked at him.

"I'm very happy for both of you." He reached for her hand, and she allowed it.

"Thank you, Wesley. If you really want to do something for me, a couple of pancakes would be great." She gifted him with a wide smile.

"Come, I'll make you some fresh ones," he said and took her elbow, when somebody bumped into him from behind. He lost his balance and stumbled forward, toward Leila. She caught him, and in the process of steadying himself, his hand slipped to her stomach. There was no noticeable bump yet, but there was something else he picked up. Though he wasn't a hundred percent certain, since the contact had been so brief.

Wes straightened.

"Everything okay?" Aiden said behind him.

Wes nodded, but didn't turn, and instead looked at Leila. "Leila, I know this might sound like an odd request, but do you mind if I put my hand on your stomach?"

"Why?" Aiden walked to stand beside his wife, though he didn't put his arm around her like he normally did when Wes saw them together.

"I noticed something about the pregnancy when we bumped into each other just now. I want to make sure."

Leila and Aiden exchanged a look, then Leila nodded. "Okay."

Wes looked at Aiden, making sure he too was giving his permission. A barely perceivable nod told him it was fine, so Wes laid his palm on Leila's stomach, then closed his eyes and concentrated.

A moment later he opened his eyes and removed his hand. "I can hear two heartbeats."

"Of course, mine and the baby's," Leila said.

Wes smiled and shook his head. "Two heartbeats coming from your womb. You're having twins. Congratulations."

"Twins?" Leila murmured and looked at her husband. "Oh, Aiden." It looked like she wanted to put her arms around him, but she didn't, and neither did he.

"Come on, Aiden, what is wrong with you today? Aren't you even gonna hug your wife?"

Aiden sighed. "Could somebody please explain to Wes why I can't do that?" He looked around. "Logan?"

"Sure thing," Logan immediately said and put his arm around Wesley's shoulder, leading him toward the living room.

"What is all this?" Wes asked, getting a little annoyed about all the secrecy.

"Listen, maybe Virginia should explain this to you, but clearly you guys aren't at that stage in your relationship yet," Logan said carefully and rather quietly.

Wes lifted an eyebrow but didn't contradict him.

"Anyway. Between couples there's sex and then there's sex the

Stealth Guardian way."

"The Stealth Guardian way?"

"Yeah. It's intense. In their case"—Logan motioned in Aiden's and Leila's direction—"Aiden poured his *virta*, his life force, into Leila while they made love. That's what makes her shimmer golden for hours afterwards. But what it also does is make her climax every time he touches her."

"But everybody else hugged her, and I touched her too."

"It only happens if the person touching her is the same one who gave her his *virta*."

Wes shook his head in stunned disbelief. "Wow, that's wild. Does that work the other way around too?"

Logan chuckled. "You mean when the Stealth Guardian is a female?"

Wes cleared his throat. "Yes, just, you know, out of interest."

"I'll leave that for Virginia to explain to you." He smirked.

"Come on, be a friend."

"Hey, not my place," Logan said, lifting his hands. "If she wants you to know what happens to a guy if and when she does it, she'll tell you." He turned and walked back to the kitchen island.

Wes sighed. Now that he knew about this particular Stealth Guardian practice, he couldn't wait to be alone with Virginia to ask her about it. Alas, the occasion didn't present itself right away. Leila was asking for pancakes, and the rest of the gang wanted seconds, too. So for the next half hour he was glued to the stove, filling orders as if he were a short-order cook at a busy diner.

And just as everybody finished breakfast, and Manus and Tessa volunteered to clean up, somebody switched on the sound on the TV, drawing everybody's attention to the news report that was unfolding on the screen. The reporter from the previous night spoke into the camera, while a red banner reading *Breaking News* scrolled along the bottom of the screen.

"Police have arrested two suspects during a raid in West Baltimore last night. They are being held in connection with the brutal murder of

Baltimore businessman Anton Faldo, who was found bludgeoned to death yesterday."

The screen split, and the mugshots of two thugs appeared on one side, while the reporter continued, *"Michael Brown and James Brown are the nephews of Carol Jefferson, Mr. Faldo's housekeeper. The police found items belonging to Mr. Faldo in the suspects' apartment, as well as forensic evidence that may directly link the two to Mr. Faldo's death. A police source also confirmed that Mrs. Jefferson, whom we interviewed on this program yesterday, has become a person of interest, and it hasn't been ruled out that she may have given her nephews access to the house. Police are currently waiting for DNA evidence to be analyzed, but a source close to the investigation has told us that both suspects will be charged with murder and an array of other crimes."*

Somebody muted the TV.

Wes looked at the assembled. He'd been witness to plenty of criminal cases and worked with the San Francisco Police Department enough times to understand what the Baltimore police must have in terms of evidence. "If the police are willing to leak that they'll be charging those two with murder, then they have enough evidence even without the DNA results to make a case. Once they have that, it'll be a slam dunk."

Virginia met his gaze. "I agree. So that's a dead end for us. The demons didn't get to Faldo, a bunch of thugs did."

"So, what now?" Wesley asked.

"We'll have to wait for Deirdre to make a move," Virginia said.

"Sit around and wait?" He didn't like that at all. "We've gotta do *something.*"

"Virginia is right," Hamish said. "We need to wait. In the meantime, we'll check in with the other compounds. See if they have any news for us. Everybody's got their eyes and ears open."

Though Wes nodded to agree with Hamish, he knew he couldn't just sit around. He had to think of what else there could be done. Maybe it was time to convince the Stealth Guardians that they didn't have to fight this battle alone.

26

———

Vintoq placed a stack of papers on Zoltan's desk. "The reports you were looking for, oh Great One."

Zoltan nodded. "For the entire last four weeks?"

"Yes. It includes every possible Stealth Guardian sighting as recorded by our spies as well as our own men."

"Worldwide?"

"As you requested."

"Good. Pull up a chair and sit down. You can help me go through them."

Vintoq pulled the chair closer and sat down. "What am I looking for?"

"Names."

"Names?"

"Yes, take down the names of anybody mentioned in the reports, note whether they are human or Stealth Guardian, and the location they were spotted at."

Vintoq nodded dutifully. Then he looked at the stack again. "And, if I may ask, what is the purpose of it? These reports have already been acted upon, with no result. The Stealth Guardians spotted are long gone from wherever they were seen, and the humans are no use to us at this point."

Zoltan cast a long assessing look at his underling. "On the contrary." He reached for the cell phone next to him. "Do you remember this? Ulric brought it to me. It belongs to a Stealth Guardian, and its contact list is full of names." He slammed his hand on the stack of reports. "There must be someone in here who matches a contact in this phone. I only need to find one, and we're in the game. Now, start."

"Of course, oh Great One." Vintoq took a part of the stack and placed it in front of him, then started leafing through the reports. "This will take a while."

Zoltan grunted. "Hmm. Perseverance leads to success." And patience. Though the latter he had in short supply. He was running out of time. He needed to make a move soon, or this window of opportunity would close just like others had closed before.

He glanced back at the dagger that rested on the side table again, next to his other trophies. It had outlived its usefulness, but he kept it as a reminder that he couldn't fail again. He had sold the destruction of the Stealth Guardian compound as a win to his subjects, even though he knew it had been a failure, because it hadn't achieved the most important goal: destroying the guardians from within. Destruction of only one compound when they could have gotten to so many more, had his advance team not screwed up, was a failure of epic proportions. But to his demons he would never admit it. They had to believe that it was a success.

Propaganda was important. The wrong kind could topple a leader. The right kind could empower him.

~

THE ENTIRE DAY, there had been a sense of calm before the storm at the Baltimore compound. Wesley had watched the guardians as they went about their work: doing perimeter checks every hour, monitoring communications with other compounds, watching the news for anything odd, and in general, just waiting for something to happen. But nothing stirred.

By the time the sun had set and dinner was over, Wes was on edge.

"We can't just sit around and wait," he said to the guardians lounging in the living area.

Pearce looked up from his tablet, with which he was still monitoring Deirdre's movements. "Sorry, pal, but what do you want us to do? If you have an idea, let us have it." He shrugged and dropped his gaze back to his device.

Maybe this was as good an invitation as he'd ever get. Wes took a deep breath, then braced himself for the opposition his idea would garner.

"It's time to bring Scanguards in on this. The vampires can help us."

Every head spun in his direction. Well, at least he had everybody's attention. Now he just had to make his case.

"The council won't authorize it, not in a time like this," Hamish said calmly.

"I'm not asking the council, I'm asking you guys," Wes said. When several of them opened their mouths to protest, he lifted his hand. "Hear me out, before you object. It's not like you're doing anything else important right now."

A few glares answered his words, but Wes ignored them. Instead, he looked at Virginia. At least she wasn't glaring at him.

"Fine, we'll listen," Virginia said.

He couldn't help but notice that even Enya looked surprised at this, though Virginia didn't seem to notice it.

"As an outsider, I'm looking at all of this and wondering what we're missing," Wesley started. "I've been wracking my brain all day. And I think I found it."

A few skeptical gazes landed on him.

"Now, I don't presume to know more about demons than you, but not being a guardian myself, I think I might have a different perspective on a few things. So, the demons seem to be everywhere, right? I mean they have their own network of spies—humans and demons—in the world, watching us, presumably reporting to their boss, right?"

Hamish shrugged. "Yeah, so? We know that already. That's why we're extremely careful when we go out there and remain invisible whenever we can."

Wes nodded. "That's what I thought. But when you're not invisible, they can recognize you by your aura, whereas the demons themselves don't have a preternatural aura you or I could see. It puts you at a disadvantage."

"You forget their green eyes," Enya said, almost bored.

He acknowledged her comment with a nod. "No, I'm not forgetting. But eyes can be shielded, either with sunglasses, or with colored lenses."

"We know that," Enya said, "but a lot of the demons we encounter don't seem to take that precaution."

"Enya is right," Virginia added. "Though I've been confronted with more and more demons that seemed to go the sunglasses route in the last few months."

"Exactly. If they truly want to hide from you, they can disguise themselves. And then you have no way of recognizing them until it's too late. They could be following you anywhere and you wouldn't know it." Like they'd followed Virginia so many decades ago.

Virginia's chest seemed to rise as if she was afraid that he would disclose her secret. "What's your point, Wesley?"

"What if there was another way of recognizing a demon, even if they've disguised themselves?"

"You mean like when they plunge a dagger into one of us?" Logan asked dryly.

Wes smirked. "It would be a little too late by then, wouldn't it? No. But the demons have a scent. Not something I would be able to distinguish, nor you, but there's one species that can recognize anybody by scent."

"Vampires," Virginia murmured.

"Yes, and I just happen to be good friends with a whole bunch of them. And not only that: they're highly trained bodyguards, used to fighting evil."

"And why would a bunch of bloodsuckers help us?" Enya asked, her voice full of disgust.

"You probably shouldn't call them bloodsuckers," Wes cautioned. "They might get offended."

Logan stood. "I've got the same question as Enya. Why help us? Vampires never ally themselves with anybody. They don't make friends with others. Hell, they fight among themselves enough as is."

"I'm the living example that they do make friends. They are loyal. Half my family are vampires. My brother is one, my sister is bonded to one. I have a niece and a nephew, both hybrids. I know these people. I've lived with them for over twenty years. They are just. They are brave. And they fight for the same thing you do: to eradicate evil. And right now, they're probably worried sick because they haven't heard from me in nearly two weeks. If I return to them now, they'll be so happy to see that I'm alive that they'll agree to anything I propose. Let them help you fight the demons, and you'll see you can trust them, too. Let them prove to you that an alliance between our two species is in the best interest of all of us."

"What if you're wrong?" Hamish asked, exchanging a look with Aiden, who looked doubtful, too.

Aiden added, "We can't afford to lose anybody, Wes. The demons already outnumber us. We can't take the risk of meeting with vampires. We might be running into an ambush." He glanced at his wife who sat on the couch next to him.

"I'm not asking for the whole compound to come with me," Wesley said quickly. "I just need one person to trust me. One of you to come with me and demonstrate to Scanguards what you're capable of, and that you come in peace, and I can guarantee you that they'll be more than eager to join forces. Just one person."

Silence fell over the room. The guardians exchanged looks. Wes couldn't blame Aiden and Hamish for not wanting to come with him. They had women to take care of. They had the most to lose.

"Come on guys," he urged the others. "Why are you suddenly all chickening out?"

Manus huffed. "We're not. But there are rules." He slanted a glance at Virginia. "The council will have our hide if they find out. And they will find out."

Laughing, Virginia suddenly rose. "Now you're touting the rules? That's rich, Manus, particularly for you. According to your file, you've broken just about every rule there is."

"I take offense at that, *counselor*," Manus said with a red face.

Virginia shook her head. "Don't all pretend that you suddenly love following rules, just because I'm here, watching you. What would you do if I weren't here? If you weren't under scrutiny?"

The looks the guardians exchanged gave away their true feelings. Wes could see that. And apparently Virginia could, too.

"Just as I thought." She let out a breath. "But none of you are going to Scanguards."

Wes opened his mouth. "But—"

"I'm going with Wesley," Virginia interrupted. "And the rest of you will cover for us. Is that clear?"

Nobody contradicted her.

And Wesley couldn't be happier. Virginia had finally decided to trust him.

27

"I hope I won't regret this," Virginia whispered to Wesley an hour later.

After discussing all the details with her colleagues, and establishing certain protocols if things went wrong, Virginia and Wesley had geared up and were now standing in front of the portal, ready to transport to Scanguards. Hamish and Logan, who had outfitted both her and Wesley with weapons, were with them, waiting.

Wes slung his backpack with his witchcraft tools over his shoulder. "Trust me. Nothing is gonna happen to you. I won't leave your side." He squeezed her arm in reassurance.

"Virginia," Pearce called out as he came down the stairs.

She looked past Wesley.

"I've programmed a new cell phone for you. It's a secure line. Only use this one to contact us. And if the line rings, pick it up. It can only be us. Nobody else knows the number."

She nodded and accepted the cell phone. She slipped it into the inside pocket of her jacket, a jacket Tessa had lent her. It felt a little snug, but it was better than nothing if she didn't want to shiver. Apparently, the weather in San Francisco, where they were headed, was cold and wet at present. It was the rainy season in California, Wesley had explained.

"Are you sure you'll be able to find a portal in San Francisco?" Hamish said. "I've looked through the register of lost portals, and so far, we haven't found one yet."

"If Wesley's theory is correct, that the lost portals are remnants of old compounds, then there will be one in San Francisco. I was assigned to a compound there in the 1960s. The compound was destroyed after it was compromised." She swallowed away the bad memories. "I'm counting on the stone that encased the portal to have been reused in construction somewhere in San Francisco."

Hamish let out a breath. "Well, then good luck. Shoot us a text when you've arrived so we don't worry."

Virginia met his gaze. What she saw in Hamish's eyes surprised her. He meant what he said. "I didn't know any of you cared about what happens to me."

The three Stealth Guardians exchanged looks. Then Hamish winked. "Oh, we're not worried about you." He jerked his thumb at Wesley and grinned. "We're just getting used to having Wes make pancakes for us. Don't wanna lose the best cook we've ever had. Right, guys?"

The other two nodded.

"So, keep him safe, will you?"

Virginia caught Wes rolling his eyes.

"We'll be in touch," Virginia said and pressed her hand to the dagger carved into the stone wall of the portal. Seconds later, the portal was open. She walked inside, and Wesley followed her.

He immediately put his arm around her waist, before she could stop him. A quick glance at her three colleagues outside in the corridor confirmed that they'd noticed the intimate gesture. But to her surprise, nobody seemed to care. They wouldn't tell anybody that she, too, had broken some rules.

She nodded at them, then willed the portal to close. Darkness engulfed them.

Wesley pulled her into a closer embrace, and for an instant she resisted.

"Only so you won't leave me behind," he murmured in her ear. "Who knows where we'll land this time."

"Are you afraid?"

"Not as long as I can feel you."

She put both arms around him and leaned her head against his.

"Mmm, better," he whispered and kissed her on the cheek.

Virginia concentrated on San Francisco, on her old compound, on everything she knew about the city, its landmarks, its many hills, its streets and its buildings. She felt the air churn around her and knew they were moving. The portal was taking them away. To the place where she'd made the biggest mistake of her life. A mistake she hoped she wasn't repeating.

"We're here," she announced to Wesley.

"I can't see anything. It's too dark."

"I haven't opened the portal yet. We need to be prepared for anything." She eased out of his arms. "Have your weapon ready."

"All right," he agreed. "I'm ready."

"Let's do it," she murmured and willed the portal to open.

Loud noise immediately pierced her eardrums, as bright lights rushed past the opening. It took a second for her brain to make sense of it. A train was whizzing past them.

"We're in a subway tunnel," Wesley said next to her.

With the train having passed, Wes now inched his head out of the portal and looked down the tunnel. "There's a station only a few hundred yards down."

Virginia looked in the same direction and saw the lights of the subway station, where the train had stopped. "Let's get there before the next train comes." She glanced down the other end of the tunnel, but saw no lights around the bend.

"Agreed," Wes said. "But let's put our weapons away. We don't want to look suspicious when we reach the station."

She put her dagger back into its sheath.

"Watch your step," he advised. "There's only a slim ledge."

"Go, I'm following you."

Carefully walking along the edge of the tunnel, she followed Wesley toward the station. The train was getting ready to leave, its doors closing now. There were plenty of people on the other side of the platform, though this side of it was clearing out. Still, too many people would see her and Wesley emerge from the tunnel.

Wes looked over his shoulder. "This is Sixteenth Street BART station. We're in the middle of the Mission. Scanguards' HQ is right around the corner."

"My old compound was in this neighborhood." So they hadn't moved the debris too far from its original site and reused it in the building of the BART system, the intra-city rapid transit system that connected the South Bay cities with Oakland and the East Bay, via San Francisco.

Just before they reached the spot where the station lights fell into the tunnel and could expose them, Virginia put her hand on Wesley's shoulder.

"Wait," she murmured. "I'm going to make us invisible."

"Good idea." He reached back and took her hand, and slowly they walked out of the tunnel and onto the platform.

Wesley navigated them past the few people waiting for the next train and followed those heading up the escalators, careful not to get too close to anybody in case some unsuspecting citizen suddenly bumped into an invisible obstacle.

When they reached the next level, where the turnstiles and ticket booths were located, it was busier. Wes pointed to the turnstiles and leaned in to whisper in Virginia's ear, "Without tickets we can't get out. Can you keep me invisible while I jump over it and then help you?"

"No problem."

The hurdle was an easy one, and moments later, they emerged outside the station, at a busy intersection in the Mission district. It was raining and it was dark here too. Based on the traffic and the amount of people on the sidewalk, they were in the middle of rush hour.

"Shit!" Wes cursed. "The rain is gonna make us look like Chevy Chase in *The Invisible Man*."

Virginia understood immediately. Their silhouettes would become visible. "This way." She dragged Wesley to an alley, where several trash containers shielded them from view. "I need to make us visible, or the jig is up."

"Do it," Wesley agreed.

Assuring herself that nobody could see them, she uncloaked Wesley and herself. "Okay, we're good. Let me tell the others that we've arrived safely." She quickly typed a text message and sent it. The reply came immediately. *Keep us posted,* it said.

"Where to now?"

Wes took her hand. "This way."

He led her along a busy sidewalk, took several turns, and crossed the street on two occasions. All in all, they probably walked four or five blocks until Wes stopped at the back of a large building that seemed to take up half of the block.

"That's our parking garage. Now, we could go in the front, but there'll be lots of humans too, and who knows how the vampire guards are going to react to your presence. I'd rather take the back entrance and go straight up to the executive floor. If that's alright with you?"

For a moment she thought about it. "You know your people best." Then she pointed to the gate that blocked entry to an underground garage. "How do we get in?"

Wes pulled something from a pocket in his backpack and waved it at her. "With an access card." He held it over the card reader. The light on it went green, but the gate didn't lift.

Virginia was about to make a comment, when she saw Wesley press his thumb on the reader. He glanced back at her. "Security procedure, just in case somebody steals our cards."

"I like it."

The gate lifted, and Wes took her hand again and led her inside.

Behind them the gate lowered. Virginia looked around. It was indeed a garage, well-lit and clean.

Wes pointed to the other end of the large space. "The elevators are back there."

As they walked toward them, Virginia instinctively held Wesley closer. He stopped and turned to her, gripping her biceps. "Are you okay, babe?"

She could feel her heart pounding. And why shouldn't it pound? She was about to enter a vampire nest. "Are you sure they'll listen to you?"

"They will. Besides, I meant what I said: I won't leave your side. I'll protect you from anybody who wants to harm you."

"Why? You've been friends with them longer than you've known me."

At that, he chuckled. "Virginia, do I really need to spell it out for you?"

"Spell what out?"

He took her face into both hands. "I'm falling in love with you."

"In love?" she gasped. "But—"

"I admit, at first it was all physical and I couldn't wait to get into your pants, but things have changed. I mean, I still want to get into your pants, believe me. But surviving a trip to the demon world with you has given me a different perspective. Life is too precious, and I'm not going to waste it any longer chasing after some skirt. I want something real."

Virginia's jaw dropped. Wesley wanted more than just sex? She was saved from having to answer by a sudden sound from the elevator. Her gaze whipped toward it, and her pulse kicked up. "Somebody's coming."

She reached for her dagger.

The elevator doors opened, and two men rushed out. Two vampires. Both armed with handguns, both tall creatures, one with long dark hair, the other with short hair.

Instinctively, she gripped her dagger tighter, when she felt Wesley's hand wrap around her wrist. She shot him a look. Was this where he would betray her?

Her heart leapt into her throat and threatened to suffocate her.

"Son of a gun!" the long-haired vampire said and grinned. "It's really you."

The other vampire simply marched toward him and pulled Wesley into a bear hug, lifting him off his feet. "Bro, you could've called." He slapped Wesley over the back of his head. "Your sister is beside herself with worry."

"Good to see you too, Blake."

The vampire, Blake, dropped him back on his feet. "We got an alert, when you used your access card. Figured we'd better make sure you weren't being forced by anybody. But looks like you're good." He turned his gaze on Virginia. "And this must be one of the Stealth Guardians you were looking for."

Wes reached for Virginia's hand and squeezed it. "This is Virginia Robson, one of the nine members of their governing council."

Both vampires looked at their clasped hands, then stared back at Wesley, an unspoken question on their lips.

Wesley smirked. "And my girlfriend."

"Only Wesley." The long-haired vampire with the Southern drawl shook his head. "Pleasure meeting you, Virginia."

"Virginia, this is John Grant," he introduced the man who'd spoken. "And this is Blake Bond."

Blake offered his hand for a shake. "So, you fell for this womanizer's charm, and nobody was there to warn you about him. My apologies."

She spun her head to Wesley, who was already punching his friend in the arm. "Would you stop that? Virginia has a good opinion of me, and I'd like it to stay that way."

Blake laughed. "Yeah, good luck with that." Then he winked at Virginia. "You could have done worse. He's not all that bad."

"You're helping a lot," Wes said dryly. Then he pulled her closer.

"Don't listen to anything he's saying. He's been the bane of my existence ever since I joined Scanguards."

John cleared his throat. "We should go up. Samson will want to see you."

Virginia took a deep breath. Now that she'd seen Wesley interact with the two impressive vampires, she was a little less worried. They seemed to share genuine affection and friendship. Cross-species friendship. For the first time since she'd heard about Wesley and his association with Scanguards, hope blossomed in her chest that maybe her own kind could overcome their prejudices when it came to vampires.

28

———————

It felt good to be back.

"So, what's new?" Wes asked his colleagues. "Anything happen while I was gone?"

John and Blake exchanged a look. Both grinned.

"What? Spit it out already."

"Roxanne got hitched," Blake said.

"You're shitting me! The ice princess?"

Blake chuckled. "It gets better. Her man's a witch. A pretty powerful one too."

"What? Roxanne hates witches."

John and Blake both laughed out loud.

"Well, apparently not," Blake said.

John added, "Looks like she just didn't—"

With a glare, Wes stopped John from finishing his sentence. Because he knew exactly what John had wanted to say: *didn't like you.*

John cleared his throat. "—didn't know she liked witches."

Wes glanced at Virginia, feeling he should explain. After all he'd only moments earlier confessed to Virginia that he was falling in love with her. And now he and his colleagues were going on about another woman. A redhead he'd once had the hots for. Bad form. "She's a colleague. Scanguards employs both female and male vampires."

The diversionary tactic seemed to work, because Virginia asked, "How many are there?"

"We employ about—"

Blake's hand on Wesley's shoulder stopped him.

"A whole bunch," Blake said and smiled at Virginia. "I'll let Samson, our boss, fill you in on whatever you need to know about us."

"I see." She nodded tightly.

The elevator stopped, and the doors opened.

Wes ushered Virginia into the hallway and leaned closer as they walked toward Samson's office. "Don't take it personal, but they don't know you the way I know you. They have to learn to trust you first."

To his surprise, she turned her head and gave him a soft smile. "I know that. But you can't blame me for trying to get the lay of the land. After all, I'm the one walking into a vampire nest."

"We don't call it nest here," Blake said from behind them.

Virginia looked over her shoulder. "I forgot that your species' senses are heightened."

"I didn't mean to eavesdrop," Blake said. "But it's hard not to."

"I'll keep that in mind."

Arrived at the door to Samson's office, Wes knocked briefly.

"Enter."

"We'll see you later," Blake said, and he and John marched into another office.

"Here we go," Wesley murmured to Virginia and gave her a reassuring look, before opening the door and entering.

Samson wasn't alone. Amaury was with him, leaning his butt against Samson's desk.

Samson rose from his chair, then froze in mid-movement, his gaze pinned on Virginia. "They alerted me that you were back. They didn't mention you brought a... guest."

Wes felt Virginia stiffen next to him, while her eyes ping-ponged between Samson and Amaury, who was now standing in front of the desk, equally motionless.

"This is Virginia Robson, member of the Council of Nine, the governing body of the Stealth Guardians. I've guaranteed her safety."

Finally, Samson moved toward them. "And I'll honor that guarantee." He stretched out his hand to Virginia. "Samson Woodford. I'm the owner of Scanguards. Please call me Samson. We're not very formal here."

Virginia shook his hand. "Thank you."

Samson motioned to Amaury, the linebacker-sized vampire who was also his best friend. "Amaury LeSang, my associate."

"Enchanté," Amaury said and shook Virginia's hand. Then he grinned at Wesley. "You made it back. We were putting up bets you know." Amaury patted him on the shoulder and winked. "I lost that one. You cost me twenty bucks."

Wes laughed. "You should learn not to bet against a winner." Then he looked at Samson. "Good to be back."

Samson put his hand on Wesley's shoulder and squeezed. "Glad you made it. We were worried." He motioned to Amaury. "Even those who bet against you."

"I can't wait to see everybody," Wes said. "Where's Haven?"

"He's on assignment tonight. By now Blake will have informed him that you're back. I'm sure he'll show up as soon as Blake assigns somebody to take over for him."

Wes looked at Virginia. "Haven is my brother. A vampire." Then he looked at Samson and Amaury. "I've told Virginia a bit about us already, but there's a lot to get her caught up on. And there's a lot I need to tell you about their race."

"Judging by the fact that you, Virginia, have agreed to come to us," Samson started, "I assume Wesley has been able to convince your people that an alliance between our two species would be beneficial to all of us."

"Actually," Wes said, cringing, "we didn't get that far."

Samson and Amaury exchanged a look, then Samson said, "You've been gone nearly two weeks. Without a word."

Wes sighed. "Yeah, about that..." He glanced at Virginia. "It's complicated. First, I was locked up, then I was helping a group of them fight demons. Then Virginia showed up and locked me up again, and I was brought before the council. Who locked me up again."

Samson raised his eyebrows.

Wes shrugged. "I was locked up a lot. And then demons attacked and one of the Stealth Guardians' compounds blew up. And Virginia and I landed in the Underworld and barely escaped with our lives. The council doesn't know we're here."

Samson raised his eyebrows and addressed Virginia. "So, you're not an official envoy of your people?"

Virginia shook her head. "Not right now. In fact, I'm not authorized to negotiate with you, but I'm here to ask for your help."

"I think I'd first like to hear the long version of what happened."

"I figured you'd say that." Wes took a breath. "Maybe we should sit down for that."

Samson motioned to the seating area consisting of a large couch and two armchairs with a coffee table in the middle. As they sat, Samson said, "Where are my manners? Would you like something to eat or drink, Virginia?"

"Actually, maybe something to drink."

"Amaury?"

Amaury walked back to the desk and picked up the phone. "I'll order a selection from the lounge."

By the time the drinks arrived, Wesley was already retelling his first encounter with the Stealth Guardians from the Baltimore compound. It took a good two hours for Wes to fill his bosses in on the full details of his adventure. The only thing he left out was how he and Virginia had become lovers. That wasn't anybody's business. However, he wasn't blind: he knew that Samson and Amaury had seen him holding Virginia's hand upon entering the office. They could draw their own conclusions.

When Wes had finished, Samson leaned back in his chair and nodded slowly. "Demons, huh? We haven't had any in San Francisco in a long time. I remember encountering some when I first moved here in the early 90s. But they disappeared."

Virginia, who'd helped Wesley tell his story, reminding him of details he'd almost forgotten, said, "I have a feeling I know why."

"Yes?" Samson asked eagerly.

"I'm assuming you weren't the only vampire who moved to San Francisco in the 90s?"

"I brought several of my associates, and we established a subsidiary here. A couple of decades later, we moved HQ from New York to here. So, yes, there were lots of us by then."

"Then it makes sense. Even demons fear vampires because of their speed and ferocious fighting skills. Plus, they figure that a city swarming with vampires already has plenty of evil and fear to go around. So, their work is done."

Wesley chuckled at that. "Guess the demons are in for a surprise. Thanks to Scanguards, this city is one of the safest in the country."

Virginia met his gaze, before she swung it back to Samson and Amaury. "Despite our initial issues, I've come to trust Wesley. And from his interactions with you and the other vampires I've met tonight, I can see that you are the honorable men he promised you would be. That's why I'm going to take a leap of faith and ask you for help."

"In defeating the demons?" Samson asked, though it sounded more like a statement.

"I can't ask you for that much, no. That is a discussion for the council and yourselves. What I'm asking is that you help me find the traitor who sold out our council compound to the demons. Wesley has suggested that you'd be able to detect the demons in a way we can't. By their scent."

Samson and Amaury exchanged a look. A silent conversation seemed to pass between them, though even Wesley knew that they couldn't communicate telepathically. But their bond as lifelong friends made them understand each other without words.

Amaury nodded. "We can put together a task force, fill them in on what they need to know about the demons, and send them out on patrol. It sounds like Baltimore is a bit like demon central, huh?"

"Looks like it," Virginia said, "though I think we need eyes and ears in every major city where we've previously detected demon activity. They're attracted to places where crime can flourish. They use it to stir up more unrest."

"That's not a problem," Samson said. "We have subsidiaries in lots of cities."

"As for payment for these services," Virginia added. "While I'm currently not authorized to compensate you for—"

Samson lifted his hand. "At this point, please accept our services as a helping hand from one friend to another."

"That's very generous of you."

"Thank you, Samson," Wes added.

"Don't thank me yet." Samson looked at Virginia. "If we're indeed able to help you, I want your word that you'll get me a sit-down with your council to negotiate an alliance. An understanding that we'll come to each other's aid whenever necessary."

"I promise you that," Virginia said and reached her hand over the coffee table.

Samson shook it. "Welcome to our world, Virginia."

Wes put his arms around Virginia and squeezed her.

Samson rose. "Let's call a meeting, and fill everybody in."

Amaury stood. "I'll get Quinn to give me the schedules, and mobilize everybody who's currently on leave."

"Do that, and then—"

The door was ripped open. Wesley shot a look toward it, but the vampire entering barreled toward him at vampire speed, lifting him off the couch and into the air as if he were a ragdoll.

"You could have called to let us know you were okay," Haven

grunted. "Do you have any idea how worried we were? No, because you only think of yourself, you idiot! Don't you ever do that again!"

Wes slapped his brother on the shoulder. "You can put me down now. And I would have called if I hadn't been locked up half the time I was gone."

With another grunt, Haven put him back on his feet, then looked past him to the couch. He nodded at Virginia who had shrunk back into a corner of the sofa. "Blake tells me you had time to get yourself a girlfriend. But no time to tell your family that you're alive. Figures."

Wes glared at his brother. "Could you be civil for a moment?" He tossed an apologetic look to Virginia, hoping to ease her worry. "Virginia, this big oaf is my brother. Haven. I have to apologize for him. He's obviously forgotten his manners."

Haven cleared his throat, then seemed to calm down a bit. "Excuse the outburst, Virginia, but I'm afraid years of saving my brother from himself have taken their toll on my patience." With a sideways glance at Wesley, he added, "And it would have been nice if he had shown a little consideration for his family and at least sent word that he was alive."

Virginia jumped up. "That's entirely my fault, Haven. Wesley begged me constantly to let him call you, but I couldn't allow it. We had to establish first who he was and that he wasn't planning to betray our location to anybody. It was a security measure. Please forgive me for causing you and your family such anxiety."

Wes stared at Virginia. While he'd asked the guardians at the Baltimore compound to let him make a phone call, he'd never repeated the request. And he'd certainly never begged. Virginia had lied. Lied for him so Haven wouldn't be mad at him. Nobody had ever done that for him. There could be only one reason: Virginia cared about him.

"He begged you to let him make a call?" Haven asked, chin dropping.

"Several times," Virginia lied. "He said he didn't want you or your sister Katie to worry."

"Mmm-hmm."

"He was so upset, he barely ate or slept."

Haven slanted Wesley a look, then grinned. "She's good. What did you have to do to get her to cover for you?"

Wes winked at his brother. "It's my charm."

Virginia started to protest. "But—"

Haven cut her off with a look. "I almost believed you. But when you said he barely ate..." He shook his head and chuckled. "My brother never loses his appetite for any reason."

Wes slapped Haven on the shoulder. "It's good to see you, bro."

Haven turned fully to Wesley, his back now to Virginia. "I'm glad you're alive." Then he winked and dropped his voice. "A redhead, huh?"

Wes grinned from one ear to the other. "Everything I ever wanted."

"Lucky bastard. I'm proud of you, Wes, really proud."

Wes met Haven's gaze, choking up at the heartfelt praise. No words were necessary to convey to his brother what this meant to him.

29

Virginia felt like she'd landed in a different world. With every new vampire she was introduced to, she wondered more and more why her own people had such prejudices against them. They seemed perfectly civilized, though at times a little rambunctious.

Haven had scared her at first when he'd entered Samson's office, and though she'd been prepared to make herself invisible to escape, she'd quickly recognized that Haven was only reacting out of love and worry for his brother. She could sense the trust between all of them like glue that held them together as one big family. Just like her own kind, sworn to defend each other against their common enemy.

While a meeting was hastily organized, Virginia stood next to Wesley in the corner of a large conference room.

"Sorry about my brother earlier." Wes shrugged. "He practically raised me after our mother was killed by a vampire, and sometimes he still acts like my father. Older brothers can be a pain in the butt sometimes."

"Your mother was killed by a vampire? Then how can you and your brother work with them? I mean, knowing it was one of their kind?" It was unfathomable to her.

Wesley's kind smile didn't falter. "Would you say the same if it had been a witch who killed my mother, or a human? Or a Stealth Guardian who killed another Stealth Guardian? You can't condemn an entire race for the actions of one individual. It's not fair to blame others for what he did. He alone was responsible, not his friends, not his family, and not other members of his species." He sighed. "The vampire who killed her did it to protect his own race. He thought it was for the good of his people. I can't fault him for that. He's a good man. He did what he thought was necessary."

"You know who he is?"

Wes nodded.

Stunned, she asked, "Didn't you want to take revenge? To do to him what he did to your mother?"

"An eye for an eye? Yes, I wanted that. When I was young and foolish. Both Haven and I wanted to avenge her. Haven became a vampire slayer. He killed many. I would have too, but I wasn't very good at it. Haven constantly had to help me out of one jam or another. But no matter what he or I did, it didn't give me the peace I sought. This was before I understood the reason why my mother had to die. Only then was I able to make peace with myself."

There was a sadness in Wesley's eyes that she wished she could wipe away. "I'm so sorry."

"Don't be. Things happen for a reason. My mother was possessed with lust for power. She robbed me and my siblings of our powers, hoping to harness the Power of Three for herself. Haven and I never knew that we were witches. And Katie..." A pained looked crossed his face. "The vampire kidnapped her to make sure the Power of Three could never be resurrected. For a long time we thought Katie was dead." He suddenly smiled. "But we found her. And Scanguards helped us. My mother's attempt to steal our power was foolish. Had the vampire who killed her not taken action, she would have destroyed the world as we know it. And I would have never become the man I am today. Nor would my siblings be as happy as they are now: bonded to their vampire mates."

"You truly bear no ill will toward the vampires?"

"They're my family now. They would die for me. And I for them."

Virginia swallowed away the lump in her throat. Such honor. Such pride. How could she have ever mistrusted this man? Every bone in his body spoke of truth. Of peace. And of love.

"Wes," she murmured.

"Hmm?"

"What you said in the garage when we arrived..."

"Yeah?"

"Did you mean it?"

His baby-blue eyes sparkled even brighter than before, or maybe it was just the way the light from the ceiling reflected in his irises.

"Why don't we talk about that later when we're at my house?" He made a motion with his head. "I'd rather not be overheard by my colleagues."

She cast a look at the vampires who'd started filling the room, and saw indeed a few who were now turning their heads.

"I get it."

"Besides," Wesley added and leaned closer, "there's something I wanted to ask you about that golden shimmer."

Her breath hitched. She'd known that he would eventually ask. But was she ready for it? Was she ready to give that much of herself to a man she barely knew? Even if that man was turning out to be everything she'd never dared to hope for. Could she take that risk?

"Don't look so scared, babe," Wes whispered. "It's just a question, not the Spanish inquisition."

Easy for him to say. In fact, everything seemed so easy for Wesley: the way he'd introduced her as his girlfriend to Blake and John, the way he possessively held her hand, not caring if anybody saw it, the way he seemed to accept this fledgling relationship between them. As if it were entirely natural and normal. When she knew that it was anything but. They were from different worlds. There was so much they didn't know about each other. So much baggage in both their lives. Yet it appeared that Wesley had managed to throw off the shackles of his past and find a way to live freely. Could she achieve the same thing with his help? To free herself of her guilt and finally accept that everybody made mistakes?

Wes squeezed her arm, and Virginia nodded. "Okay, we'll talk later."

From the corner of her eye, she noticed Blake approaching them. She turned halfway, and he stopped in front of her and Wesley.

"Hey," Blake said. "We'll get started in a minute. I called Katie earlier."

"Where is she?" Wesley asked.

"She and Luther are on their way back from Grass Valley. They should be here in a few hours. Traffic is bad because of the rain. Couple of roads are washed out."

"Hope they drive carefully." Then Wes addressed her, "My brother-in-law, Luther, splits his time between Scanguards and the vampire prison in the Sierras. He's a consultant on security there."

Surprise flooded her. "Vampire prison?"

"Yeah, the vampire council runs it. And there's never a shortage of inmates. It's a way for us to keep humankind safe from the worst and most violent offenders among the vampire population," Wes answered.

"It sounds so... normal," she admitted. "Almost human."

Blake smiled. "We try to fit in as much as we can. Having a bunch of rogue vampires out there is bad for all of us. It could expose us, and nobody wants that. So we take care of those problems before they turn into disasters."

"Is Scanguards involved in running the prison? I thought you were private security guards and bodyguards."

"We are," Blake said. "And we have a contract with the city to patrol the streets at night. The only connection to the vampire prison is Luther. And only because he was an inmate there for over twenty years."

Virginia's eyes widened as she stared at Wesley. "Your brother-in-law is an ex-con? A violent vampire? How can you trust him not to hurt your sister?"

Wes and Blake exchanged a chuckle.

"Even vampires get second chances. Luther has paid for his crimes. As for Katie: she's got him wrapped so tightly around her little finger that I'm surprised he's not suffocating."

Blake jabbed Wesley in the side. "You'd better not let him hear that. Luther thinks he wears the pants in that relationship."

"Then we'd better not destroy his illusion."

In disbelief, Virginia shook her head. "You're an odd bunch. I never thought I'd say this, but you're not that different from us."

Blake laughed. "In character maybe, but I hear that your kind has some pretty cool skills that some of us here would kill for." When she stiffened, he quickly added, "Figuratively speaking of course."

She nodded.

"Now, let's get this show started. Excuse me." Blake walked to the front of the room, where he joined Samson, Amaury, and another vampire with his hair in a ponytail and a large scar across his cheek.

"That's Gabriel; he's second in command at Scanguards," Wesley explained.

The meeting took a good two hours during which Samson and Amaury relayed some of the information that Wes and Virginia had provided them with. They focused mainly on the demons, their motivation, their fighting skills, their tactics, how they moved from place to place via their vortexes, and first and foremost, how to recognize them by their green eyes.

"As vampires," Samson now said, "we have an advantage, because we'll be able to recognize the demons by their smell, even if they're disguising their eyes by wearing sunglasses or colored lenses. That's why the Stealth Guardians have asked us for help." He motioned to Virginia now. "Virginia has agreed to give us a quick demonstration of the powers of her race, so that we're prepared for it. Virginia, would you?"

Everybody's head turned to her. She stood at the back of the room. "I'm able to make myself invisible." She did just that, and gasps went through the assembled. "But making myself invisible doesn't mean you can't hear me," she continued, still invisible. "Plus, you can still smell me."

A few of the vampires sniffed, then nodded.

"In the past the demons have used dogs to ferret us out when we're invisible, because the dogs can smell us. This tells us that the demons themselves don't have that sense of smell. That's your advantage."

She made herself visible again, then grasped Wesley's arm. "We can also make others invisible." Wes disappeared in front of everybody's eyes.

"Whoa!" several of the vampires choked out.

"Either through our touch, or through our minds, which takes more energy."

She made Wesley visible and he bowed in front of his colleagues as if he'd been the one performing the trick.

"Showoff!" Blake called out to Wes.

Virginia smiled, then continued, "In order to get out of tricky situations, we can walk through walls, doors, anything solid." She left out that a Stealth Guardian couldn't walk through anything lined with lead. It was best not to give away their one weakness. "Let me demonstrate."

She walked to the nearest wall, and reached her hand through it, then followed with her body. In the room next to the conference room, she materialized.

A female vampire shrieked and shot up from her desk.

"Sorry," Virginia said quickly, then marched back through the wall into the conference room and materialized again. She jerked her thumb toward the wall behind her. "I think I just scared somebody."

A few vampires chuckled.

"Any questions?"

Everybody's hands shot up.

30

"You made quite an impression on my colleagues," Wesley said, sliding his hand onto Virginia's thigh.

He was driving toward his home in the Corona Heights neighborhood of San Francisco with Virginia in the passenger seat.

Virginia put her hand on his. "Tonight's been a revelation for all of us, I think. I never thought vampires like your colleagues existed. They seem to abide by a code of honor. I never expected that from a creature who's defined by its lust for blood."

"Defined?" Wes cast her a sideways look.

"Well, they are, aren't they? I'm assuming they still drink human blood."

"They do. The vampires who're bonded to humans drink from their human partner." He winked at her. "And it's quite a high, for both partners. But many of the others drink bottled blood. You know, donated blood. Scanguards buys blood via a medical supply company and then sells it to its employees at cost."

"At cost? That's generous."

"Samson is extremely wealthy, as are many of Scanguards' directors. He's not in it for the money. He wants peace. And a future for his children."

"About the biting…"

"Yes?"

"Have you ever been bitten?"

Wesley sighed. He should have expected the question. "Well…"

"If you don't want to answer the question—"

He squeezed her thigh. "No, I do. I don't have any secrets from you." He shrugged. "I've been bitten. By male and female vampires."

He felt her surprised gaze on him.

"I volunteered."

"What do you mean?"

"There was a newly turned vampire, he was in dire need of human blood to survive. Samson asked me if I would let him drink from me. So I agreed—in exchange for being allowed into the bodyguard training program at Scanguards." He looked at her. "And before you ask, no, it didn't feel sexual, though I have to admit that I can see how it can turn sexual if you open your mind to it. But I'm not wired that way. It was a deal I made."

"And the women?"

Wesley cleared his throat. Those incidents he couldn't explain away as business. "Virginia, I want you to know that whatever is in my past will remain there."

"You don't have to—"

"I do. I dated a few vampire women, and I let them bite me, because I wanted to experience what everybody was talking about. When you live with vampires, that's your world. Those are the people you hang out with, the company you keep." He caressed her thigh. "But no matter how exciting it was, it pales in comparison to how I feel when I'm with you."

"Wes, you…"

"Wait until we're in bed. I'll say it again, and then you'll believe me, won't you?"

He pulled into the driveway of his home and pressed the garage door opener. While the gate lifted, he looked at Virginia.

"I believe you," she said softly and lifted her hand to his cheek. "Even when we're not in bed."

He slid his hand higher up her thigh. "I think we should still go to bed. We need our rest."

Virginia brushed her lips against his. "Why do I get the feeling that we won't get much rest in bed?"

"It's not my fault. Well, not entirely anyway." He kissed her. "You can't look like you do, and then expect a guy to keep his hands to himself."

"So, you're blaming me now?"

"Yep. That's my story, and I'm sticking to it."

Amidst Virginia's soft laughter, Wes drove into the garage, lowered the gate behind them, and switched off the engine. Before the gate had even fully closed, his mouth was already on Virginia's lips, silencing her. She molded to him immediately, and he loved the feel of it. Reluctantly, he released her.

"Let's go upstairs, before I forget all my manners."

He exited the car and then helped Virginia out of it. Then he led her up a flight of stairs and pushed the door to the foyer open. To his surprise the light in the hallway was burning. Had he left it on two weeks earlier?

"Wesley! Oh my God, you're finally here!" Katie came running from the living room and threw herself into his arms, nearly knocking him off his feet.

"Hey, little sis!" He hugged her tightly and kissed her on the cheek. "See, I told you I'd come back in one piece."

Katie rolled her eyes. "You promise a lot of things. I was worried."

Luther appeared in the arch that led into the living room. "Worried is an understatement."

"Hey, Luther, good to see you." Wes released Katie and reached for Virginia's hand. "Katie, Luther, this is Virginia." And then, just because he wanted to, he added, "My girlfriend."

Luther and Katie exchanged a knowing look. Apparently, that explanation wasn't needed. Somebody had already told them.

Nothing remained a secret for long at Scanguards, just like in any family.

Katie stretched her hand out to Virginia, who shook it. "Blake already filled us in. I'm really happy to meet you."

"Thank you, Katie, that's very kind," Virginia replied.

"Pleasure," Luther said and reached for Virginia's hand.

There was the tiniest of hesitations, before she shook it. "Nice to meet you, too, Luther."

"So, you're a Stealth Guardian," Luther said. "Invisible and all, huh?"

Virginia nodded. "You missed the demonstration I gave at Scanguards' offices."

"I'm afraid so, but there were a few washed out roads in the foothills. We've had a lot of rain recently. Traffic was murder," Luther explained.

"I'm glad you all made it. Wesley has told me lots about his family."

Luther cast a sideways look at Wesley. "I'm sure he has."

Wes tilted his head a little. "Just the bad stuff, you know."

"Figures," his brother-in-law grunted.

"Now, now, you two," Katie said in a soft tone. "Let's not give Virginia the wrong impression." She gave Virginia a sweet smile. "Not hearing from Wes for so long really put us on edge."

"Well, now I'm back," Wes said. "And everything turned out fine as you can see."

Luther smirked. "Looks like it."

Wesley suddenly yawned in an exaggerated manner. "Virginia and I have had a long day and need to rest."

Luther put his arm around Katie and dipped his head to her. "I think we're being asked to leave."

Katie sighed. "So much for rushing back from Grass Valley to see my brother."

Wesley rolled his eyes. "We'll have plenty of time to catch up in the next few days. I promise you. I'm not planning on going anywhere soon." Then he motioned to Luther. "Besides, it's your husband who can't wait to leave so he can have you to himself."

Luther growled.

"Oh please, Luther." Wes clicked his tongue. "I'm doing you a favor here."

Luther slanted a look at Virginia, then back at Wes. "Just as I'm doing you one. Guess we're even."

As soon as Wesley shut the door behind Katie and Luther, he heard Virginia let out a breath. He turned to her.

"What?"

"You have an interesting relationship with your family."

He chuckled. "Don't get me wrong, we love each other, and we'd fight to the death to protect each other, but there are moments when I'd rather see the back of them." He put his arm around Virginia's waist and pulled her to him. "And now is one of those moments. Because I think you and I have something important to discuss."

He noticed how she swallowed and recognized it as a sign of nervousness. "Um..."

"Logan told me why Leila was shimmering golden."

"I figured he did."

"But he didn't tell me everything. He only said that a female Stealth Guardian could do the same to a man. To someone like me."

"Mmm-hmm." She bit her lip.

"But he said it works differently for a man. So, are you gonna tell me what Logan didn't wanna tell me?"

She avoided his gaze and instead focused her eyes on his chest. "Wesley, I'm sure... I don't... It's—"

The doorbell interrupted her. She sighed with visible relief.

"You're not off the hook," he said, and released her.

He opened the front door, and was almost mowed over by his twenty-one-year-old niece Lydia.

"Uncle Wesley! You're back! I'm so relieved." She hugged him tightly.

Almost eighteen-year-old Cooper was right behind her, patting him on the shoulder. "Hey Uncle Wes. Cool that you're back. You've gotta tell me about the demons. Dad just called and said you were in the Underworld. Wow, that's just awesome!"

Wes released his niece and grinned at his nephew. "Well, it wasn't all that awesome when we thought we'd never get out of there."

"But you made it!" Cooper insisted. "You're the best!"

Wes ruffled his nephew's hair, and another person appeared in the door.

"Sorry, Wes, but they insisted," Yvette said as she entered, carrying a few shopping bags.

"Hey Yvette, good to see you." Wes turned to Virginia and reached for her hand. "Guess you get to meet my entire family today." He pointed to the children. "My niece Lydia, my nephew Cooper. And this is Yvette, their mother, and Haven's mate. Guys, this is Virginia."

This time he didn't add *my girlfriend*. Because they already knew.

After an exchange of greetings, Yvette said, "We really don't want to disturb you for long. I just wanted to bring this for Virginia." She lifted the shopping bags.

"For me?" Virginia asked, a surprised look on her face.

"I was told you arrived without luggage. So, I went out to get you a few essentials."

Virginia pressed her hand to her chest, clearly touched by the gesture. "I don't know how to thank you."

Yvette handed her the bags. "Don't thank me." She winked. "I used Wesley's credit card." She pointed to the bags. "There's lingerie, toiletries, a couple of tops, and some pants."

"Wow." She looked into the bags and pulled out a pair of jeans. "They're my size!"

Yvette laughed softly. "My husband has an eye for that kind of thing."

Wes leaned in and gave Yvette a kiss on the cheek. "You're the best sister-in-law."

"I'm your *only* sister-in-law." Then she turned to her children. "Let's go home."

"But I want to hear about the demons!" Cooper protested.

"Another day," Yvette said.

"Why don't you come by tomorrow afternoon and I'll tell you all about it?" Wes asked.

"During daylight?" Virginia asked and stared at him.

"I'm a hybrid," Cooper said proudly. "Half vampire, half human. I don't burn in the sun like a pureblood vampire."

"Oh, that's what it is." She shook her head. "I was wondering why your aura and your sister's were a little off from a vampire's."

Cooper looked at her with pride in his eyes. "Yeah, we're pretty cool, aren't we?" Then he nodded at her. "But you're cool, too. Dad said he saw you make yourself invisible and walk through a wall. I'd like to learn that."

Virginia laughed. "I'm afraid that's not something anybody can teach you. It's genetic."

"Bummer!"

"Well, maybe," Wesley hedged with a sideways glance at Virginia, "Virginia will give you a demonstration tomorrow if you're coming to visit."

Cooper's eyes lit up. "Yeah!"

Yvette smiled at him. "Thanks, Wes. Good night, Virginia. I'm sure we'll see you soon."

Then she ushered her children outside, and silence fell over the house again.

Wesley turned slowly, facing Virginia. "I believe we were interrupted just as you were about to tell me more about that golden shimmer."

~

VIRGINIA FELT her heart pound into her throat. Wesley deserved an answer. After all, he'd been open with her, confessed that he'd experienced a vampire's bite as part of a sexual encounter. So why was she still hesitating? Was it because once she told him what it would do to him, Wes would ask her to make love to him that way? And what then? Was she prepared for it? Was she prepared to give so much of herself to him?

"It's the *virta*, our life force, that makes you shimmer golden. It's a connection that we only seek with those we love. Nobody would perform that ritual with a casual acquaintance, or a one-night stand."

She noticed Wesley's expression suddenly turn serious. "I understand. It's okay."

He dropped his arms, preparing to step away, but she gripped his biceps.

"It's very intimate. It's like sharing your soul with another being. And it heightens the sexual experience. Logan probably told you that when Leila shimmers golden, all Aiden has to do is touch her and she'll climax again."

Wes nodded in silence.

"It's different for men. If a female guardian pours her *virta* into a man, any man, no matter the species, he'll start to shimmer golden just like Leila did. And when that same female touches him again while his skin glows,"—she blushed a little—"he'll get an instant erection."

Wesley's chin dropped and his eyes widened. "You're kidding me."

"No."

"How long does the shimmer last?"

"Hours, depending on the amount of *virta*. Six, eight, even ten hours isn't uncommon."

"Fuck me!" he murmured and stared at her, his eyes now full of interest, full of eager anticipation. "You mean if you, just hypothetically, were to pour your *virta* into me, I'd have a hard-on for ten hours?"

She cleared her throat. "Well, hypothetically, yes. Though, of course, if we were to have sex again, and again, you'd orgasm each time. And then you would instantly get hard again, because I'd still be touching you. It's a vicious cycle that only stops when the shimmer subsides."

A broad grin spread over Wesley's face. "I wouldn't call it a vicious cycle. I'd call it paradise."

"You would, wouldn't you?"

Wes tipped his chin up. "So, you're saying this is only for those in a serious relationship."

She nodded.

"You asked me earlier whether what I said in the garage was true."

"Yes?"

"I'm afraid that when I said that I was falling in love with you, I wasn't being entirely truthful."

Her breath hitched, and her heart stopped. She knew it had to be too good to be true. She braced herself for the blow to come, her chest tightening.

"I've already fallen too deep and too hard." He slid his arms around her and pulled her closer. "Virginia, I'm hopelessly in love with you. There's no halfway, no doubt. I was fooling myself when I thought that I still had any control over my heart. I don't. It belongs to you. Whether you want it or not. And I'm not gonna give up until you feel the same. I don't care how long it takes, or what I have to do. But I'm never gonna pressure you to do anything you're not ready for. You don't have to share the golden shimmer with me. Just make love to me like we did last night. I don't want anything else. Just you in my arms."

She felt tears well in her eyes. She couldn't have hoped for a more sincere declaration of love from Wesley. Her heart felt like bursting with the emotions she never thought she could express. But Wesley made her brave.

"Wesley, what if I wanted to pour my *virta* into you? Would you let me?" A tear rolled down her cheek.

"Let you? Tonight?"

She nodded, too choked up to say anything else.

He lifted her into his arms and spun them both in a circle until she thought the entire world was spinning around them. His eyes sparkled a vibrant blue, more vibrant than she'd ever seen them. When he stopped turning, he pulled her head close to his.

"Are you sure, babe?"

"I've never been so sure of anything in my life." Just as she was sure of her feelings now. "I love you, my wonderful witch."

"Make that insatiable witch."

She laughed, but Wesley cut off her laughter with a kiss.

31

———

Naked, Wesley leaned back against the headboard of his bed and watched the door to his ensuite bathroom open. His mouth dropped open. Virginia walked into the bedroom looking like an angel. She wore a white silk Kimono-style robe with a belt loosely tied at her waist. Her hair hung loose over her shoulders, its red color emphasized by the white fabric, strands of it caressing her breasts like flames licking at her skin.

He lifted his lids to look at Virginia's face and saw the same kind of fire in her eyes.

"Remind me to thank my sister-in-law for getting you those clothes."

Virginia walked toward the bed, her gaze roaming over him. "It seems she knows what you like." Her eyes focused on his groin, where his cock was already standing to attention.

Wes leaned forward and reached for her hand, pulling her on top of him so she straddled him. "I like a lot of things. In particular, I like you, naked, wet, and panting." He untied her robe, and it fell open, revealing that Virginia wore not a stitch beneath the silk. Slowly, he slid his hand between her legs and caressed her pussy. Warmth and wetness greeted him. "Well, two out of three isn't a bad start."

Virginia pulled her lower lip between her teeth. "Neither is this." She wrapped her hand around his cock and squeezed it.

A groan escaped him. "I like a woman who knows what she wants. And I'm more than happy to oblige."

A smile stole onto her lips. "I hope you still say that tomorrow morning."

Wes slid his hands onto her breasts and caressed them. "Don't you worry about that."

He leaned in to capture one hard nipple between his lips and sucked gently, and felt Virginia's hands on his shoulders, gripping him for balance. Then she rubbed her pussy against his cock, making circular motions.

He let her nipple pop from his mouth, then moved to the other breast and licked the hard nub there, while he massaged the firm flesh with his hands. He'd always been a breast man, but even more so with Virginia. Hers were perfect in size and firmness, like two giant grapefruits, juicy and overflowing in his palms. He licked them more eagerly now and pressed them together, then swiped his tongue along the middle.

"I love your tits, babe." He gazed up at her and met her eyes.

"You want to fuck them?" She shrugged off the robe completely.

"Fuck, yeah."

Placing his hands on her hips, he lifted her off him and lowered her to lie on the duvet. Her hair spread out around her head like flames. Her lips parted, she lay there, waiting for him. He dipped his head to her cleavage and licked it generously, before he moved over her, one knee to either side of her torso.

Without needing any instruction, Virginia placed her hands on the outside of her breasts and squeezed them together. The sight made his cock spasm. He took his erection into his hand and guided it to her cleavage, pushing it between her breasts, where his saliva had created a smooth path.

With a groan, he sank between her gorgeous tits and felt Virginia squeeze them together around him.

"Fuck!"

Virginia licked her lips. "You like that, huh?"

Wes withdrew then sliced back into the soft shelter she'd created for him. "Babe, you're so hot."

A sinful smile curved her lips upward. "You haven't experienced anything yet."

"Oh yeah?" He started sliding back and forth with increased tempo, his balls tightening, while he roamed his gaze over her. Her face was flushed, her eyes dilated, her lips parted. Soft sighs rolled over her lips confirming that she was also enjoying their passionate foreplay. But this was just an appetizer to tonight's main course, and he shouldn't get greedy.

With another thrust he stopped and pulled back, nudging backward, and sliding down her body.

"I think it's time I thanked you for this sexy treat," Wes said and pushed her thighs apart to slide into the place between them. He lowered his head and spread her farther, exposing her wet folds to his hungry gaze. "Oh my, you *are* wet."

"Your fault," Virginia murmured, her voice thick with passion.

"In that case, I'd better lick up all this mess I created."

"You should."

Wes brought his mouth to her nether lips and swiped his tongue over her slit, gathering up her juices. "Mmm." He scooped his hands underneath her ass and tilted her pelvis up for better access, and did it again, this time licking all the way up so the tip of his tongue touched her clit.

Virginia moaned, and he noticed her hands claw the duvet.

Loving her taste, he continued to lick and suck, bringing his fingers to aid in caressing her, sliding one into her tight channel and feeling her muscles tighten around his digit. Soon, she would do the same thing to his cock. Soon, she'd do a lot of things to him, things he couldn't wait to experience. But he wanted to show her first how much he worshipped her, how eager he was for her to find pleasure.

Wes lovingly licked her center of pleasure, feeling how the little organ swelled with blood, and how Virginia started twisting beneath him. He clamped his hands down on her hips, holding her so he could continue to bring her closer and closer to her climax.

"Wes, please!" she choked out, her breath coming in heavy pants.

He sucked her clit between his lips and pressed down.

A strangled moan ripped from Virginia's throat, and a second later, her body trembled. Wes felt the waves of her orgasm reach his lips and groaned. Slowly he released her and lifted his head.

Tiny beads of sweat were running down Virginia's chest, which rose and fell in even breaths now.

"I love it when you come," he said.

She opened her eyes and reached for him. "I need to feel you. Now. Deep inside me."

He didn't lose a moment. He rolled over her, adjusted his cock, and plunged into her. "Like that?" he murmured, staring into her eyes.

"Just like that," she said and pulled his head down to kiss him.

The moment he parted his lips to accept her kiss and felt her tongue slide into his mouth to play with him, everything around him changed.

The bedside lamps flickered like bulbs about to burn out. The floor beneath them shook with tremors as if an earthquake was striking San Francisco. The air began to churn around them like a storm was brewing. Fog filled the room as if the windows had opened and let in the moist air from the ocean. Yet there was nothing cold or unpleasant about the elements going wild around them. Instead, they formed a cocoon that swept them up, causing them to float as if on a bed of cotton wool.

But what was happening around them was nothing in comparison to what was going on inside him. Virginia was sharing herself with him, filling him with her life force, her *virta*, the energy that made a Stealth Guardian. Though she had warned him about the intimacy of this act, he wasn't prepared for it. It hit him like an avalanche. An avalanche of lust, passion, bliss—yet it was so much more.

Every cell in Wesley's body was permeated with new life, new strength and energy. And a newfound sense of purpose, of understanding. His senses went into overdrive, feeling, smelling, seeing, hearing more intensely than ever before. In his core, a fire ignited and sent flames shooting through his veins. His skin began to tingle, the tiny hairs rising all over his body. Beneath him, Virginia was writhing, welcoming his thrusting cock. A cock that seemed to now take on its own life, driving deeper and harder, thrusting faster, plunging with more power. Untamed and unbridled.

Virginia's lips fused with his, just as their bodies seemed to fuse, to melt together into one being. Yet two hearts were beating, two pairs of hands touching.

Wesley's sense of time and place vanished. All that remained was the two of them. Loving each other. Reveling in carnal pleasure. Bathing in a sea of lust. The source of it seemed never-ending. As if Virginia's life force was without limits. Just like his love for her had no limits.

And now he could show her his love: with his mind, his body, his every move.

Every thrust drove him closer to the edge. Closer to the point of ecstasy. A few more seconds, and he would be there, tumbling into the abyss.

Wes ripped his lips from hers and locked eyes with her. "I love you, Virginia. With all my heart."

His control snapped, and his seed burst from his cock. He continued to move inside her, unable to stop. That's when he knew it was happening. He glanced at his arms and saw it: his skin shimmered golden. And with their bodies still touching, his cock wasn't softening. Despite his release, he was just as hard as before. And just as horny.

But even though his cock was demanding another orgasm, he pulled out of Virginia's drenched sheath and instead rubbed his cock over her clit. It only took a few moments, and she erupted, climaxing for him.

"Good girl," he praised, and plunged back into her and continued to ride her. He started slowly, gently, giving her time to enjoy her orgasm, but the moment her spasms eased, he increased his tempo and fucked her harder.

Their sweat-covered bodies slammed together, sending sounds of passion bouncing against the walls of his bedroom. Walls he couldn't even see for the fog and air that churned around them, still cocooning them in a protective shield. And though *he* was fucking *her* like a wild beast, he was at Virginia's mercy. *She* was the one in charge, the one who held the reins, the one who made his world turn.

He gave himself over to her, letting himself fall, ceasing all control and giving her what they both craved: trust.

Virginia looked at him then, her eyes wide in wonder, her lips parted. "Oh Wes..."

He stroked his fingers over her cheek. "I'm yours."

When a tear ran down her cheek, his cock spasmed again, and another orgasm washed over him like a continuous ocean wave. Yet his cock remained hard and ready for more.

"I don't know how to thank you for this," he murmured at her lips. "This is better than any vampire bite, better than anything I've ever experienced." He kissed her long and deep, then leaned his forehead to hers. "Tell me you're not getting tired of this."

"Never." She lifted her pelvis in invitation. "I'm made for this. For you."

"Then I won't stop."

Because even if he wanted to, he wasn't sure he'd be able to. Virginia had ignited something in him. It wasn't just the golden shimmer that made him want to remain connected to her. It wasn't his constant hard-on that drove him to make love to her again and again. It was the need to cement their love and trust.

He'd finally found his mate.

32

―――――

Virginia stirred and felt something hard slide along her buttocks. A heavy arm was slung across her midsection and now tightened around her.

"Morning, babe," Wes whispered at her nape and pulled her into the curve of his body, his hard-on sliding between her thighs.

"Oh God, you can't still be glowing," she said in disbelief and opened her eyes.

"I'm not." He chuckled. "That's just me when I wake up." With his hand on her hip, he shifted his angle and slowly drove into her. "Oh, you feel good."

"You still haven't had enough?" She'd lost count of how many times they'd made love before they'd finally fallen asleep.

"Are you kidding me?"

He withdrew and thrust back inside her, instantly making her want more. She loved the feel of his thick, long cock filling her and stretching her.

"I've created a monster," she teased him and drove her ass back against his groin to impale herself fully.

"If this is you protesting, then you're not doing it right." He gripped her hip and started thrusting in an easy rhythm. Less frantic than the night before, yet no less exciting.

"Shouldn't we get up and go back to Scanguards?"

"It's still daytime," Wesley said. He started caressing her breasts, while he dipped his head to her neck and kissed her there. "Virtually nobody will be at the office."

She glanced at the clock. It was early afternoon, still a few hours away from sunset, so she eased back against Wesley's chest and moved in rhythm with him. "I guess we have a little time."

"I'll make it worth your while."

She didn't doubt that and sighed with joy.

The sound of a doorbell made her freeze.

"Oh crap," Wes cursed. He slid out of her and turned to his side of the bed. "It's Cooper."

She turned and looked over his shoulder. The screen on the telephone on the bedside table showed an image from the camera at the front door. The young hybrid stood close to the camera, waiting impatiently.

Wesley looked at her. "I have an idea that'll buy us a few minutes." He pressed the button for the intercom. "Hey, Cooper."

"Hey, Uncle Wesley."

"Can you do us a favor? Virginia and I overslept. Can you go to the store and get us some food for breakfast? My fridge is empty. I'll buzz you in. There's cash in the first drawer in the kitchen."

"Okay," Cooper agreed, and Wesley pressed the button to open the front door.

Then he turned back to her. "Now where were we?"

She laughed and jumped out of bed. "I think we were about to get up and take a shower, so your half-vampire, half-human nephew won't smell what we've been doing for the last eight hours."

Virginia snatched the white silk Kimono from the floor and slipped it on.

Wes grunted and got out of bed. "Okay, sex in the shower it is. Your wish is my command."

She looked over her shoulder and shook her head, laughing. "I said nothing about sex."

He pointed to his cock, which stood erect and curved toward his belly button. "You tell him that. I don't think he'll listen."

She laughed and ran into the bathroom, but Wes caught up with her at the sink and put his arms around her from behind. She met his gaze in the mirror. Damn, this man could get her hot with just one look. When he lifted her robe and pulled her ass back toward his groin, she let it happen and bent over the sink. A moment later, he was inside her, his hard cock thrusting deep into her.

"You need this just as much as I do," Wes said. "Just admit it."

She lifted her head. "I do."

For the next few minutes, no more words were spoken, and moans and sighs were the only sounds that bounced off the bathroom tiles.

Less than half an hour later, Wesley, showered and dressed, headed downstairs to let his nephew in a second time, while Virginia pulled her clothes on, her legs still shaking from her last orgasm, her pussy tender to the touch. With each memory of her lovemaking with Wesley another hot flame shot through her core. She looked in the mirror. Her cheeks were still flushed, and her entire body felt hot. There was no way she'd be able to hide from the young hybrid what was going on inside her. She was a woman in love.

Fully dressed, her hair dried, Virginia walked downstairs a few minutes later. She heard voices from the back of the house and found the kitchen, where Wesley and Cooper were busy preparing breakfast.

Cooper turned his head when she entered and smiled at her. "Hey, Virginia. We're making pancakes."

"Hi, Cooper. Thanks for going grocery shopping for us," she said and slid onto one of the barstools at the bar.

For a bachelor Wesley had a large and well-equipped kitchen. Cooking for the guardians at the compound had clearly not just been an act to gain their confidence. He seemed to enjoy cooking. She cast him a glance, and he turned his head and smiled at her.

"Hope you're hungry." He winked at her.

Of course, she was hungry. Starving in fact. No wonder after the amount of calories she'd burned the previous night. But she refrained from mentioning that in front of the impressionable teenager in their company. "I could eat a bite."

"So, my dad said last night," Cooper said, coming closer, "that you showed everybody at Scanguards how you can walk through walls and make yourself invisible."

Virginia suppressed a chuckle. The young hybrid definitely had an agenda. She couldn't really blame him. When she'd been his age, she'd been curious about a lot of things too.

"So, you want to see it?"

He nodded eagerly.

Wes tossed her a look from the stove. "I have to warn you: if you indulge him, you'll never get rid of him."

"Must run in the family then," she replied.

Wesley winked at her.

Virginia hopped off the barstool and walked to the nearest interior wall. She placed her hand on it, then pushed it through, so part of her arm vanished as if it had been chopped off right where it touched the wall.

Cooper's mouth fell open. "Whoa!"

"Watch," she said and lifted one leg, took a step and walked through the wall. She found herself in the dining room, a cozy room with dark wood paneling.

From the kitchen, she heard Cooper say, "Wow, that's so cool!"

She turned around and walked back into the kitchen.

Wesley smiled at her and piled several pancakes onto a plate. "Thanks for showing him." Then he placed the plate on the counter.

"And turning invisible, how do you do that?" Cooper asked.

"Cooper, let her eat first, please," Wes demanded.

"It's okay, Wes," Virginia said. "I can do both at the same time." She slid back onto the barstool, then, as Cooper watched eagerly, cloaked herself.

When she saw Cooper's stunned look, she reached for a fork and started eating a pancake. She knew what Wesley and the young hybrid would see: pieces of pancake simply disappearing as she put them into her mouth and ate them.

"That is awesome!"

Virginia laughed, but her cell phone ringing interrupted the carefree moment. She turned visible in an instant and pulled the phone from her back pocket. She pressed the talk button.

"Yes?"

"It's Logan. Deirdre is on the move. We just found out that she's at the Portland airport. She's about to board a plane to San Francisco."

"San Francisco?"

Wes tossed her a questioning look, and she pressed the speaker button. "Logan, I'm here with Wesley. You're on speaker."

"Hey," Logan said quickly. "Deirdre will be landing at San Francisco International Airport in about an hour and a half. I'll text you the flight details. You know what she looks like, right, or do you need me to send you a picture?"

"I know her face from the files, but send a picture for Wesley."

"Will do."

"Do you have any idea what she's doing in San Francisco?"

"None. There were no phone calls, no conversations with anybody. We have no idea what made her book this flight so suddenly."

"Okay, we'll head to the airport and follow her when she arrives to see what she's up to."

"Be careful."

"Thanks, Logan."

She disconnected the call and stared at Wesley.

"Eat. I'll call Scanguards in the meantime to get backup."

She pointed to the window. "The sun won't be down by the time she lands."

"Doesn't matter. They have blackout vans." Then he looked at Cooper. "Sorry to cut our visit short. You'd better go home."

"Can't I come? I'm a hybrid. I can help."

Wesley shook his head. "And give your mother a reason to rip my head off? Not a chance, buddy."

"That sucks. I never get to do anything exciting!" He growled with displeasure, and for the first time Virginia could see the tips of his fangs as they slowly descended. "I can't wait until they let me join the bodyguard training program."

"I know, but until then, your parents call the shots. So, get out of here." Wes patted the teenager on the shoulder.

Cooper cast them both a suffering look, said his goodbyes, and left.

When the door fell shut behind him, Wes sighed. "Well, so much for a lazy breakfast, huh?"

"Let's get this over with."

Maybe soon they would know who had given away the council compound's position to the demons.

33

Sitting in the passenger seat of Wesley's car, Virginia pointed to the curb on the arrivals level of one of the six domestic terminals at San Francisco International Airport.

"There she is."

Wesley directed his gaze toward the woman now crossing the street. He slowed the car even more, pretending to look for a spot to pull alongside the curb to pick up a passenger, since parking and waiting weren't allowed here. Luckily, the tracker in Deirdre's handbag was still working, and Pearce had been able to send them real-time updates on her location so they wouldn't miss her when she exited the arrivals hall.

Deirdre looked around as if searching for something. She was casually dressed in slacks and a light jacket, her oversized handbag slung over her shoulder.

"She looks younger than in the photo," Wes commented.

"She's older than I am."

"Being immortal does have its advantages."

"She's not immortal anymore. She'll start aging now."

"Where's she going? Taxi?"

"She's not taking a taxi," Virginia said. "Look."

Deirdre had reached the other side of the street and was now walking toward a shuttle stop. "She must have booked a rental car," Wes said.

Behind him a horn sounded. He looked in the rearview mirror. An airport employee was signaling him to move along.

"I can't stay here any longer."

"The stop she's waiting at only services Hertz rental cars. Do you know where their lot is?"

Wes nodded. "Yes."

"Good. Meet us there."

Before he could respond, Virginia had cloaked herself and, judging by the sound of rustling fabric from the passenger seat, was passing through the closed car door.

"No parking here, move along," somebody called out through a bullhorn.

Wesley sighed and merged back into the outside lane, driving away slowly, trusting that Virginia had reached the spot where Deirdre was waiting for the rental car shuttle. There was nothing he could do right now, other than make his way to the rental car lot.

It took about ten minutes before the shuttle arrived at the Hertz rental center on North McDonnell Road. Wesley watched it pull into the parking lot, letting the passengers disembark outside the office. Only a handful of passengers exited, and Deirdre was easy to spot. She had no luggage to speak of, only her handbag.

Wesley was parked and waited by the exit from the rental car lot. Nobody paid him any notice. He watched every car that exited, checking to make sure he didn't miss Deirdre. Suddenly, he heard a sound inside the car.

"I'm back," Virginia said.

He sighed with relief and turned his head, as she appeared next to him in the passenger seat.

"She's rented a Toyota Corolla. It's white. She should be the next one out. I've memorized the license plate just in case."

"Good. Did she sense you following her?"

"No. She's fully human now. None of her Stealth Guardian senses remain. It was easy to follow her. Just stay far enough back so she doesn't realize a car is tailing her."

"Don't worry, I'm trained." After all, Scanguards had trained him well in all kinds of disciplines, including surveillance.

"Here she comes."

After briefly stopping at the security hut at the gate, the white Toyota exited the car rental lot and merged into traffic. Wesley started the car and followed.

He exchanged a quick look with Virginia. "Looks like she's heading into San Francisco."

The white Toyota merged onto I-380. Wes fell back a little and kept his eyes on Deirdre's car. Interstate 380 was a short connector to Interstate 280. To his surprise, Deirdre merged over to the far left lane, which led not to I-280 North, but South.

"She's heading for San Jose." He glanced at Virginia. "Anything down there that you can think of?"

"Nothing that comes to mind."

"Well, we'll stick to her." He reached for his cell phone, which he'd mounted on the dashboard, and tapped on it.

A moment later, Blake's voice echoed in the car. "Hey, did she arrive?"

"We're on her tail. White Toyota Corolla rental car. California license plate 7KL895G. She's heading south on I-280 toward San Jose."

"Got it. I'm tapped into your GPS. We've got eyes on you."

"Great." He tapped the phone once more to disconnect.

"Are they ready?" Virginia asked.

"They will be," Wesley assured her. He glanced to his right. "Sun will be down soon."

"Did you notice that Deirdre had no luggage?"

"Yeah. Guess this trip wasn't planned much in advance, was it?"

"And it doesn't look like she's staying long, wherever she's going," Virginia added.

He took his eyes off the road for a moment. "Don't worry, whatever she's up to, we'll figure it out."

Virginia nodded, then pointed out the windshield. "Where's she going now?"

Wes noticed that the white Toyota was merging into the far right lane.

"There's an exit coming up," Wes said. He crossed two lanes to get into the same lane as Deirdre and continued following her. The white Toyota left the freeway at the next exit. Wesley did the same, taking the Skyline Boulevard/Highway 35 exit.

"Guess she's not going to San Jose after all," Wesley murmured.

"Where does Skyline Boulevard lead to?"

"Nowhere really. It's just a minor highway going south into the hills that run between the freeway and the coast. It also connects to Highway 92, which leads directly to the coast."

"The coast?" Virginia snapped her head in his direction. "Which town?"

"Half Moon Bay."

"Shit!" Virginia cursed.

Alarmed, Wesley stared at her. "What's in Half Moon Bay?"

"Cinead's private compound. It's a little north of Half Moon Bay just before El Granada."

"You think she's going there?"

"That's the only Stealth Guardian compound in the area." Virginia clenched her hand into a fist. "And it makes sense. She's selling out her half-brother for not sticking up for her, for voting to exile her."

"You believe she's leading the demons there? I haven't noticed anybody following her. Trust me, I would have."

"I'm certain of it," Virginia insisted. "We can't let her get any closer. We need to stop her now."

"Okay, there's a sinkhole repair in process about three miles ahead of us. The construction workers will have left for the day, and the locals are avoiding the road at the moment because of the delays. We might be in luck. I'll try and cut her off at the construction site."

Wesley sped up and caught up with Deirdre's Toyota. He pulled over to the middle of the road to look ahead. In the distance, he saw a car coming toward them. He punched the gas pedal and sped past the Toyota, then pulled to the right again just a couple of seconds before the oncoming car reached them. Not slowing the car, he raced ahead, leaving the Toyota behind.

As he sped along the wet road, the drizzle turned to rain, Wes connected with Blake again.

"We're on CA-92. Cutting Deirdre off before the sinkhole repair around Nuff Creek. She's heading toward a council member's compound. We think she might be leading the demons there."

"Got it."

"Thanks!" He disconnected the call.

"There it is," Virginia said, and pointed to the signs alerting drivers to the repair site.

One side of the street had been blocked off, turning the highway into a one-lane road. Wes slowed the car, and at the point where the road narrowed to one lane, he stopped and put his hazard lights on, while putting the car into park.

"Okay, so far so good," he said and looked at Virginia. "Will Deirdre recognize you?"

"Most likely yes. I brought many suspects before the council while she was a member. She'll know who I am."

"Well, I guess that's good. She'll know the jig is up when she sees you." He looked into the rearview mirror. "Here she comes."

Virginia looked over her shoulder and saw the white Toyota with Deirdre at the wheel stop behind them. Virginia opened the door and got out. Wesley did the same on the driver's side.

The rain was getting heavier, but Virginia ignored it and marched toward the white rental car. At least the rain would make it harder for Deirdre to recognize her from the distance. She walked to the passenger side and tried the door. It was locked. Deirdre whipped her head in her direction. Her eyes widened. She'd recognized Virginia.

Virginia passed through the closed door, entering the car.

Deirdre shrieked and reached for the door handle. She managed to push the door open, and Virginia let it happen. Deirdre got out of the car in a hurry, while Virginia turned the key in the ignition and stopped the engine. Then slowly, she exited and looked over the roof toward the driver's side.

Wesley was holding Deirdre's hands behind her back, and Deirdre was struggling against him. Unsuccessfully. When Virginia approached, Deirdre tossed her a scared look.

"You!" She fought against Wesley, but couldn't free herself. "Let go of me!"

A few more steps, and Virginia was face to face with the former council member. "So, you remember me. Good."

"What do you want from me?" Deirdre spat, defiance spewing from her eyes, venom in her voice.

"What are you doing in California?"

"I don't see how that's any of your business!"

"Oh, you don't?" Virginia took a step closer. "Well, that's where you're wrong, Deirdre. Who sent you?"

Deirdre pressed her lips together and glared at her, while she tried to free her arms from Wesley's grip.

"You know I can make you talk," Virginia threatened.

Deirdre tipped her chin up in defiance.

"Cinead was wrong about you," Virginia said. "You never saw the error of your ways. You never repented. Even a year in a lead cell hasn't made you understand how wrong you were. Once a traitor, always a traitor."

"I'm not a traitor!" Deirdre protested with a raised voice, her hair now matted to her head from the continuing rain. "But you wouldn't understand that."

"Oh, I understand. You're so full of hatred for your half-brother and the council that you're trying to wipe us out, aren't you?"

Deirdre's eyes widened.

"Yes, I'm onto you. Your first attempt failed. The demons didn't manage to kill any of us. And we destroyed the council compound before they could get to the portal."

"What?" Stunned, Deirdre stilled.

"So, what's the plan this time?" Virginia continued. "Get inside Cinead's compound and then call for the demons? Is that what you're planning?"

"You're wrong! I would never help the demons. Never!"

"Liar!"

Deirdre shook her head and fought against Wesley's hold. "You're the one who's with the demons. Cinead warned me not to trust anybody."

Now it was Virginia's turn to be surprised. "You spoke to Cinead?" She glanced past her at Wesley who looked equally stunned.

But Deirdre pressed her lips together again, unwilling to answer.

"Damn it, Deirdre, answer me! Cinead would never risk contacting you after the attack on the council compound."

Deirdre narrowed her eyes. "You can say whatever you want, but I'm not going to believe you. He said there are traitors among the guardians. And that they'll try to stop me from getting to him."

"That's bullshit!" Wesley hissed at Deirdre's ears.

She jolted and whipped her head to him, as if she'd almost forgotten that he was still restraining her. She gave him a long look. "You're a demon, aren't you?"

Wesley shook his head. "No green eyes. Sorry."

She snorted. "So, you disguised them with colored lenses. I know your tricks."

Virginia combed several wet strands of her hair out of her face and cursed. "Listen to me, Deirdre. Wesley isn't a demon. He's a witch, and neither of us are in league with the demons. So don't try to distract us from the truth. You're the one who's leading the demons to Cinead's compound." She'd had enough of Deirdre's stalling tactics. In one swift move, she gripped the other woman by the throat. "And now you're gonna tell me everything you know about the demons' plan, or I swear, I'll crush your windpipe."

Virginia tightened her hand around Deirdre's neck to make her understand that she meant business. An expression of panic spread over Deirdre's face. She began to choke.

"No. Please," Deirdre pressed out, and Virginia loosened her grip. "There's no plan."

When Virginia squeezed again, Deirdre said breathlessly, "My phone." Her eyes dropped to her jacket.

Virginia let go of her neck.

"I can prove that Cinead asked me for help. In my right pocket. My cell phone. You'll see the text message."

Virginia reached into Deirdre's pocket and pulled out a cell phone. "Unlock it," she ordered Deirdre and motioned Wesley to release her arms.

"Here," Deirdre said and, after unlocking the phone, navigated to the text messages. "This is the message I receive from Cinead, asking me to come."

Virginia read it.

"I need your help. Come to my place immediately. There's no time to lose. I'm in danger. Trust no one. We have a traitor in our midst. Be careful."

"It's from Cinead," Deirdre said and pointed to the top of the display. "It's his number. I know it by heart. And I programmed it in when he settled me in Portland."

Virginia shook her head. "This isn't from him. It can't be. He would never risk summoning a human to his compound. A human who can be followed by demons."

Deirdre pointed to the cell phone again. "But it's him. Damn it, he needs me. He's in danger." A sob tore from her chest.

Virginia exchanged a look with Wesley.

"They're using her," Wesley said.

"I know, but I'm pretty sure that this is Cinead's number," Virginia said. Then she shook her head. "I'll have to get Pearce or

Logan to check on it, though. I had his number, but my phone blew up with the compound, so..."

The moment she said it, her eyes locked with Wesley's, and she knew they were thinking the same thing.

"Shit!" Wes cursed. "Outside the council chamber. All those phones."

Virginia nodded. "The demons must have gotten the phones. The council members all ran for their lives. I didn't see anybody trying to grab their phone. I sure didn't."

Deirdre's mouth dropped open. "You mean that text isn't from Cinead?" Disbelief and fear collided in her face. "Oh no! What have I done?" She looked over her shoulder, panic now joining her fear. "The demons, they could be anywhere. We have to get far away from here. Far away from Cinead. If anything happens to him..." Another sob tore from her throat.

Virginia put a hand on her shoulder. "We'll take care of it." She looked to Wesley, seeking reassurance, when she saw lights flicker behind him. "Oh shit, police."

Wes looked over his shoulder. A police cruiser, its blue and red lights flashing, stopped a few feet behind Deirdre's white Toyota. The driver's door opened, showing the emblem of the San Mateo Police, and a tall police officer stepped out.

Wes looked back at Virginia. "Let me handle this. We'll be out of here in a couple of minutes. Just stay calm. We don't want to arouse suspicion."

34

Wesley pasted a smile on his face and approached the cruiser. The police officer, dressed in a black police uniform and Aviator sunglasses, was already heading toward them. His rain jacket was open in the front, the broad rim of his hat shielding his face from the rain.

"What's going on here?" the policeman asked with a booming voice, one hand on his belt where his gun was holstered.

Wes spread his arms to the sides, making sure the policeman knew that he wasn't armed. "I'm so sorry, officer, we're already on our way. We got lost and had to ask for directions."

The policeman looked past Wesley to where Virginia and Deirdre were standing. He tipped his chin in their direction. "Are you with those two women?"

"Uh, yeah."

"In two cars? Whom were you asking for directions?" He glanced around, presumably to see if anybody else was in the area.

"Yes, our friend was following us, but I think we took a wrong turn. So, we stopped to confer which way to go."

"You can't just park in the middle of the road," the police officer chastised him. "There's only one lane open."

"I understand. And I'm really sorry. We'll be on our way."

Wesley was about to turn and walk away, when the policeman said, "I didn't say you could leave. I'm gonna have to write you a ticket."

At the words, the hairs on Wesley's nape rose. He'd dealt with a lot of policemen in his life, and a little traffic holdup had never landed him a ticket. Apparently, this policeman was in a bad mood and ready to take it out on him.

Sighing, he said, "Very well."

"Wait here," the cop said and turned slowly to walk back to his police car.

Wes sighed and looked over his shoulder. Virginia and Deirdre were still standing next to the Toyota, waiting. He shrugged, then looked back to the cruiser. That's when he realized it: the police officer hadn't asked him for his license and registration. He'd been in traffic stops before, and the first thing a cop would do was ask for papers, so he could verify that he wasn't dealing with a criminal on the run.

Wesley's heartbeat kicked up a notch. Something was wrong. He watched the cop turn to enter the car, his profile showing now. There was nothing unusual about it—except for the fact that even in the rain and with sunset imminent, the man was wearing dark sunglasses. Who would do such a thing?

"Shit," Wes cursed under his breath.

The cop, his body shielded by the open car door, snapped his head toward Wes and froze. At the same time a large truck appeared on the road behind the police car and pulled alongside it, coming to a stop.

Wes whirled around. "Demons!" he yelled at Virginia and Deirdre. "Get in my car!"

Without waiting for Virginia's reaction, Wes spun back around. The cop was charging toward him, wielding a dagger, while the doors of the truck opened, and several more men jumped out. They, too, were armed with daggers and swords. But unlike the faux cop, they hadn't bothered wearing sunglasses. As clear as day, their green eyes broadcasted what they were: demons. The demon cop had been waiting for reinforcements, stalling Wesley with irrelevant questions. Well, they were here now.

"Fuck!" Wes cursed and threw up his hands, calling his powers to him. With the sun still a few minutes from setting, he'd have to hold the demons off long enough for help from Scanguards to arrive. He knew his friends had to be close. But just how close?

With his arms raised, he began chanting in Latin, "Aqua undaliquidum..." A wall of water rose before him, cutting off the demons' approach.

"Kill them!" the demon cop, clearly their leader, ordered. "Get me the human alive!"

Wes pushed the wall toward them, letting it crash against them and collapse. The force of the water threw several of the demons on their asses, but the rest of them approached, including the faux cop. Ferocious battle cries came from them, and fury blazed in their eyes.

Three demons rushed him, their daggers aimed at his heart. Again, Wesley called on his powers, using another incantation, and created a spear of water. He launched it at one of his attackers, hitting him square in the chest with it. It tossed him backward onto the pavement. But the other two kept coming.

"Shit!"

Wes pulled out the dagger the Stealth Guardians of Baltimore had outfitted him with and squared his stance, ready to fight. The demon charging toward him was massive. Still, he had no choice. He had to make sure Virginia and Deirdre got away.

"Time to die, fucker!" he yelled, when suddenly, a dagger whizzed past him and lodged in the demon's throat.

The demon's eyes widened. He reached for the dagger in his throat and pulled it out. Green blood spewed from his neck like soda from a fountain. He staggered forward a couple of paces.

"Duck left, Wesley!" Virginia yelled from somewhere behind him.

Without questioning, he followed her command, and a second dagger whizzed past him, hitting the other demon, felling him like a dead tree.

"Damn it, Virginia, run, save Deirdre and yourself!"

But she didn't listen to him, didn't even reply.

More demons were rushing toward them now, the demons he'd temporarily disabled with his wall of water. They'd recovered and were running to help their brethren.

"Fuck!" Virginia cursed.

Wesley saw it, too: from the back of the truck, more demons were emerging, a veritable army was descending on them.

"We're fucked!" Wes let out.

All around them, demons were approaching, some trying to break in from their right flank, others charging straight ahead.

A scream made him spin his head. Next to the Toyota, the faux cop had grabbed Deirdre.

Wes sent a spear of water toward him, causing him to lose his grip on the woman, but a moment later, the demon regained his balance again. Sneering, he snatched Deirdre again.

"Out of daggers," Virginia called out next to him. From the corner of his eye, he saw her vanish, cloaking herself as she lunged for the demons on the ground to retrieve her weapons. Despite her power, the rain made her silhouette visible.

A demon jumped on her. Wesley flung himself toward them and drove his dagger into the asshole's back, then kicked him off Virginia. But more demons were coming at them like an endless stream.

The sound of motorcycles suddenly roared over the shouts and grunts of the demons.

Wesley whipped his head around and saw four figures on motorcycles charging toward them. Three of them he recognized immediately. The hybrids: Amaury's twins, Damian and Benjamin, and Grayson, Samson's son. The fourth motorcyclist was clad in thick Kevlar gear and a dark headshield that, unlike a regular helmet, covered not only his face, but also his throat and nape from UV-rays: this could only be Luther, in his prison uniform.

All four charged into the melee, their engines revving, attacking the demons from behind simply by mowing them down. Grayson and one of the twins slithered to the ground, letting their motorcycles slam into a group of demons, while they rolled off and pulled their guns from their holsters, aiming into the crowd. Yet their guns did little damage. Bullets could injure demons, but they couldn't kill them, and despite their wounds, many continued fighting.

The second twin and Luther drove straight through the crowd and swerved to meet Wesley, then let their bikes slide to the ground and drew their weapons too.

"About time!" Wes grunted.

"Sorry, bro, bit of an accident back at the exit ramp," Luther replied and barreled toward a demon, firing at him.

"Bullets can't kill them!" Wesley yelled after him.

Virginia was on her feet again, having recovered her daggers. She resumed her fighting stance, ready to re-engage the enemy, when another scream sounded from behind them.

Wes spun his head in the direction of the scream. "Shit, he's got Deirdre."

"I'm on it!" Virginia yelled and kicked a demon out of her way, before charging in the direction of the Toyota.

Wesley tried to follow, but the demon Virginia had leveled rose back up before him and attacked furiously.

"Fucking demon, die already!" Wesley gripped his dagger more tightly and lunged for his attacker. But another one came at him from the side.

"Shit!"

Fighting against two demons now, Wes held his attackers off as best he could, drawing on his magic whenever he could to launch walls of water to distract and disorient them. For a while, it seemed to work. But the demons kept coming.

"Rip their heads off!" Wes yelled toward Luther and the hybrids. The Scanguards men were valiant fighters, but they were outnumbered. However, with vampire speed on their side, they were able to at least hold the demons back, wounding and even killing several of their adversaries.

Green blood spurted everywhere. The hybrids were getting the hang of it, using their sharp claws to inflict damage on the demons. But they were being driven back now. And Luther, hindered by his heavy Kevlar uniform couldn't even use his claws to fight. He had to rely on pure brute strength to battle his attackers.

Then all of the sudden, more men swarmed in. It took Wesley a split-second to recognize them through the rain: Scanguards.

The sun had finally set.

The vampires charged into the fray: Amaury came up behind one of his twin sons and ripped a demon's head clear off, dowsing himself in green demon blood in the process. Zane, the bald vampire, and the meanest fighting machine among them, took it a step farther. He barreled into a demon and slammed his claws into his chest, cutting through sinew and muscle. With a ferocious growl, he ripped the demon's heart right out of his chest cavity. Unsurprisingly, several of the demons nearest to him panicked and started running, but Zane, Gabriel and Samson by his side, gave chase. Meanwhile, Haven, John, and Amaury charged through the battle, heading straight for the demons surrounding Wesley.

"Need help, little brother?" Haven called to him.

He'd never been so happy to see his brother. Or the rest of Scanguards. "Took your bloody time!"

Wes continued to use all the powers at his disposal to hold off his attackers.

The sound of another car engine roared into the scene. With a whoop, Wes saw Thomas, Eddie, Blake, and Quinn jump out and swoop into the fight. With the sudden arrival of four more vampires, more demons turned tail and ran.

With Haven, Amaury, and John fighting off the demons surrounding Wesley, he was finally free to come to Virginia's aid. He spun on his heel, but when his gaze found the spot he'd last seen Deirdre and the demon cop, they were gone.

"Virginia?" he called out, but he got no answer.

Oh God, had the demons gotten to her before the vampires had arrived? He whirled around on his own axis, searching, hoping, praying. The battle raged on, and the vampires took full advantage of their superior speed, disarming the demons and using their own weapons against them. More demons were fleeing, and in the distance, Wesley saw them casting their vortexes and disappearing.

For the first time since the fight started, Wesley started to panic. Terrified that something bad had happened to Virginia, Wes ran through the fighting adversaries, dodging accidental blows and jumping over dead bodies.

Then a familiar scream made him spin to the left. There, on the other side of the Toyota, Virginia was fighting two demons, one of them the demon cop. She was trying to shield Deirdre from them, but was close to losing the fight.

"Zane! Amaury! Anybody! Virginia needs help. Behind the white Toyota!" Wes cried out for help, already charging toward the scene. Before he reached it, another demon hit him from the side, and he slammed onto the wet asphalt. He lost his dagger on impact and snapped his head to the side. Frantic, he reached for it, managing to grip the handle, but the demon was already upon him, his dagger aimed at Wesley's chest.

"Fuck!"

Before the dagger could reach its mark, two hands with razor-sharp claws wrapped around the demons neck, slicing through it and ripping the head clear off. Green blood rained down on Wesley, blinding him for an instant.

"You're welcome," Zane said with an almost smile and helped him up.

Knowing Zane, this kind of fight was right up his alley.

"Virginia?" Wes managed to say, still out of breath, and turned his head in the direction of the Toyota.

Amaury and John were charging toward the two women. But two more demons had joined the fight, and now the faux cop was backing away from the vampires, dragging Deirdre with him, while leaving his demons to fight off Virginia and the vampires. Virginia tried to follow, but the demons were preventing her from going after Deirdre. She couldn't get past them.

"Fuck!" Wesley hissed.

He couldn't let Deirdre fall into the demons' hands. She knew everything about the Stealth Guardians, and eventually, torture would make her spill her secrets.

Wesley raced around the other side of the car and chased after the demon cop and the struggling Deirdre. He reached them just as the demon cast a vortex. Desperately, Wesley jumped toward them and managed to push Deirdre to the side. The demon lost his grip on her, and she tumbled to the ground.

The demon cast a quick look past Wesley, and judging by the expression on his face, he knew he'd lost the battle. He jumped into the vortex.

"Not so fast, buddy!" Wes lunged after him, and the vortex engulfed him.

Darkness surrounded him, but his hands found purchase: he'd caught the demon's leg and ripped him backward, making him stumble.

Together they fell, fighting, punching, kicking.

Wes concentrated on his witch powers and pushed against the demon, kicking him off. But the demon wouldn't give up, wouldn't relent.

"Fucking witch! I'll teach you to mind your own fucking business!"

Suddenly pain like piercing shards of glass assaulted his head. Wes pressed his hands against his head to prevent it from exploding, as the demon's thoughts penetrated his mind like daggers. The pain was blinding, excruciating.

Images and words swirled together in a vicious mental attack as the demon sought to overpower him. As the pain grew, he sensed a dagger coming closer, knew it was the end. But instead of feeling the blade pierce his flesh, he heard an explosive clattering sound as it hit something hard. The weapon shattered, splitting into two parts, the blade and the hilt.

Everything was turning around Wesley. He was tumbling, grasping blindly at thin air. Trying to hold on to something.

"Wesley, don't leave me!"

The voice wasn't the demon's.

"Virginia..."

A hand gripped his shoulder, then another one hooked under his armpit. Suddenly and forcefully, he was yanked backward. For an instant, there was a flash of light.

Then everything went dark. Silent.

35

Aided by John, Virginia finally managed to pull Wesley from the demon's vortex. The moment his body was free of the swirling fog and dark mist, the force of her action made her stumble backward and lose her footing on the wet ground. Quickly she found her balance and looked at Wesley who was sprawled on the muddy shoulder of the road. Blood was seeping from a head wound, and his eyes were closed. He wasn't moving.

"Oh no! Wesley, no!"

Had she been too late?

Panicked, she scrambled toward him, fear pushing tears into her eyes. She gripped his shoulders. "Please, Wesley, don't leave me! You can't do this to me!"

Next to her, John reached over and laid his hand on Wesley's chest, then sat back on his heels.

"Virginia, he's alive."

She snapped her head to him, but through her tears she could barely see him. "His head, he's bleeding."

"That's a strange wound."

"What do you mean?"

John shrugged. "Don't know. Just looks weird, almost as if it came from the inside." Then he stopped himself and shook his head. "I'll make it stop. Trust me." John bent over Wesley's head and brought his mouth to the open wound.

Virginia shrieked and ripped him back. "No!"

John snatched her hand and held her immobile. "Listen to me: I'll close his wound with my saliva. It'll stop the bleeding."

Shaking, she locked eyes with John. Slowly, she nodded. She had to trust him.

John brought his mouth to Wesley's head and licked over the wound, licking up the blood that oozed from it. Then he pulled back. When he looked back at her, she noticed his fangs. They'd extended to full length and were peeking from his lips.

She gasped at the sight, but forced herself to relax, and looked at Wesley instead.

"He's still bleeding," John said, concern evident in his voice. "I need to give him vampire blood to heal."

"Won't that turn him into a vampire?"

"No. His heartbeat is strong. He'd have to be at the point of death to be turned." John lifted his wrist to his lips and pricked the skin with his fangs. "Hold his mouth open."

She followed John's instructions and watched him drip blood into Wesley's mouth. For a moment nothing happened, but then she saw Wesley, still unconscious, swallow.

"He'll be fine," John said calmly.

Virginia was about to let out a sigh of relief, when a scream sounded behind her. She whirled around and to her horror saw a badly wounded demon lunge for her, dagger glinting in his hand. In her crouched position, she couldn't move fast enough, could only raise her arms to ward off the worst.

But before the demon's dagger could reach her heart, a woman threw herself between her and her attacker. Deirdre. It had been her scream that had warned Virginia. Now Deirdre screamed again, this time in pain. The demon's dagger had hit her in the chest. Virginia caught her and stared at the demon. His green eyes flickered with hatred. Virginia reached for her own dagger, but never got the chance to use it.

From behind the demon the bald vampire, Zane, appeared and gripped the demon's head, twisted it so hard that a snapping sound could be heard, then yanked it in the opposite direction, before using his sharp claws to slice the head right off the demon's neck.

Green blood spurted everywhere. Zane nodded at her as if to acknowledge Virginia's unspoken thanks. There was no time for words now.

"Deirdre, stay with me," Virginia urged the former council member who now lay in her arms, bleeding profusely from a chest wound.

A gurgling sound came from her. Her eyes were open, but the light seemed to dim in them.

"No, Deirdre, you can't die." Tears shot into Virginia's eyes. Deirdre had saved her life. She couldn't let her die. Desperately, she pressed her hand over the wound, trying to stop the bleeding, but the sticky red liquid kept flowing. "Please, Deirdre." She met the dying woman's gaze.

"Never wanted to hurt anybody..." Deirdre murmured.

"Don't talk now. We'll get you a doctor." Or a vampire to heal her.

"Too late... Watch over Cinead... keep him safe..."

"Deirdre, no you can't leave us." She looked up at Zane. "Help her. Heal her."

The vampire crouched down. "She's dying. She can't be healed. She can only be turned."

Virginia felt a hand on her shoulder and snapped her head to the side.

John looked at her. "I'll do it, if that's what you want. I'll make her a vampire."

Virginia stared back down at Deirdre. Her eyes were starting to close.

"So tired," she murmured, almost inaudibly.

"Do it, John. I won't let anybody else die on my watch ever again." Too many had died in the past because of her mistakes. "Save her."

"I'll hold her," Zane offered and gently took Deirdre from Virginia's arms. Then he motioned to Wesley. "Stay with Wes."

Virginia moved to Wesley's side, taking his hand, and looked to where the battle had taken place. The fighting had stopped. Demon bodies were strewn over the entire street. Streaks of green blood painted the ground, making it look like fresh grass. At least two dozen vampires were busy checking the demon bodies, making sure they were really dead, while others were loading bodies into their truck.

There was red blood among the green, too. Some of her rescuers had been injured. She searched for the wounded, and found a few of them sitting by the side of the street, gulping down bottles of red liquid, while a beautiful woman with long dark hair and a doctor's bag tended to them.

"That's Maya," Haven said. She looked up. He was walking toward her. "She's our in-house doctor."

Haven crouched down next to Wesley, opposite her.

"He jumped after the demon. They fought in the vortex," she said to Haven.

"He'll be all right." Haven ran his hand over Wesley's head, where the wound was already closing.

"John gave him his blood."

Haven nodded. "It's healing him. He'll be as good as new." Haven chuckled unexpectedly. "He's probably just playing unconscious so he won't have to help with the cleanup."

Virginia met Haven's eyes, and despite the lighthearted words, she saw worry in them. "I don't know how to thank you all. You and your colleagues have done more than I ever expected."

He smiled and glanced at his brother. "Family is everything to us." He lifted his hand to wave at somebody.

Virginia looked over her shoulder. Samson was heading toward them. There were green and red blood splatters on his jacket, but he appeared uninjured.

Virginia rose and stretched her hand out to him. "Thank you, Samson. You saved our lives. Without your people we wouldn't have made it."

Samson shook her hand and glanced past her. "Is Wes all right?"

"He's good," Haven said. "We'll have Maya check him out at HQ."

Samson nodded, then swung his gaze back to Virginia. "Sorry that it took us so long to get here. There were a couple of accidents on the freeway due to the rain, one right at the exit ramp. The hybrids' car got stuck there, so we had to send them ahead on motorcycles. Together with Luther."

"That was Luther? In that dark suit? But it was still daylight when he got here."

"It's a special Kevlar suit they use at the vampire prison. It shields him from the sun," Samson explained. Then he motioned to where John and Zane were taking care of Deirdre. "That's the human you were tracking?"

Virginia nodded.

"Since you saved her, I'm assuming she wasn't a traitor?"

"They used her. She didn't know. At the destruction of our council compound, the demons got hold of a council member's cell phone and used it to send her a message. She thought it was from the council member—her brother. She was leading them straight to his compound without knowing it." Virginia swallowed hard. "The cell phones; we don't know how many more names and numbers the demons have. I have to call the Baltimore compound."

Samson nodded. "Let me know what else you need, okay?"

"Thank you." She pulled her cell phone from her pocket and pressed the only number that was programmed into it.

It rang once, then the call was answered. "Virginia, it's Logan."

"Listen carefully, I need you to act quickly." She hoped it wasn't already too late. "The council members' cell phones have been compromised. That's how they got to Deirdre. They used Cinead's cell phone to send her a message. She was on her way to his compound in Northern California."

"Fuck!" Logan cursed. "Is he okay?"

"I think so. But I haven't been able to confirm it. It's too risky to go there now. We were able to intercept Deirdre before she got anywhere close to his compound, but demons attacked."

"Shit! What happened?"

"I'll fill you in later. But I need you to do something right now. The cell phones. The demons who attacked the council compound got a hold of Cinead's. We have to assume that they may also have the other members' phones. Any number that was programmed into those devices is compromised. They need to be disconnected. You need to contact every compound and have them set up new secure lines for everybody affected. Can you do that?"

"We'll get right on it."

"Is my line safe?"

"It probably is, but we can't be a hundred percent sure. Is there another number we can reach you at?"

She glanced at Samson, who nodded immediately. "Samson, the owner of Scanguards, will give you a secure number in a minute. I'll be at Scanguards headquarters within an hour. Once our communication lines are secure again, I need to talk to Cinead and the other council members. Thanks, Logan."

She handed the phone to Samson and turned to look back at Wesley. Haven was lifting him up.

"Where are you taking him?"

"We'll transport him back to HQ in one of the vans." He motioned to the large vans parked behind the demons' truck.

"And the cars? We can't leave them here and block the street. The police—"

"It's in hand," Haven interrupted. "Our guys will drive the cars back the HQ."

"Okay." Her gaze drifted to Deirdre. John and Zane were lifting her up and carrying her away. Her heart constricted. Deirdre had sacrificed her life for Virginia's.

"We'll know soon if the turning is taking," Haven said as if he sensed her unspoken question.

She looked at him. "I hope she'll forgive me when she wakes up."

"Forgive you?"

"Deirdre hated... uh hates, vampires. She, like so many of us, believed that there was no honor, no good in them." She dropped her lids, ashamed that she had made those assumptions without knowing all the facts, without even meeting a vampire face to face. "We didn't know any better."

"She'll find out very soon that we're not so different from your kind. We fight for those we love just as fiercely as you do." Haven looked down at his brother as he carried him toward the van. "No matter what species they are, witch, vampire, human, or Stealth Guardian. Love connects us."

Hope spread in her chest. "It makes us family."

36

———

Zoltan cursed. "Vampires!"

He slammed the door to his private chamber, furious at this latest failure. How had the Stealth Guardians been able to enlist the help of vampires? Those bloodsuckers didn't ally themselves with anybody. They kept to themselves, didn't even look out for each other as a species. And now suddenly they were coming to the guardians' aid?

"What the fuck!"

Still dressed in the uniform of the police officer he'd first fed off, then killed to take his car, Zoltan began to undress. He tossed the blood-and-mud-stained clothes in a corner. So much for his foolproof plan! Everything had worked perfectly at first. The human woman had followed the text message without questioning it, her concern for the sender evident in her reply. He'd expected a few Stealth Guardians to show up and had prepared for it, bringing an abundance of demons with him to crush any attempt at foiling his well-planned operation.

But his demons had been no match for the unexpected appearance of the vampires. Vampires who, despite their lack of weapons forged in the Dark Days, had been able to inflict mortal wounds using their speed, their fangs, and their claws.

He'd had to watch as several of his subjects' heads were ripped from their bodies. One vampire had even gone so far as to tear their hearts out, tossing the demon to the side like a ragdoll. Although the demons had fought valiantly, they had been unable to inflict any lethal wounds. The only metal that could kill a vampire was silver, and none of the weapons from the Dark Days were forged of it. Even Zoltan had been unable to kill a single bloodsucker. It appeared he would need to procure new weapons for his men, now that they had to fight two very different enemies.

And then that witch! He'd had the gall to jump into the vortex with him. But Zoltan had shown him and unleashed a barrage of mind blasts at his enemy. It should have turned his brain to mush immediately, but the witch had been strong, too strong, and somebody had helped him. Pulled him out just before Zoltan had been able to conjure up more of his power to destroy the witch once and for all.

But this wouldn't be their last encounter. Now that he knew what kinds of allies the Stealth Guardians had managed to enlist, he would be better prepared for the next fight. Brute force wasn't going to cut it any longer. He needed to find another way to get at the Stealth Guardians. Get at them from the inside.

A DULL PAIN made Wesley groan and sit up suddenly. Sterile lights gleamed around him, hurting his eyes. It took a second or two for his eyes to adjust and for him to realize where he was: in Scanguards' onsite medical center, a small wing at HQ with exam rooms, an operating theater, a lab, an x-ray room, and a large refrigerated vault with blood and medication for a variety of illnesses, most of which were meant for human staff members.

Wesley lay on a gurney in one of the large exam rooms. "Virginia?" It was the first thought that came to his mind.

"Well, there's our patient."

The voice belonged to Maya, who now came around the curtain

that separated the treatment areas in the room. She pulled the curtain back.

"Where is she? Is she all right?"

Maya smiled. "She's perfectly fine. But we were a bit worried about you." She reached for his wrist and felt for his pulse.

"I'm fine. Where is she?"

Maya sighed. "She's with Samson and Gabriel." She pulled her cell phone from her pocket and typed a quick message. "I just let them know you're awake. Now let me look at you. I want to make sure you don't have a concussion."

"I'm a witch, Maya."

She rolled her eyes. "That doesn't make you invincible."

She pointed to his head, reminding him of the dull pain he could still feel on one side of his skull.

"You can thank John for closing the wound and giving you vampire blood. You could have lost a lot more blood than you did, if he hadn't acted so quickly."

"I'll make sure to thank him."

He was grateful, but right now his need to see Virginia was greater than his concern for his injuries. He had to reassure himself that she was well. After the experience he'd had in the vortex, fighting the demon, he needed to see with his own eyes that Virginia hadn't been hurt. And he refused to have her see him lying on a gurney like some loser.

He swung his legs off the hospital bed and stood. Instantly, he swayed.

"Whoa!" Maya caught him and pressed him back down to the bed. "Head wounds are no joke."

Wes pressed his hand to the spot where the pain was the worst, but he couldn't feel any actual wound or scar. Vampire blood had ensured that he healed perfectly. So why was his head still hurting?

"That demon must have gotten me with his dagger," he murmured.

Maya shook her head. "Not according to John. He said the wound on your head wasn't caused by a blade. He said it looked more like something had burst from the inside."

"What?"

"You know like a bird trying to hatch from an egg, knocking through the shell from the inside."

"That's impossible. He must be wrong."

Maya shrugged. "Can't verify it since it's already healed. But he's sticking to his story. Does it still hurt?"

"I've felt worse."

"Hmm. So, what happened in that vortex?"

The door swung open without warning and Virginia rushed in. "You're awake." She marched to the gurney and put her arms around him.

Wesley pulled her to his chest and kissed her. "And you? You didn't get hurt?"

"I'm fine."

"And the others?" He glanced at Maya, but knew that he would have seen it in her face if anybody from Scanguards had gotten hurt.

"Just a few scrapes," Maya confirmed.

Turning to Maya, Virginia released him. "Is he okay again?"

Maya shook her head, and Wesley wanted to protest, but she cut him off. "His head is still aching. It shouldn't, not after the blood John gave him. So, I can only assume that whatever happened to him in the vortex has a lasting effect."

"Can't you find out what it is? Can't you give him something?" Virginia asked, her concern evident.

"Hey, ladies, I'm right here. No need to talk about me like I can't hear you."

Still ignoring him, Maya continued, "I was just trying to find out what happened to him in the vortex."

Both women turned their gazes on him.

"Oh, now you want to talk to me."

Both rolled their eyes as if they'd rehearsed it a hundred times.

"What did the demon do to you?" Virginia asked.

"It was different this time."

"What do you mean?"

"You know how we were able to read the other demon's mind when we piggy-backed on his vortex?"

She nodded.

"It wasn't really like that. It was painful. He launched a barrage of thoughts and images at me. I can't really describe it. It wasn't anything concrete. I tried to fight him. I used my witchcraft, but it made it worse, as if it allowed him to get into my mind." It had felt like an invasion.

A concerned look on her face, Virginia said, "Demons can influence others with their minds. They try to make us do things, try to manipulate us with their thoughts. The weaker the personality, the more easily they can bring them to their side." She shook her head. "But you shouldn't have felt it that intensely. You would've been able to fight it. To push him out of your mind."

Wesley contemplated her words. "I think... when I tried to use my witchcraft... I think it made me vulnerable."

"How?"

"I had to open my mind to collect my powers and—"

"—the demon slipped in," Virginia finished his sentence. "Oh my God." She clasped his hands. "But it's over now. It must be."

He met her worried gaze. "I'm not sure."

"Wes... maybe it's just the aftermath of the injury."

"There's something else." He hesitated, because he wasn't sure himself.

Virginia held her breath.

"It feels like he left something behind."

Both Virginia and Maya gasped and stared at him, panicked.

"I think some of his memories are still there." He tapped at his skull. "Somewhere in there, there's something important. Something that I figured out in the vortex." He sighed. "But I can't remember it. I just know it's important."

Virginia's cell phone rang. She pulled it from her pocket, but before she answered it, she said, "We'll figure it out, we will." Then she connected the call. "Yes?" A moment later she said, "We'll be up in two minutes." She disconnected the call and tucked the cell phone away.

"What is it?" Wesley asked.

"Cinead and Barclay have arrived."

"The council members? They're here? At Scanguards?"

"I had to tell Cinead what happened to Deirdre. I convinced him to come."

Recalling the frantic battle, Wes held his breath as he asked, "Did she get hurt?" He tossed a quick look around the room, but there was no second patient. "Oh my God, is she dead?"

"I'll fill you in on the way up," Virginia said and helped him up.

37

———————

Still worried that whatever Wesley had experienced with the demon in the portal could have a lasting effect, Virginia opened the door to the small conference room where the meeting with her fellow council members was taking place.

Everybody was already assembled when she and Wesley entered.

Samson, Amaury, and Gabriel were standing near the head of the table, while Cinead and Barclay were waiting close to the door. They looked relieved when they saw her.

"Cinead, Barclay, I'm so glad you came," she greeted them.

Barclay nodded and glanced at Wesley. "We didn't really have a choice. I'm happy to see that you're okay." He motioned to the three vampires. "We've been introduced. Your, uh, new friends have given us more details about what happened."

Cinead seemed on edge, his voice shaking slightly, when he spoke. "There's so much I can't quite grasp yet. Deirdre... she must be frightened..."

"She's being taken care of," Virginia assured him.

"She hasn't come out of it yet," Samson added. "We'll know more in a few hours. My people are making sure she has everything she needs when she comes to."

Cinead nodded gratefully. Then he took a step toward Wesley. "I suppose I owe you and your friends a debt of gratitude."

"You owe us nothing," Wesley said quickly. "All we want is a chance to meet with you and make a proposal."

"Shall we sit?" Samson asked and pointed to the table and chairs.

Cinead turned toward the table when Wesley suddenly put his hand on his shoulder. "Counselor?"

Cinead looked over his shoulder, a surprised look on his face. "Yes?"

Wesley pointed to Cinead's hip. "This dagger. I've seen it before."

Virginia followed Wesley's gaze. On Cinead's hip, an ancient ceremonial dagger was sheathed.

"I doubt that very much. Only the counselors have this type of dagger. And the last time you saw me, we were all seated. You wouldn't have been able to see the daggers. You must be mistaken."

Wes shook his head. "No, I've seen it. I remember the nine intertwined rings on the hilt. They look like they're made of seashells with gold inlay. I'm sure I've seen a dagger like this before."

Virginia put her hand on Wesley's arm and made him look at her. "Like Cinead said, that's not possible. Only nine of those daggers exist. They were made especially for the original members of the Council of Nine and then handed down from counselor to counselor."

He sighed, looking confused and almost disappointed. "Then I must have seen you with one when you arrested me and brought me before the council. That's it."

He turned toward the table, but Virginia stopped him. "I never had the same dagger as Cinead and Barclay and the other council members."

"But—"

"She's correct," Barclay said and stepped closer. "Virginia's predecessor's dagger was never recovered."

"Was that Finlay?" Wes asked.

Barclay jolted. "How do you know about Finlay?"

"Doesn't matter now. But if Virginia never had the same dagger, then I couldn't have seen it on her. But I know I've seen it. Somewhere. Broken apart." He looked away from Barclay and sought Virginia's eyes. "You have to believe me. I've seen this exact dagger." He lifted his hand to the healed wound on his head. "It's in here. I know it."

She stared at him, recalling his words from earlier. "The demon..."

"I think so," Wesley said.

"But you can't remember where it was?" she asked.

"No. But I saw it break apart. The demon saw it." He turned to the three vampires. "When I was in the vortex with the demon, I saw things. I felt and heard things that I couldn't possibly have seen or heard or felt. But I did. Something happened to me when the demon tried to invade my mind. I tried to repel him with witchcraft, but somehow, I must have accessed his memories instead."

The three vampires looked at each other, concern and worry traveling across their faces.

"Do you still feel him?" Amaury asked.

"No. I'm not connected to him anymore, if that's what you're worried about," Wesley said quickly. "But I know I saw something important. I just can't remember it. The injury, you know. Maybe Maya is right and I do have a concussion."

"Or maybe you just need help remembering," Gabriel interjected.

Virginia saw Wesley and Gabriel exchange a look.

"I think I do. Would you?"

"If you think it's important."

Wesley nodded.

The hairs on Virginia's nape rose. "What's going on?"

Wes took her hand. "Gabriel has a gift. He can unlock people's memories and help them remember what they've forgotten."

She sucked in a breath. "How?" Her gaze snapped to the scary-looking vampire with the ponytail and the large scar that marred one side of his face.

"Don't be alarmed, Virginia," Gabriel said. "It's absolutely noninvasive. Wesley won't feel anything, but it'll help him figure out what he's forgotten."

She looked back at Wesley.

"Trust me," Wesley said.

She'd done a lot of that in the last few days: trusting Wesley, trusting his friends. Slowly, she nodded.

"It'll only take a few minutes," Gabriel promised and walked to Wesley, stopping only a foot away from him. "Just close your eyes and relax."

Virginia watched with bated breath as Wesley followed the vampire's instruction, and Gabriel laid his hands on Wesley's head. From the corner of her eye, she noticed Cinead and Barclay exchange a doubtful look. She couldn't help but agree with them. Who'd ever heard of a vampire restoring memories?

But when she looked at Samson and Amaury, she saw no such doubt in their faces. They were simply waiting in anticipation, as if they were one hundred percent certain that their fellow vampire could deliver what he'd promised.

When a gasp suddenly came from Wesley, Virginia snapped her eyes back to him. Gabriel's hands were still on Wesley's head, and he too had his eyes closed, but both seemed to jolt several times as if they were reliving something frightening.

Suddenly, both stumbled back, severing the connection, and opened their eyes.

"That was intense," Wesley let out.

Gabriel moved his head from side to side. "Never experienced anything like it. You were right about the demon. You managed to extract some of his memories while you tried to fight against him with your witchcraft."

"It was close."

"A few seconds more in his mind and you wouldn't be standing here," Gabriel said. "You were lucky."

"What?" Her heart pounding, Virginia gripped Wesley's arm and made him look at her. "What does Gabriel mean by that?"

Wesley took her hand and squeezed. "I think he's telling me that if you and John hadn't pulled me out when you did, Zoltan would have turned my brain to mush."

A shaky breath tore from her throat.

"So, you know it was Zoltan, their leader?" Barclay interjected, stepping closer.

"Yes, Gabriel helped me remember." Wesley touched his skull. "And my headache is gone. No concussion after all. It was just Zoltan's memories trying to break through."

"Tell us what you saw," Cinead demanded.

Wesley pointed to Cinead's and Barclay's daggers. "It was the same dagger. I'm sure. It was in Zoltan's possession. I saw it break into two pieces. The handle split off. It was hollow, and inside it, there was a picture. Old. Black and white."

Cinead gasped. "A picture?"

"What did it show?" Barclay asked.

"A couple, dressed in the style of the early 1900s. It fit with the way the photograph looked," Wes explained. "You know, like one of these old sepia photos?"

"Did you recognize the couple?" Barclay asked.

"No. But there was something else. On the back of it, something was written: *First day at the council.*"

Virginia exchanged an alarmed look with Cinead and Barclay, but Wesley continued, "But it makes no sense, because there was no building in the photograph. Just a bunch of old stones."

"Stones?" Cinead asked.

"Yeah, a bit like Stonehenge, but different. Not as neatly arranged as Stonehenge, and the stones were of different sizes."

"Oh God," Virginia murmured and met Cinead's gaze.

"I need a computer, quickly," Barclay demanded, looking at the three vampires.

Amaury snatched one from a side table and booted it up. "Here you go."

Barclay slid onto the chair and pulled up a browser, while

everybody crowded around him. His fingers flew over the keyboard as he typed something into the search box. Virginia didn't have to look at what he'd written, because she knew what he was searching for.

Images finally filled the screen. Barclay clicked on one of them to enlarge it and looked over his shoulder to Wesley. "Is this what you saw in the picture?"

Stunned, Wesley stared at the image, then at Barclay. "That's it. How did you know?"

Barclay swiveled in his chair. "These are the Callanish Stones. In our native language we call them Clachan Chalanais. A ring of stones located on the Isle of Lewis in the Outer Hebrides in Scotland." He looked straight at Wesley. "You were there."

"Trust me, I've never been to Scotland."

"You were there, because that's where our council compound was located until the demons attacked us and we had to destroy it."

Wesley's mouth fell open, and the three vampires also let out gasps. "That's how the demons knew. Zoltan found the picture in the dagger and put two and two together."

Cinead nodded. "That dagger can only have belonged to one person."

"Finlay," Virginia said. "And because of his betrayal, Zoltan knew that Finlay was a member of the council, and what he looked like. It would have been easy for him to figure out that the picture showed Finlay and his wife not far from the compound."

Barclay nodded. "Finlay joined the council in 1903. I can have a photo of Finlay sent to us so Wesley can identify him."

Cinead nodded and pulled his cell phone from his pocket. "I'll contact the council." Then he looked at Virginia. "Don't worry, this is a new phone with a new number."

"Good." Virginia moved her gaze to Barclay. "So, there was no leak then. It was more fallout from Finlay's betrayal."

Barclay nodded slowly. "It appears that way."

"I've got it," Cinead said and held up his phone, motioning to Wesley. "Is this him?"

Wesley took the phone from Cinead's hand and stared at the display. "Without a doubt. In the picture he looked a little younger, but not by much." He returned the cell phone to Cinead.

Cinead sighed and shook his head. "How can we be sure that Zoltan doesn't retain any more of Finlay's possessions?"

"Zoltan was frustrated," Wesley said.

"What?" Cinead asked.

"When I was in the vortex with him and felt his thoughts, I knew he had nothing else. The dagger with the photo only led him to the council compound. It would have ended there, had one of his demons not brought back your cell phone. I don't know whether they got any of the others, but it doesn't matter. All compromised numbers have been disconnected. Even if he got the other council members' phones, they're now useless."

"But how did he find Deirdre?" Cinead asked.

"I have a theory about that," Samson suddenly said.

Everybody looked at him.

"Go ahead," Cinead said.

"If the demons are smart, and we must assume that they are, or that at least their leader is, they'll keep records of confirmed Stealth Guardian sightings. It's what I would do: try to isolate a pattern of appearances so I could anticipate where you'll turn up next. It would be easy to review those reports and cross reference them with contacts in your phones."

"I helped Deirdre settle in Portland a couple of weeks ago. I wasn't always invisible," Cinead admitted.

Samson nodded. "If somebody saw you, they could have easily figured out Deirdre's name and yours too. They could have overheard a conversation. Anything. And when they managed to get your cell phone during the attack on the compound, all they had to do was find that name and send Deirdre a message in the hopes that she would come to you. Then all they had to do was follow her to get to you."

Virginia nodded to herself. It all made sense. But it was also disheartening. It meant that no matter how careful they were, there was always a chance that the demons would find them.

"I think you're right, Samson," Cinead said. "It was my fault."

"No," Virginia protested. "It was nobody's fault. It's just the nature of the game. The demons can spot us by our aura, but we can't spot them unless they reveal their eyes—"

"—which brings us to what Scanguards can offer you," Wesley cut in. "While this threat may be over, it won't be the last one. Zoltan won't give up. But next time, you'll be better prepared. With Scanguards by your side."

Barclay and Cinead exchanged a look. Then Barclay said, "I suppose it wouldn't hurt to discuss a possible collaboration."

Samson motioned to the large conference table. "Shall we take our seats at the table, gentlemen?"

When both Cinead and Barclay nodded, Virginia looked at Wesley and smiled. He took her hand and stepped closer.

"We're going to make a great team," he whispered to her.

"A perfect team."

Because they complemented each other perfectly.

38

____

The negotiations between the vampires and the Stealth Guardians were going well, when a knock sounded at the door.

Wesley turned his head as the door was ripped open.

Maya charged in. "We have a problem," she announced. "Deirdre won't drink human blood."

"Shit," Wesley cursed and looked at Cinead, whose expression was one of panic.

Cinead jumped up. "How long can she survive without it?"

"A few days, but we can't let it come to that. We need to do something," Maya replied.

Wes was already on his feet. "Cinead, come with me." He motioned to Maya. "Where is she?"

"We had to lock her in one of the holding cells. She's turning violent."

"Oh God, no!" Cinead choked out.

As they dashed to the door, Virginia called out, "I'm coming with you."

Wesley looked over his shoulder. "No, babe, it's too dangerous. As a newly turned vampire she can't control herself. She's liable to attack you, and I can't risk that." To protect Virginia, he would kill anybody —even the woman who'd saved her life. "Please stay here."

He didn't wait for her reply. Instead, he followed Maya and Cinead.

"Is anybody with her?" he asked Maya while they rushed to the elevator.

"John is trying to keep her calm."

The elevator doors opened, and they got in. Maya pressed the button for sublevel three, where the interrogation room and the cells were located.

"Is it normal for a new vampire to refuse blood?" Cinead asked, looking at Maya, his concern for his half-sister evident.

Maya sighed. "There've been cases, where the vampire refused the blood offered. I'm one of those cases."

"But you're alive," Cinead said.

"Because I drank another vampire's blood. I craved his, because there was something in his blood that I needed."

"What if that's the case with Deirdre?"

Maya shook her head. "I don't think so. In mine and Gabriel's case it was because we were never fully human before we were turned. We have the genes of another species in us."

"But couldn't that apply to Deirdre too? I mean, she was Stealth Guardian for centuries."

"But she was fully human when John turned her. There's no doubt about it. I don't think it's something physical that's preventing her from drinking human blood."

"Then what is it?" Cinead asked, his voice more agitated now.

"She's rejecting her new nature. I think the very thought of what she's become repels her."

Hearing Maya's explanation, Wesley stared at Cinead. "Your race hates vampires, don't they? Does Deirdre?"

The elevator doors opened and there was a brief break in the conversation, while they stepped into the corridor.

Cinead hesitated and looked at Maya. "It's nothing personal, you must understand that. You and your colleagues have shown us nothing but kindness, and provided us with more help than we could have ever hoped for. But for so long we believed that all vampires were violent and evil. We didn't quite toss them into the same bucket as demons, but we never held them in high regard or believed we could even live peacefully side by side." He sighed. "Deirdre had some particularly bad experiences with them. She hates them with a passion."

"She hates herself now," Wesley murmured.

Cinead met his gaze. "I believe so."

"Do you still love your sister, even knowing what she's become?"

"How could I not? She is my flesh and blood, and what happened to her is my fault, not hers."

"Then you have to convince her that she's still deserving of love," Wes said firmly. "Or she will starve herself to death."

In front of the cell, they stopped. Maya pressed the intercom next to the cell door and said, "John? It's Maya. I'm with Wes and Cinead. We're coming in."

The intercom crackled, then John's voice could be heard. "Okay. I'm restraining her." There was a high-pitched scream, then the intercom went silent.

"Stay close to us," Maya warned Cinead, then unlocked the door.

The room was larger than the lead cell Wesley had been in, but not any more welcoming. It was generally only used for hostile and dangerous vampires, and in this case, Deirdre was considered a danger —to herself.

John was trying to keep Deirdre from lunging toward her visitors, holding her from behind, one hand restraining her arms behind her back, the other arm slung like a vise around her torso. She was fighting against his grip, and by the looks of it she'd managed to inflict some wounds: there were cuts on John's face, and also on his exposed forearm. Blood had dried over the wounds, which had most likely been caused by Deirdre's claws.

Even now, her fingers curved into sharp barbs and her fangs were fully extended. Her eyes glowed red with rage, and she growled like a caged beast.

But John was well fed and stronger, whereas Deirdre had to be feeling the pangs of hunger by now, which weakened her.

"Deirdre, oh my God," Cinead choked out and stretched his arms toward her as if wanting to embrace her, but Deirdre hissed at him, and he jerked backward.

"It's me, Deirdre, it's Cinead, your brother," he tried again.

She shook her head violently left and right, sending her hair flying.

Undeterred, Cinead took a few steps toward her. Deirdre suddenly stopped moving and stared at Cinead.

Her eyes changed. The red glare dissipated. "Cinead?" She took a breath. "Help me. They've locked me up. They're trying to hurt me."

"They're here to help you. You're not well right now."

Deirdre glanced at Wesley and Maya, then looked back at Cinead. "Don't trust them. They're vampires. They want to hurt us. Save yourself."

Cinead continued to approach until he was only a couple of feet away from her. "Listen to me, Deirdre. Everything will be fine." He reached out and swept a few strands of her hair behind her ear. "It's a big change. But you're alive. You sacrificed so much for me, for us. You saved Virginia's life."

Wesley noticed tears rim Deirdre's eyes, red tears.

"I love you even more now. You've proven that redemption is truly possible. You've redeemed yourself in all our eyes. The entire council will hear of it. And I know they'll praise you."

A red tear dislodged from one eye and ran down her cheek. "Cinead," she whimpered. "But look at me. Look at this."

Cinead gently stroked his hand over Deirdre's head. "You're strong, my little sister. You can do this. You can *be* this." Cinead's voice was thick with emotion. "These people are our friends. They've promised to protect you now. To help you accept this. And I'll be here for as long as you need me. I'm still your brother, no matter what form you've taken. Because I know that inside this new body of yours, your heart is still the same."

Tears were now rolling down Cinead's face, but he didn't seem to notice, or didn't seem to care.

"Please don't leave me, Deirdre. Please don't give up." He motioned to John. "John is going to release you now."

John hesitated and looked at Wesley.

Wesley nodded. "Do it."

Slowly, John released his grip on Deirdre. At first, she didn't move. Everybody in the room held their breath.

All of a sudden, there was a movement so fast Wesley couldn't even follow it. When he blinked, Deirdre was embracing her half-brother, sobbing at his chest, and Cinead was holding her and stroking his hand over her back as if she were a little child.

"I'm so hungry," she murmured.

"We'll get you some nourishment, won't we?" Cinead said with a look at John.

John turned to the table where several bottles of blood stood, picked up a bottle and unscrewed the top.

The scent of the blood seemed to reach Deirdre, because she suddenly released her brother and turned to look at John.

"It's all for you. As much as you like," John offered and held the bottle out to her.

Her movements hesitant, she reached for it and took it. As if she was ashamed of her need, she dropped her lids and turned away.

Seconds later she lifted the bottle to her lips and drank.

Cinead let out a relieved breath.

"Everything will turn out all right, little sister. You'll see."

Deirdre had accepted her second chance at life. And Wesley knew that his friends at Scanguards would make sure she was safe. Not only because she was a vampire now, and one of them, or because she had saved Virginia's life, but also because as a former council member, Deirdre knew too much. That knowledge could never fall into the demons' hands.

39

It took over a week for Scanguards and the Stealth Guardians to hammer out the details of their alliance and secure the approval of the principals on both sides. But finally, each side was happy and ready to work together. Virginia and Wesley were chosen as the respective liaisons for their parties, something Virginia couldn't be happier about. It meant that despite the fact that she'd broken about a million rules when she'd trusted Wesley, the council wasn't going to punish her. On the contrary. They had granted their permission to continue the relationship. Privately, however, the council had urged her to make the union official. But just how did a woman approach the man she loved and ask him to marry her? Wasn't that the man's prerogative?

"Penny for your thoughts."

Virginia snapped her head to the bathroom door, where Wesley was leaning against the frame with only a short towel covering his groin. Her breath instantly hitched, and her heartbeat accelerated. She'd thought that after more than ten days of seeing him like this, she'd be used to it, and her reaction would be less explosive. But that sculpted chest, those strong abdominal muscles, and those muscled thighs dusted with dark hair sent a wave of fire through her body every time.

Under her negligee, her nipples pebbled, and farther south, the flesh between her thighs began to tingle in anticipation. Every day since coming to San Francisco, they'd made love until nearly midday, then slept until sunset, before returning to Scanguards. For that whole time, she'd refrained from making love to Wesley the Stealth Guardian way, because they had to take part in the negotiations and needed to be rested, but now that all of it was done, there were no more excuses. This weekend, there would be no work. And apart from a family get-together, she and Wesley would be alone.

"A penny isn't nearly enough," she said and pulled the duvet back. "I'd rather make a trade."

Wesley smirked and loosened the towel around his waist, then tossed it back into the bathroom. "Now you're talking, babe."

He walked toward her without hurry. His cock hung heavy between his legs, already filling with blood and getting harder before her eyes. She loved the way he got aroused so quickly. But what she loved even more was the way Wesley looked at her: with love and passion. And that look hadn't faltered once, but seemed to grow more intense every day.

The mattress depressed next to her as Wesley slid beneath the covers to join her. His eager hands were already touching her, shoving her white negligee over her head to free her from it.

"I don't know why you even bother wearing this, when you know I'm going to undress you anyway."

She chuckled. "Maybe I like the way you undress me."

"Point taken." Then he pulled her closer and locked eyes with her. "Anything else you like?"

"Yes, I'd like you to be mine forever."

The words were out before she knew she'd said them. She sucked in a breath.

There was a flicker in Wesley's baby-blue eyes. "Are you saying what I think you're saying?"

Cautiously, she asked, "What do you think I'm saying?"

"Forever is a long time for an immortal. So, you think you'd like to have me around for that long?" He pulled her pelvis to him and pressed his erection to her stomach. "Knowing what I'm like? How insatiable I am?"

"I like insatiable."

He rolled over her, shoving her thighs apart to make space for himself, while he took her wrists and pinned her arms to either side of her head. "I hope you know what you're getting into." He plunged his cock into her pussy with one perfect thrust.

Virginia let out a moan and tilted her pelvis toward Wesley's groin, welcoming the invasion.

"I'm not the mild-mannered witch everybody thinks I am."

"I know who you are. I've seen what's inside you. And I love every part of you."

He withdrew his cock then thrust again. "How about this part?"

"What are you trying to do, torture me?"

He brought his lips to hover over hers. "Just a little. Just to make sure you mean it." He kissed her passionately, then severed his lips from hers. "Now please tell me your kind has a bonding ritual that involves sex. Because I'm afraid the witches don't."

She smiled up at him. "You're in luck."

"Perfect," he murmured.

"I need to explain a few things."

He put his finger over her lips, stopping her. "Surprise me."

"It could be dangerous," she warned him.

"We've been through a lot of danger together. I think we can survive a bonding ritual, don't you?"

"As long as our love is true."

"It is."

Then they had nothing to fear.

Virginia pulled his head to her and kissed him. Wesley responded to her, sliding his tongue against hers, exploring her like she explored him, caressing her. Farther below, his hips moved back and forth, his cock sliding in and out of her in a steady rhythm.

Using her powers, she spun a cocoon around them. Fog and mist engulfed them, shielding them from the world and the dangers outside their four walls. They were invisible to everybody now, as if they didn't exist. Because at this moment, they only existed for each other.

Virginia felt her life force bubble to the surface, and knew she couldn't hold it back any longer. She allowed her *virta* to flow outward and seep into Wesley's body at each point where they were connected.

They were floating now. Not on air, but on their love, a love that was stronger than any power known to mankind. It alone held them up and supported them, kept them safe.

She took her lips off Wesley's and stared into his eyes. Love and adoration reflected back at her.

"Are you ready?" she murmured.

"I've been ready from the moment I met you."

She took his hand and placed it on her heart. "Do you feel the *virta* inside you?"

"It's like fire."

"Send it back to me. Let it flow into my heart."

"I love you, Virginia," he whispered, when suddenly a visible glow traveled through him. It reached his shoulder, then slithered down his arm toward his wrist.

Virginia held her breath.

Wesley's fingers turned golden, and from its tips, golden tendrils flowed outward and fused with her skin. A bolt of electricity shot through her and pierced her heart. A wave of passion washed over it, soothing the pain away. What it left behind was a bond so powerful that only death could break it.

Virginia put her hand over Wesley's heart. It beat into her palm. And it beat for her. There would never again be any doubt about it.

"You're mine now," Virginia murmured.

A soft smile spread over Wesley's face and he stroked his knuckles over her cheek. "I was already yours a long time ago, babe. It just took me a while to find you."

Tears swam in her eyes, the happiness in her heart too much to contain. "Oh, Wes..."

"Now let your witch husband show you what he meant by insatiable."

His lips descended on hers and took her to a place where only love and passion existed. Where only the two of them existed. Where they were one.

40

Zoltan followed the man as he turned toward the floor-to-ceiling windows of the elegant condo.

"The view from here is the best in the city."

"Indeed," Zoltan said and stopped next to his host. "And you're willing to give this up, Mr. Vaughn?"

"Only for a few months." Vaughn cast him a sideways glance. "Like I said in the advertisement, it's only a short-term rental. I'm going hiking in the Himalayas, and the rent will help me finance my lifelong dream."

"Ah, I understand. So, four months only then?" Zoltan asked.

Vaughn nodded. "Is that a problem?"

Quickly, Zoltan said, "No, no. Not a problem at all. It's just what I need. And the furniture remains?" He glanced around. The man had good taste. Most of the pieces looked new and barely used, and the color scheme of dark tones interspersed with colorful accents made the entire place look elegant. So very different from his abode in the Underworld.

"Yes, everything stays. I'll of course have to take a damage deposit, just in case anything is stained or broken during your stay."

"Of course. I expected as much." He glanced around again. "And while you're hiking, is there anybody I should contact in case of an emergency like an overflowing toilet, a relative maybe? Or a close friend?"

"I'm afraid you'll be on your own. I have no relatives in the area. As for friends, I moved here only recently."

Perfect. "So, I should contact the condo board then? You'll let them know that I'll be staying in your absence?"

A concerned look passed over Vaughn's face. "Uh, well." He hesitated. "Thing is, the board doesn't allow short term rentals. I only found out after I bought the place. So, I'd rather you not tell them that you're renting from me. They'll just give me trouble."

Zoltan knew that already. After all, that was why he'd picked this building. Anybody renting out a condo on a short-term lease would have to do so without the association's approval, and therefore there would be no record of Zoltan being a tenant. "I see."

"If there are any issues that concern the condo association such as a water leak or something similar, just tell them you're me."

"Oh? Isn't that a bit high risk?"

"This building has such a high turnover, nobody knows anybody here. I'm sure you won't have any issues."

Zoltan didn't think so either. In fact, this place was perfect, for so many reasons.

"One more thing," Zoltan said.

"Yes?"

"Are you scared?"

"Excuse me?"

Zoltan snatched the man by the throat and pinned him against the wall. "I asked: are you scared?"

Panic rolled off the man, and he struggled, trying to punch Zoltan. But the human was weak.

Zoltan laughed. "Time to succumb to your fear, human."

He slammed the man to the ground and pinned him there, then brought his face close to his victim's.

"Come to me," Zoltan urged. "Give me your fear and make me strong."

Mist started to escape from his victim's nostrils and mouth. Greedily, Zoltan sucked it in and swallowed it. And again. He took it all, took the fear, the pain, the anguish.

Zoltan rose and looked out through the windows to admire the view from his new abode. This would be his hideout. And not just for the next four months, because Vaughn would never return from his hiking trip to demand his condo back. He looked over his shoulder at the man whose empty shell lay motionless on the pristine wooden floor. Vaughn had already left the building, never to return.

ABOUT THE AUTHOR

Tina Folsom was born in Germany and has been living in English speaking countries since 1991. Tina has always been a bit of a globe trotter.

She lived in Munich, Lausanne, London, New York City, Los Angeles, San Francisco, and Sacramento. She has now made a beach town in Southern California her permanent home with her American husband and her dog.

She's written 50 romance novels in English most of which are translated into German, French, and Spanish.

https://tinawritesromance.com
tina@tinawritesromance.com

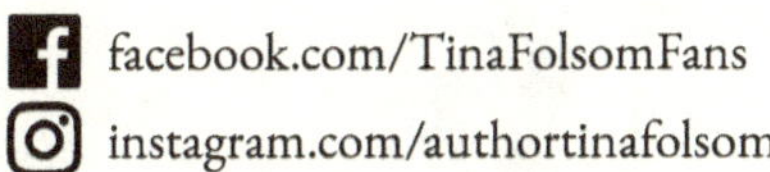

facebook.com/TinaFolsomFans
instagram.com/authortinafolsom